Going, Going, Gone

A Jonathan Benjamin Franklin Mystery

David L. Gersh

Durban House

Printed in the United States of America.

For information address:

Durban House Press, Inc.
5001 LBJ Freeway, Suite 700
Dallas, Texas 75244

Library of Congress Cataloging-in-Publication Data

Gersh, David L.

Going, Going, Gone/David L. Gersh

Library of Congress Control Number: 2008937984

p. cm.

ISBN: 978-0-9818486-4-8

First Edition

10 9 8 7 6 5 4 3 2 1

Visit our Web site at
http://www.durbanhouse.com

For Stella

Acknowledgments

I always thought writing was a solitary and internal process. In fact, if it doesn't take a village, at least it takes a very extended family. So let me try to set about giving my thanks to some of the people who helped.

First and foremost, to my late wife, Stella Zadeh, my love and gratitude for all the help she gave me in her comments from the endless reading of endless drafts, and for her astute and insightful advice in getting the book sold.

When Stella passed away, it tore my heart out. Anne Cooper Ready put it back. She also read and edited the last (of many) versions of this book. I thank her for her insights and her encouragement.

Again, Bob Middlemiss, my editor at Durban House, is a gem. Bob is thoughtful, encouraging and tough. What a guy. My dear friend Harvey Champlin has read every draft of every book that I've written and always gives me useful comments. He has helped me immeasurably. Fanny Pereire was my muse. She is the delightful young French woman who talked to me about her work at Christie's and the art auction business and started me thinking about the subject of the art world, which has fascinated me for the last 15 years.

David Rintels is not only a great writer; he has been a source of constant encouragement. I needed that.

Many of my friends took their time to read my manuscript and make helpful comments. Their enthusiasm spurred me on. In alphabetical order, barring any more useful arrangement, I want to give my thanks to Meg Barbour, Noah benShea, Jerry Cohen, Richard Cohen, Stan Cornyn, Janc DeHart, Dawn Dyer, Mark and Missy Gersh, Allan Ghitterman, Micalyn Harris, Lauren Lucier, Clark Miller, Bob Temkin, Joe Tumbler and Tom Weinberger. Bless their hearts.

Also by David Gersh:

Art Is Dead

Prologue

Paris, 1940

Rain dampened the sounds. Jean-Claude Fernaud didn't hear the boots clicking on the wet cobblestones in time. They were very close.

He quickly hunched into the darkness between two buildings, clutching the cumbersome package to his chest. His knuckles whitened with the pressure. A bead of sweat slid down the side of his face in spite of the cold.

The Germans passed near enough for him to smell their cigarette smoke. One snickered. The sound chilled him. He waited an eternity after they passed, listening. He hardly breathed. Then he warily started out again, glancing over his shoulder. He strained to hear any sound.

The old building he sought out stood in a side street in the Porte de Clingancourt. The flea market was still allowed to operate, and the comings and goings of shopkeepers and poor artists provided some cover. Rain splashed on the sidewalks, turning the dirt into streaks of mud.

The pattern had been the same for more than a year. Use a banker to get at a wealthy Jew. Squeeze him for his gold, his art, anything of value. Make him believe he was safe as long as he cooperated. Then the Jew was gone.

S.S. Colonel Eugen Kurtzmann smiled to himself as he relaxed before the fire in his suite at the Ritz Hotel, turning the tumbler of cognac in his hand. Things were proceeding well. This young DeSant had been useful. He was pliable and had been easier to handle than the old banker might have been. The bill of sale for the Matisse he'd made DeSant demand from the Jew Rosenberg had been a nice touch. Kurtzmann laughed aloud when he recalled the shocked look on Georges DeSant's face. Reichsmarschall Goering would be pleased.

"LeClerc, why is he not here?" George DeSant asked. He had been pacing the small, cold room for an hour. His breath clouded in front of him.

"DeSant, you are a fool," LeClerc muttered, brushing aside the smoke from his Gauloises. "It is dangerous to be in the streets after curfew."

"This is unbearable." DeSant's hand shook as he reached for the pack LeClerc held out. His eyes looked older than his twenty years. The tap on the door startled him. He dropped the match he was trying to hold to the end of his cigarette.

"*Merde*," LeClerc said, barely concealing his disdain. "Turn out the light." He pointed to the light switch.

LeClerc opened the door a crack, and the tall young man slipped into the dark room. Fernaud carried a large rectangular package under his arm. A puddle of water formed on the floor under him. He wiped the rain from his face with the back of his sleeve.

DeSant grabbed away the package. "Is it dry?" he asked, anxiously unwrapping it. "Let me see." He held the painting up to the dim light. "My God, this is magnificent. Such perfection," he said, shaking his head.

He turned back to Fernaud. "Please hurry. Wrap it back up. I must get to Kurtzmann right away. I wish this accursed rain would stop. Will it harm the picture?"

"No. No. Of course not. Just keep it wrapped as I have it."

"Thank you, Fernaud." Gripping the picture to him with both hands, he turned. "Say goodbye to Rosenberg for me, LeClerc. He will give you the rest of your money when you get them safely into Vichy."

LeClerc seized DeSant's arm. DeSant struggled to hold on to the picture. Fernaud lunged forward to keep it from falling.

LeClerc stepped in front of DeSant, getting into his face. "Why must I wait for my money? I was told I would have it now. I am risking my life, not playing the Nazi whore, like you two." He moved his head to take in both of them. The corner of his mouth turned up as he looked from DeSant to Fernaud.

DeSant shrugged off LeClerc's hand with an angry gesture, looking directly into his eyes. "Now you are being the fool, Le-Clerc," he said, turning toward the door. "Get them to safety and you will have your money."

LeClerc looked down. He spat on the floor as the door closed behind Georges DeSant.

One

New York, 1998

George Desant was furious. The small, white-haired man sat bent over the papers on the breakfast table, slowly reading the report. His long, straight nose and thin face gave him an imperious look. The index finger of his left hand absently played with the corner of the typewritten page as if anxious to get on with it. Light flooded in through the large windows of his apartment, making his pink scalp shine through the precise part in his thin hair.

He muttered to himself as he turned the pages, making notes in the margin with his small gold pencil. A stab of sunlight caused him to squint his pale gray eyes. He got up painfully and crossed the room. He reached across and drew the curtains, closing off the view of Central Park.

DeSant had been upset for three weeks now. Since he had received the last bill from Parks & Ellwood. He was a meticulous man. Precise. Every time he'd spoken to that lawyer, Cunningham, he had made a little note in his calendar, in his small, precise, copperplate handwriting.

He was worried about the market, and he had been considering a reallocation of the trust assets again. But he also had become concerned about his legal fees. Something was wrong. DeSant had spoken to his accountant, who had referred him to Tumbler & Rose, a forensic accounting firm that specialized in analyzing lawyer's bills. He had made an appointment with Joseph Tumbler and delivered the Parks & Ellwood bills for the last year. He expressed his doubts to the young man, Tumbler, but he wasn't sure he had gotten his point across. He was never comfortable with strangers.

The accountant's draft report had arrived yesterday. DeSant had spent an hour skimming through it. Then he called Samuel Cunningham's office to make an appointment. Now he was reviewing the report again carefully to prepare for the meeting. His mouth was a thin line as he read the words before him.

Mid-October is usually pleasant in New York, but the hot weather had persisted unnaturally. It was already muggy when Sam Cunningham left his building on East 71st Street. Cunningham was short and overweight. He didn't like the heat. He always tried to dress well, but the sticky weather rumpled him and put him on edge.

It appeared that today would be hot again. The tympani roll of thunder in the distance suggested the possibility of some relief, although Cunningham wasn't inclined to be optimistic.

His shirt stuck to his back as he walked toward the subway. The sky was a tangible weight on his shoulders. He hated New York in the summer, but he hadn't been able to afford a summer house, even though Sandra had been pushing him for one. Cunningham had tried to explain what was happening at the firm, but she didn't want to listen.

Damn it, I'm doing my best, he thought as he battled the heat. He wiped beads of sweat away from his upper lip with his wrist.

Parks & Ellwood was a pillar of the New York bar. Both founders were past presidents of the Bar Association of the City of New York. And when they finally died, the firm had remained about the same. No lawyer ever moved to another firm back then. Not unless he was fired.

Somehow, in the '80s, things changed. Maybe it was the legal recruiters. Maybe it was because law firms started to expand nationally and began to cherry-pick partners. Or maybe it was because the *American Lawyer* started to publish competitive information on all the law firms. Maybe it was just the way the kids who came into the firm had been brought up. But all of a sudden, the good ones wanted it all, now, or they would move to the hot new firm across town that would give it to them.

He had to step aside to avoid a woman with a tiny dog on a leash.

"This is a business, not just a profession," they said. "Unless we raise the firm's profits, the firm is going to be vulnerable," they said. "Even more than that, we need to attract good people, or the firm won't survive in the long run."

Of course, everything they said was in their own best interest too. Thinking back on it, Cunningham realized it was all inevitable. It was the perfect example of Gresham's law. Bad currency always drives out the good.

Competition had raised associate salaries. The small businesses that were the core of Parks & Ellwood's practice fiercely fought every fee increase. The firm had pushed a few through, but it left them skittish about raising fees, and the partners' profits were dropping. Naturally, everyone had started looking around for "deadwood." Cunningham hated that term, "deadwood." He was a good lawyer.

"No, I'm a damned good lawyer," he said aloud. Several people on the street turned to look at him. *That's all the firm expected of me and that's what I am*, he resumed musing silently. He still had two blocks to go to the subway station. He struggled with the weight of his scuffed brown briefcase and shifted hands. He fiddled with his grip to get it more comfortable in his sweaty palm. *It's just wrong to change the rules in the middle of the game, isn't it?*

The management committee had already had two meetings with him. They called it constructive criticism. Sure. After the first one, they'd cut his compensation by 15 percent. Why wasn't he meeting his billing goals? Well, they had raised the billing goals to an impossible level. Why wasn't he out developing business? The average partner was now originating $1.5 million a year in fees, they said. He had tried to explain the estate planning practice to them, but they'd told him it was his problem.

The last meeting was a week ago. It had been bad. The chairman of the firm had suggested that he step down from his partnership at the end of the year. Or else. Effectively, he had been fired. Where could he get another job at 61? He told them that, but it didn't make any difference. And his call to a lawyer friend over at Shaikawitz, Rosenblatt & Howe had been discouraging. The age discrimination rules, it seemed, didn't apply to partners, only to employees.

Well, thank God for the DeSant trust. He had been the trustee for several years now. The fees last year had been $250,000. He would get them up to at least $400,000 this year. It would be tough, but he would do it. It was a good thing he got along with old DeSant. He could be prickly, with his stiff manner and reserved demeanor.

I wonder why he wants to come and see me today? Cunningham mused as he reached his subway station. The air was cooler as he descended into the darkening underground. *It's not time for our annual review of the trust. I should make it a point to ask him to dinner.*

"Mr. DeSant, how nice to see you," Sam Cunningham said, sticking out his hand. "Please sit down." Cunningham gestured toward a client chair as he made his way around his desk.

Those pale gray eyes always seemed to look through him. They made him uncomfortable. Cunningham couldn't imagine how DeSant looked so fresh in his starched, high-collared shirt and his blue bow tie. He felt wilted. Perhaps it was because DeSant was so small and thin. Maybe the heat didn't affect him in the same way.

He smiled at DeSant. It was an effort. "Can I get you some coffee or a cold drink? This weather is just awful, isn't it?"

DeSant waved away the offer with a small, curt gesture. Something in his posture made Cunningham uneasy.

"How can I be of help to you, Mr. DeSant? Is there a problem with any of the investments?"

DeSant opened a small leather portfolio he held across his knees and placed a document carefully on Cunningham's desk. He closed the portfolio and pushed the document across, looking straight at Cunningham.

"Mr. Cunningham, Parks & Ellwood has been cheating me."

Cunningham opened his mouth, but nothing came out.

"I have this report from an accounting firm," DeSant said, pointing at the document. "They believe you have billed the trust for unnecessary work and concluded you have billed for more time than you could have spent. There are also discrepancies in the time charges in the discussions we have had."

"Mr. DeSant, please. There must be some mistake. May I look over the report? I need to review our time records. Perhaps there was an error. I will speak to the accountants."

"I brought this copy for you, Mr. Cunningham. I am told it will be thirty days before I receive a final report." His voice was soft and cold. "I will not undertake any steps until then. But I will not tolerate disloyalty in those who serve me. Nor will I tolerate dishonesty."

It took Cunningham a moment to recover. "I'm—I'm sure there must be some error. Let me read the report, Mr. DeSant, and believe me, we will work this out. I'll call you."

"Yes, do, Mr. Cunningham." DeSant rose. "Please do." He walked out, leaving Cunningham sitting at his desk.

My God, Cunningham thought. His hands balled into fists. *I can't let this happen. I just can't.*

Three

The windows shook in the grip of a good old, full-blown Nor'easter. The rattle of the shutters woke him. Jonathan Benjamin Franklin peered over the top of his covers. At least the storm had broken the oppressive heat that had been hanging on for days. The temperature must have dropped 30 degrees overnight. He quickly settled back in, lulled into sleep by the slapping rain.

He awoke later with the spreading sense of a firm female body pressed against him. His fondness for young women might have been considered a small failing by some, but it wasn't one that endeared him to the wives of his Harvard Law School colleagues.

Besides, it was a mystery to them why pretty young women would be attracted to a middle-aged man, on the short side, a little overweight, nearsighted and losing his hair. The only exceptional feature in his otherwise ordinary face was that when he smiled, he smiled all the way to his hazel eyes. Actually, it was a mystery to Jonathan too.

"My God, Jon, what have you done?" a female voice said. "It must be 20 below in here. I'm frozen."

"Sorry, boiler must be out. You know these old houses. Anything I can do to warm you up? You already have the top of my pajamas." He lightly put his hand on her soft, firm belly. They worked that out in the most logical manner for the next half-hour.

* * *

Jonathan loved trees. Lush green, exploding with color, bare or budding, they gave him joy. Maybe it was spending so many years in a high corner office in the naked, concrete canyons of Wall Street, but he truly loved them. So when he returned to the law school to teach, he chose to live, not in Cambridge, but in a more rural place.

He had turned 47, and with his working lawyer's scars and the small fortune he had accumulated as the head of mergers and acquisitions at Whiting & Pierce, he had purchased the two-story clapboard colonial house in Concord. He loved it. Built around the early 1800s, it still had seven acres of good land, its own pond and a small copse of mixed birch and elm. His heart responded to the sense of history here, and he loved furnishing it and making it his own. But he quickly learned that a rich sense of history was expensive.

He'd have to call Harry the plumber again. Harry was the best and the busiest Yankee plumber in Concord. It was a good thing that Harry hadn't gone into law instead of plumbing, or Jonathan figured he would have had to retire with a lot less money. As it was, Harry was coming on strong in the field of wealth redistribution.

After he got Harry lined up for the weekend repairs on his woebegone boiler, naturally at double time, Jonathan turned to his young guest. "I make a wicked eggs Florentine. Can I interest you in some?"

"That would be cool," she replied.

Cindy was a gorgeous young woman of 26, slender and statuesque, a delight to the eyes and other senses. But Jonathan was feeling the burden of a discussion that was definitely one-sided. Clearly, the art of discourse was no longer required study at Smith College. He had hoped for better when he first saw her.

"Did you enjoy dinner last night?" Jonathan ventured.

"Sure, it was a terrific restaurant. I saw it written up in the paper."

"I thought the '82 Latour set off the beef perfectly, although I found it a little surprising."

"Was that the red wine?" she asked.

"Yes, the red." Silence and mere beauty would have to suffice.

He had read somewhere that women were "creatures of mystery, unknowable, like cats." But that didn't stop him from adoring them, if one could call a girl of 26 by such a name. Jonathan had become a firm adherent of Franklin's First Law of Relationships: "The first six times you sleep with a woman, it's fun. Then you have to start dealing with them as people."

Jonathan was short of people.

Four

Harvard Law School is on a sweeping bend of Mass. Avenue, where it is joined by Boylston Street, one of its major tributaries. Beside the flowing traffic, the law school spreads out like a great, deep estuary of egos and ideas.

Jonathan was passionate about the law school. Its history and tradition struck a resonant note deep inside him, stirring a sense of continuity and belonging. He loved being identified with Harvard.

The college was founded in 1636. It had been named after a Charlestown minister, John Harvard, its first benefactor, who left the school his library, worth around $150. One of the better deals for naming rights ever made. The Dutch paid less for Manhattan, but they didn't get naming rights.

Jonathan loved the little bronze plaque on the tree across the street in Cambridge Commons that announced, "This is the tree where George Washington tied his horse while accepting command of the Continental Army." That spot did seem a bit greener than the rest.

The college had gotten around to founding the law school some two centuries later. More than one of his clients had questioned whether that had been a good idea.

He pulled his yellow Porsche 356 Cabriolet into his reserved space, grabbed his umbrella and ran for Langdell Hall. The lovingly restored Porsche had been his gift to himself when he took the new job.

He was anxious to talk to Dean Cohen about an idea for a new business transactions class he wanted to develop for the joint JD/MBA program next fall. He also wanted to put in a few hours of work on the paper he had agreed to deliver in November at the London School of Economics on "The Macro Economic Effects of Highly Leveraged Merger Transactions." Besides expenses and the small honorarium, there would be three glorious days in London.

The meeting with Ben Cohen had gone well. It looked like the new class might be a go. Jonathan had been back in his little office for almost an hour. He was pleased with the progress he was making on his paper when his stomach reminded him it was lunch time.

As Jonathan walked up the ramp at Harkness Commons, the law school cafeteria, he caught a glimpse of himself in the glass panels from the corner of his eye. Man, he thought, sucking in his gut, I'm getting a potbelly. I'd better get my ass in gear and start working out again.

Randy Tilling, his classmate and a professor of constitutional law, waved Jonathan over to his table. Tilling had achieved prominence from his books and articles. He was regarded as a distinguished constitutional scholar among a group thoroughly capable of distinguishing. His problem was that he knew it. Very well.

Jonathan put his tray on the table beside Tilling's. He was facing the north wall in the high-ceilinged room that the huge windows filled with light, even through the gloomy drizzle outside. Jonathan had a sudden recollection. He shook his head and laughed.

"What?" Tilling said, looking up.

Jonathan pointed at the wall. "You know, I was in my third year of law school before I figured out that the bunch of blue tiles glued to the wall over there was an original Miro. I probably would never have figured it out if I hadn't finally seen the signature. I can't believe how dense I was back then. Probably still am."

"You've been here now, what, a year?" Tilling asked. He put down his fork.

Jonathan looked up from cutting his veal parmigiana. "A little more."

"Do you really like teaching business law?"

"It's not business law. It's business transactions. They're different." He said it a little acerbically. He didn't like the direction the conversation had taken.

"Whatever," Tilling said.

"I love it. Why?"

"I don't know," Tilling replied. "I never really found business that interesting." Tilling resumed digging at his salad.

"You're missing something, Randy. Maybe you should give it a try." Tilling raised his eyes. His face looked as if he had bitten into a sour lemon. "I like the psychology of deal-making," Jonathan continued. "And I like to see how businesses operate, how they actually make money."

Tilling shrugged. He looked down, focusing again, unenthusiastically, on his salad. He seemed to have lost his taste for it. Or the company.

What an asshole, Jonathan thought. "If there's anything I miss here at the law school, it's the high I used to get from making a deal," he said. Maybe he was pressing it a little more than necessary. "I never liked to see money wandering around aimlessly."

By the time Jonathan left the law school, it was the late afternoon of a beautiful fall day. He was still muttering to himself about what an asshole Randy Tilling could be. The rain had finally stopped. He put the top down on the Porsche to enjoy it on the drive home. The clouds were chasing each other across the sky like children.

He reached the front door of his house just in time to hear the telephone ring. Fumbling with his keys, he grabbed at the phone before the answering machine could kick in.

"Mr. Franklin, I have Simon Aaron calling from London. Would this be a convenient time?"

His chest tightened. The memories came flooding in.

Five

It seemed such a long time ago, not just a year, since Jonathan and Simon Aaron had spoken. The thought of Simon Aaron brought it all back.

Harvard Law School '74, editor of the *Harvard Law Review*, law clerk to Mr. Justice Rehnquist. Jonathan Benjamin Franklin was a *wunderkind* to everyone but himself. He had joined Whiting & Pierce in 1976 and became its youngest partner nine years later. Somehow, he had become 46.

Whiting & Pierce was the most respected and the "whitest" of the white shoe law firms on Wall Street. In Boston, the Lowells spoke only to God. For Whiting & Pierce, it was a local call. But even Whiting & Pierce had clients.

Simon Aaron's last call had definitely been long distance. "Simon, damn it, I'm trying!" Jonathan said. He pushed his glasses up onto his forehead and closed his eyes. His mouth was a straight line, and his lips were white from the pressure.

"I don't care about trying. Get it done."

Simon Aaron was being even more difficult than usual—if that was possible. He was Jonathan's most important client. Jonathan squeezed the bridge of his nose between his fingers.

"For God's sake, Simon, don't shout at me. I know you want the deal closed," Jonathan said. His voice was tinged with the weariness of weeks of unrelenting strain. "But I can't get the letter we need out of Sanford's accountants. The banks won't close without it."

"Quit giving me excuses. I'm paying you to get results."

The deal was for the acquisition of Sanford's, the large English biscuit and confections company, and it had already taken eight months out of his life.

"I'm pressing them as hard as I can. I've been on the phone at four a.m. every day this week."

"Are you completely incompetent? Do I have to fire you and get someone who can do the job?"

It was the worst possible time to be dealing with this, just as Jonathan was trying to cope with his father's death after a brief but difficult illness.

"Simon, you're being unreasonable. I'm doing everything I. . ."

He heard the phone slam down in his ear. Jonathan put his head down in his hands and took a long, deep breath.

Two months later, he rang up the firm's managing partner, Wilton McKesson, to ask for a few minutes of his time.

"Jonathan, good to see you. Sit down." McKesson smiled his famous smile and leaned back in his deep Moroccan red leather desk chair. He raised his open hand towards Jonathan. "It seems like weeks go by and we don't even get a chance to say hello. My God, we're on the same floor." Jonathan's fingers worked the cherry wood arms of the client chair. This wasn't where he wanted to go. "We need to have lunch soon. The executive committee was pleased with the Sanford's deal. You did a great job."

"Thanks, Mac, but I've got bad news." Jonathan blurted it out. He rubbed his hands together nervously. "I'm leaving the firm." There, he'd done it. He couldn't go back.

"You're what?" McKesson came forward in his chair with a thunk. His face sank into a mask. His manicured hands gripped the edge of his desk. "What the hell's going on? No one leaves Whiting & Pierce. Certainly not on his own. Are you completely out of your mind? How can you walk away from a million dollars a year?"

Jonathan's mind flashed back to his father. When Jonathan had asked him why he worked so hard. Why he couldn't spend more time with him. He remembered the pain in his father's eyes, his open hands spread in front of him—"I wish I could, Jonathan. But I have to earn a living for us. It's all or nothing. You have to choose." He hadn't understood then.

"Mac, I know. But I'm burned out."

"Is it the money? Do you want more money? I'll speak to the executive committee."

"Mac, it's not about money."

"Is it time off? Go away for a few weeks." McKesson's voice hardened. "If you leave, you know we can't take you back."

Jonathan tightened his resolve. "I know that. This is the most terrifying thing I've ever done. This job is who I've always been. But I'm 46 and I feel empty."

McKesson softened a little. "Look, Jonathan, take a couple of days and reconsider. You're part of us. The firm will do whatever it takes."

"I've been offered a teaching position in the fall at my old law school, and I'm going to take it. This is really tough for me, Mac." Jonathan blinked back tears.

McKesson's voice turned cold again. "So it's final then? There's nothing we can do to change your mind?"

"No, Mac, nothing."

"Maybe it's best, then, if you leave quickly. Can you clear out your office by Monday?" McKesson had already turned back to the papers on his desk.

Jonathan sat still. "If that's what you want."

As Jonathan got up, McKesson's phone rang. McKesson looked up at Jonathan without expression as he picked up the phone.

"Mr. Ghitterman for you, Mr. McKesson."

"Allan, how are you?" McKesson said into the phone. His client voice. "Can you hold on for one second?" He held the phone to his chest. His voice was flat again. "Oh, and drop off your key with my secretary when you leave. Good luck."

The reality of what he had done slammed into Jonathan like an errant baseball. He was out.

Six

"Jonathan, is that you? It's Simon." The deep voice startled him out of his reverie. "Where the blazes are you? I've had my secretary tracking you down the last two days. I need you to come to London right away."

"How in Christ's name did you get my unlisted telephone number?" Jonathan pushed the front door closed with his toe. "Why are you calling me at home on Saturday afternoon? I'm not coming to London to meet you. No way."

In the world of corporate finance, Simon Aaron was a serious player. In the sanctum sanctorum of many corporate boardrooms, his name had the social grace of breaking wind. He inspired real fear. In the half-dozen or so deals Jonathan had represented him in, he had made more or less a billion dollars. And a lot of enemies. He ruthlessly weeded out deadwood, sold the private jets, auctioned off the art collections, and focused attention on the bottom line. And nothing so focuses the mind of a comfortable corporate titan as the potential loss of his power, not to mention his stock options.

Jonathan had his own scars to show what a martinet Simon Aaron could be. On the other hand, Simon could as easily be just a round, affable and generous little Jewish guy who happened to have a billion dollars.

"Simon, you know I gave up practice. Why are you calling me?" Jonathan was wary.

"Calm down. When I heard you'd gone off somewhere to teach, I just couldn't believe it. You were the smartest lawyer I had. Did I ever mention that? Look, I really need you. I've got a situation here, and I'm sinking fast."

"I've got classes to teach. I have my own commitments."

"Please, just listen to me for a minute." This was definitely not classic Simon Aaron. An urgency in his voice caught Jonathan's attention. "Witten's is in serious trouble."

Witten's was the auction house Jonathan had helped Simon acquire some nine years earlier in an ugly fight with United Worldwide that became personal to both Simon and Vincent Rollins, the controlling shareholder of United.

"The Japanese art market has collapsed," Simon said. "We have serious bad debts, and our subordinated bonds come due early next year. And after the Sanford's acquisition, my liquidity is zilch. I haven't been able to turn Sanford's around yet. The Witten's stock is in the crapper, and Vincent Rollins has been making noises about our financial condition. I've been hearing rumors that some of our banks have been approached with an offer to buy up our loans. I'm in real trouble. I need you."

Vincent Rollins was a man totally driven by ambition. Jonathan had met him several times on a social basis, and the feeling he got about him wasn't good. Rollins wasn't a nice man, not even sometimes.

"Jonathan, I'm asking you. As a personal favor. Please. Come to London. Give me a hand. You're the only one I trust. Those Harvard fellows like Tilling take cases on the side, don't they? Take me on. I know money isn't important to you." *Like hell*, Jonathan thought. "But I'll make it worth your while. Please think about it. Come see me."

Jonathan was intrigued. The curl of the wave was beckoning. "Simon, let me sleep on it. I'll let you know tomorrow."

But Jonathan already knew.

Seven

Sunday was a working day, and Jonathan bounded out of bed. After dispatching Valerie, a lovely, red-headed, 28-year-old model, clutching her makeup bag to her chest and muttering about the early hour, he set off for the law school, thinking about the call from Simon Aaron.

He stepped gingerly across his small office, which spilled over with stacks of magazines, newspapers and *Law Review* articles, some of which showed the sad effects of old age. Jonathan had always agreed with Carl Jung that a messy desk was the mark of a creative mind.

A young man in torn jeans and a dirty tee shirt covered by an open flannel shirt tapped on the open door.

"Hey, Tim," Jonathan greeted the law student, who was his research assistant. The dress code had deteriorated since his own student days. "How have the interviews been going?"

"Oh, fine, Professor Franklin." It still gave Jonathan a kick to be called "Professor Franklin." "I have call-backs from Paul Hastings and Skadden in Los Angeles and Brobeck in San Francisco. I'll be going out for interviews in a couple of weeks. Is that okay?"

"Sure," said Jonathan, shedding his sweater onto his only guest chair, already piled high with papers. His sweater clung desperately to the mess. "I'll be in London, so it works out great. What are the firms paying nowadays?"

"Oh, it's pretty good. Around 140."

"Thousand?" Jonathan said, more loudly than he intended.

"Yeah, Greedy Associates.com—you know, the law firm associates website everybody looks at—says that's pretty top end, which is okay, I guess. But the associates seem to have a lot of gripes about all the pressure."

Jonathan lost interest and turned to his own project. He picked up his London School of Economics presentation and held it out. "Tim, first I need you to finish up the sub-cite check on my talk. Read all my footnotes and check the sources. Make sure you agree with all my citations."

The warbling calls of law school students tossing around a football came through the open window. Jonathan ignored it. "Then come back to me. I need you to get into the SEC online files and check out the latest 10-K, 10-Q and all the recent 8-Ks on United Worldwide. Pull any loan agreements, and I want to see the latest 10-Q balance sheet, the full 10-K with all of the exhibits, and any unusual 8-K announcements. You know what all those are?"

"Oh yeah, we reviewed them in my securities law class. The annual and quarterly reports and material announcements that public companies have to file, right? Including the financial info. All the dirt, too. Pretty cool."

"After that," Jonathan continued, loosening his tie and fiddling with the top button of his blue button-down shirt, "run United Worldwide and Vincent Rollins through the SEC files and all the Internet services for the last six years and do an online litigation search on them. I think that the Southern District of New York and the Central District of California should do it. Oh, and do Delaware too. I want to know what companies Rollins owns or has a major interest in, and any unusual information that pops up. I figure that should keep you busy for at least a while."

"Like the rest of my life."

"Okay, then, see you later."

Jonathan settled back in his creaky wooden desk chair and put his feet up on his desk, knocking over a stack of old law reviews and stirring up a puff of dust. He looked at his scuffed loafers. *Better get my shoes polished*, he thought, ignoring the magazines tumbled onto the floor. His mind quickly wandered away from his beat-up shoes.

He adjusted his glasses and closed his eyes, settling down to think some more about Simon Aaron's call. He already knew he wanted in. It would be the most fun he had had standing up in the last year. When real chips were on the table, the game was different. No matter what Randy Tilling thought. He scratched an itch on the side of his nose. Strangely enough, for all the pain Simon Aaron had caused him, he actually was fond of the man. It came as a surprise.

Jonathan reached Simon Aaron in his London flat about ten p.m. London time.

"Okay, Simon, here's the drill. I'll give you a hand on this problem, but I'm your strategic adviser. I'm not your lawyer and I'm certainly not your employee. No—hear me out.

"My fees are $1,000 an hour, with 50 percent more as a success bonus. I get a $50,000 non-refundable retainer in front. First-class air travel, and I stay at Claridge's. Oh, plus out-of-pocket costs. No—don't interrupt." He loved doing this.

"Any of your usual asshole behavior, any shouting, any unpleasantness, you get one warning, then you're toast. Okay, now you can talk."

"Jonathan, I thought we were friends." Simon chuckled. "You know I'm just a poor Jewish boy trying to scrape a living out of the dust bowl of life. Why, I'm practically a charity case."

"Oh, let me assure you, we are friends. And did you know my mother was Jewish?"

"No."

"That's why I'm giving you my pro bono rate." Jonathan paused for a beat. "Are you in or out?"

Aaron sounded as cheerful as a boy who had just copped his first feel. "It's good to see you haven't lost your edge. Welcome aboard."

"Great. I'll send you a confirming memo. Simon, I need to do a week or so of intensive research and some thinking. Then I need to see your investment bankers. You need to be there. Who are you using?"

"Aspen & Leach. Henry Kent. Do you know him?"

"Oh, shit, do I know him. That arrogant bastard. He thinks of himself as some kind of samurai warlord and the rest of us as his peasants. Why are you using that schmuck?"

"I know he's a pain in the ass, but they have great resources at Aspen & Leach, and I may need their money. Anyway, don't worry about Kent. You speak for me."

"Okay," Jonathan said. "Let's set a meeting in New York for —let me see—" He reached into his pocket and flipped open his calendar. "—how about the afternoon of Tuesday, November 10th." His words were quick and staccato. "You and I'll have lunch beforehand. Once we have some kind of strategy worked out with the investment bankers, I'll need to go to London. I want to get a feel for Witten's and see how it operates. I need to be there anyway to present a paper at the London School of Economics."

"So I won't have to pay the air fare?"

"Wrong, Simon. Nice try." Jonathan laughed. "How do we arrange London?"

"Hold on for a second. Let me get someone on the phone."

Jonathan waited as the line went dead for a few moments, and then Simon Aaron came back on. "Jonathan, I have one of my key people on the line. Someone I trust. She's been with me a long time.

"Jonathan Franklin, Nicole DeSant."

Eight

Nicole DeSant struggled out of her wet raincoat. Beastly weather.

"Damn Simon," she shouted to the empty flat. Her gray eyes flashed. She slammed her briefcase onto the couch and crossed through her dining room into the kitchen, kicking off her shoes as she went. One bounced off the pastel-colored wall, leaving a dark mark on the baseboard. "Shit," she shouted.

She opened the door to a small built-in wine cooler and uncorked a bottle of '90 Chambertin, tasted it, then poured some. She swirled the red wine around the deep crystal glass, sniffing the intense aroma as she padded back into the living room and flopped into a large chair, making her short dark hair bounce. She shook her head sharply to make it fall back into place. Then she raised the glass to her lips and took a sip.

"Damn Simon!" she said again over the lip of the raised glass. Her breath fogged the edge of the crystal. Why had he brought in that lawyer?

She remembered the man vaguely from some nine years ago at the closing dinner for the Witten's deal. She couldn't recall anything special about him. *Why him? Is Simon trying to push me aside?*

She wasn't going to let that happen. She deserved the managing directorship of Witten's he had promised her. *I've earned it, damn it.*

Why couldn't he just let go? Every time she tried to discuss it with him, he changed the subject or he snapped at her. Now this!

She needed information. She had to protect herself. She took another sip of wine, deep in thought. Then she slapped her hand on the arm of the chair. The movement sloshed a bit of red wine onto the carpet. She didn't notice. She got up and padded into her den, picked up the telephone and dialed an overseas number. The phone rang twice before Henri DeSant answered.

"Henri, it is Nicole. *Bon soir.*"

"Ah, Nicole. I was about to call you. Witten's stock fell again today. My advisors tell me that its subordinated debentures are selling at a further discount as well. I believe that this is the moment to go forward if we choose to do so."

"Yes, I believe we should. Simon is overextended, but Witten's is fundamentally sound. It appears to me these troubles will pass." She raised the wine glass to her lips and sipped.

"Nicole, are you not feeling well?" It must have been something in her voice.

"I am fine. It has been a difficult day."

"I am glad you are well. So you think we should proceed?"

"Yes, Henri. The real estate is very valuable, as is the goodwill. But perhaps we should consider buying the debentures as well as the common stock."

"That would be wise. We will be well-positioned no matter what happens. I will discuss this with your father."

"Please give him my love. Tell him I will call him soon. Thank you for this, Henri."

"*Mais non, cherie.* I believe this is a good investment, as does your father. *Au revoir* for now."

She put down the phone and sat in the den for several minutes, thinking and sipping her wine. If only Simon hadn't become so reticent. It just wasn't like him. She suddenly felt very tired. Her emotions seemed to drain all the energy out of her. It would be an early night.

She had been in bed reading for some twenty minutes when the phone rang. She ignored it.

The answering machine clicked in. The voice came faintly from the other room. "Nicole, this is Vincent Rollins. We need to pursue our discussions. Call me."

Nine

Pasquale Bastien's day, his week, his whole year picked up when he turned to page four of Sunday's *International Herald Tribune*. A thin smile creased his hollow face. Calculation brightened his green eyes. Bastien was an old man with a grudge, nurtured and matured over many years. Against the world, against the Nazis, against the Germans, the French, whomever. He reached over and turned off the radio. He needed to think.

Life had not been fair to Pasquale Bastien. He'd had to scratch and scrape a living in the low end of the jewelry trade. And London was not a city to be appreciated on a scratch-and-scrape income.

His life wasn't supposed to be that way. His uncle, Emil Rosenberg, his mother's brother, had been rich. Very rich. Uncle Emil had always told his mother that he would take care of the boy.

The memories of those early years in Paris—his uncle's wonderful chateau outside the city, its fountains and its statues, the smell of its lovely manicured gardens—were a glimpse of luxury for a little boy. And the painting that had dominated his uncle's drawing room. Even to a small boy it was breathtaking. The respectful servants. It made him feel special, not just the son of a small-town baker.

Then the war came. His mother and father fled with him to London before the Nazis occupied Paris. They inquired about the Rosenbergs. Finally they heard that his uncle and his family had been killed in Vichy, trying to escape.

And the dream was gone. Bastien was just the son of a baker again, when he should have been so much more. No education, no fine home. No income to indulge himself.

All that would change now. There on page four was a description of four paintings that had been recovered in Germany. He would know the Matisse anywhere. He had spent hours playing beneath that picture, and years since then thinking about it. Bastien rubbed his hands together as he surveyed his shabby living room.

What he needed now was to talk to a solicitor. There was that fellow he had met last year at a party. He tapped on his lips with the edge of his fist. Why couldn't he remember? He'd talked to him for a long time. Rather loud voice. He could picture him. Bit of a twit. Couldn't stop telling Bastien how important he was. Had offices in Chancery Lane somewhere. Something like Marks, or Marker. Maybe Markham. No, that wasn't it. Marking, yes, Marking. Theodore Marking. Maybe I can get him to advise me without a fee, Bastien thought.

Things had been slow for Teddy Marking for the last six months. Teddy wasn't at the top of his trade, but the last six months had been worse than usual. It was eleven on Monday morning and he was sitting in his office, chewing on his cold cigar, wondering how he was going to pay the rent again this month, not to mention the bills that were piling up in his top right hand desk drawer. It was a good thing he had let his secretary go last month.

The telephone rang. It was his first call of the day. "Offices of Theodore Marking," he answered. "Yes, Mr. Bastien, this is Theodore Marking. My secretary stepped out. Of course I remember you," he lied. "Yes, I can see you sometime this afternoon. Four p.m.? Let me check my calendar." A pause. "Yes, I can be free then. Let me give you directions to my office."

The story was intriguing. And this chap Bastien was so intent on not paying any fees out of his own pocket that he had agreed straight off to a 25% contingency fee on the value of everything he realized and had already signed the retaining letter. It was a long shot, but probably not that much work. And if that Matisse was the right one, it could be a multimillion-dollar fee. Well worth the risk, Marking thought, particularly since he had precious little else to do.

Bastien sat across from Marking in the old oak client chair, his little eyes fixed on him. "So, Mr. Bastien, what I need is for you to tell me everything you know about this painting. I need a photograph of it in your uncle's house, if you have one somewhere. That would help a great deal. And can you show that you are Emil Rosenberg's only surviving heir? Good. And are you sure there was no will? Yes. Brilliant."

He didn't much like the look of Bastien. There was something shifty about his eyes, but you took your clients as they came. At least if you were Teddy Marking.

"We're going to need an expert, Mr. Bastien, to identify the Matisse and verify that it is the one your uncle owned. I know some important chaps over at Witten's. Perhaps I can check with them to see if they can take us on. And if they'll consider deferring their fees under the circumstances." *I'm not going to front the money*, he thought. *And this chap certainly won't.* "Perhaps they'll cooperate if you'll agree to let them sell the painting when we get it back. I read somewhere that one of their fellows is interested in recovering looted art. Maybe this will appeal."

Marking ushered Bastien out of his office with a light but firm hand on his back and a handshake at the door. "Don't worry, Mr. Bastien, I'll get this sorted out. Leave it with me."

Then he went back to his desk and dug his cigar out of the side drawer where he had dumped it and popped it back into his mouth. He reached for the phone to call his old solicitor friend Albert Jerome.

"Al, you have that chum at Witten's, what's his name? I may have something for him. Good. Vetch. Right. Got his phone number? Brilliant. Cheers."

He dialed the number. "Mr. Vetch, my name is Theodore Marking. I'm a solicitor, and I have a client who believes he is the rightful owner of a very important piece of art that may have been just recovered in Germany. A Matisse. Correct, the one mentioned in the *Herald Tribune* yesterday. I'd like to meet with you to discuss engaging your services as an expert and perhaps to sell the painting once we acquire it.

"Of course," Marking continued in response to Vetch's answer, "I understand you will need to consult with your head. Who is that, please? Ah, Monsieur Fernaud. Can you spell that for me? Yes. Perhaps you can speak to Mr.—oh, sorry—*Monsieur* Fernaud, and get back to me. Yes, I'll leave it to you. Many thanks. Brilliant."

Marking was surprised when his telephone rang an hour later.

"Mr. Marking, this is Jean-Claude Fernaud." The voice was accented and dignified. "I am the head of Impressionist art at Witten's. I understand you have a client who claims to be the owner of the Matisse piece that has just been recovered in Germany. I would be very interested in meeting with you. May I suggest tomorrow? Fine. At my office then."

Marking thumped his desktop. If the head of Witten's had called back that fast to personally set up a meeting, he had been right. That Matisse was worth a lot of money.

Jean-Claude Fernaud put down the phone and flexed his hand where he had been tightly gripping the receiver. The arthritis in his gnarled fingers was acting up. He grimaced as he stretched out his hand and tried to shake away the pain. How very appropriate that this should also be such a reminder of the Nazis.

Marking's client could become important to his plans. He had also recognized the Matisse from its description in the *Herald*

Tribune. It was the picture that Georges DeSant had passed on to the Nazis. If this man's client was really the heir of Emil Rosenberg, the last thing he wanted was for this lawyer to be poking around to find out how the Nazis had gotten that picture. He certainly didn't want anyone to think that Jean-Claude Fernaud was a collaborator. And it would be worse if that lawyer found out about Georges DeSant. Far worse.

Ten

Jean-Claude Fernaud instinctively disliked the untidy, balding man sitting across from him, whose stubby fingers were still holding the cold stub of a cigar that Fernaud had insisted he put out when he entered his office. Fernaud could still smell the cigar smoke on his clothes. Heathen. One did not usually have to stoop to such a level in his work. But now it was necessary. Theodore Marking brushed away at the streaks of cigar ash on his vest as Fernaud gathered himself.

"Mr. Marking, the question you present is not as simple as one would like." Marking looked up from his tidying. "I do understand the desire of Monsieur Bastien to once again possess so important a part of his past. But it will not be easy."

"Mr.—excuse me—*Monsieur* Fernaud," which Marking pronounced in a manner that made Fernaud wince, "Mr. Bastien might consider selling the painting when it is recovered. It's something I wanted to talk to you about."

"So be it, Mr. Marking, but nonetheless, we should explore the problems. There are many issues of law. I have become something of an expert on these matters, although I am not a lawyer." He reflexively stretched out the fingers of his left hand to ease the pain.

Fernaud reached for the thin teacup on his desk and wrapped his hand gently around the steaming cup. The warmth eased the pain a little. Then he shifted his grip to take the handle of the cup and took a delicate sip. He spoke to Marking over the cup. A small gesture of disdain. The man was too boorish to notice. He paused to concentrate around the pain. It had been getting worse lately.

"This has become much more important recently. Once again, since the fall of the Iron Curtain, many looted works of art are being discovered. But this can be a most difficult and expensive legal task."

Marking frowned, as Fernaud had expected. "Please, tell me more," Marking responded.

"Are you sure that Mr. Bastien is the sole heir? It is obvious that he must have the right to the picture."

"He tells me he is. I need to check further." Naturally, the man was a clod.

"Of course. And can you be sure that this picture—you said it was a Matisse, I believe—was owned by Mr. Bastien's predecessor, what was his name?" It was best to seem to know little.

"Rosenberg, Emil Rosenberg," said Marking.

"You must be sure that the picture is the one owned by Monsieur Rosenberg. There are several Matisse paintings that could be described in much the same way. And a great deal of art was sold by people needing to raise cash at that time. Unless you can show the art was actually stolen by the Nazis, the French government will claim the painting." Fernaud took another sip of tea and put down the cup.

"Even if the painting was stolen, you may have an issue in having the piece brought here. The French are very protective of what they see as their national treasures. That, of course, may affect its value." He spread his gnarled hands. "And these are only the basic problems."

Marking blinked his eyes as if bothered by the sunlight. "Perhaps I should get some assistance," he said. Marking's stubby hands fidgeted as he spoke, the forgotten cigar stub still between his fingers.

That was not what Fernaud had hoped to hear. He certainly didn't want another lawyer involved. Perhaps a brighter one. He needed to reassure him.

"Mr. Marking, of course you may find that necessary, but I may be able to assist you. This is something that is of importance to me."

"I'd like that." Marking talked eagerly. "But Pasquale Bastien hasn't got any money, and I couldn't afford to pay you out of my pocket." He spoke in a quick voice that Fernaud found grating. "I asked Mr. Bastien if he'd let Witten's sell the picture once we recovered it. Could you, maybe, defer your consulting fees until then?"

Fernaud nodded. "It is certainly something I think we can consider. Perhaps we should talk further once you have consulted again with Mr. Bastien and established his position and the ownership of the piece. I would not advise you to rush into a lawsuit until you have established these basic facts. I, perhaps, can help you trace the provenance of the painting once you can prove Monsieur Rosenberg owned it and Mr. Bastien is his heir. Please feel free to call me when you have sufficient proof of these matters."

"Thank you," Marking said. "I'll keep you informed."

Fernaud spoke as he rose from his chair. "And thank you for coming in, Mr. Marking. We will talk further."

"I will not!" Theodore Marking was quite agitated. His voice was fluting with anger. He was sitting forward behind his old oak desk, the phone gripped so tightly in his hand his fingers were white. Pasquale Bastien was on the other end.

"Absolutely not. I've spent a great deal of time and effort on your matter already, and I've even lined up Jean-Claude Fernaud at Witten's as our expert. You signed an agreement with me." *Damn right he did.* Cigar ash spilled down his shirt. He ignored it.

"This matter is far more complicated than you think, Mr. Bastien. This could take me years." He hoped not, not with the rent due. "I refuse to reduce my fee to 15%."

It had been six days since Marking had met with Fernaud. Marking thanked goodness he had had the foresight to send a letter to the Department of French National Museums and the French Interior Minister making Bastien's claim to the Matisse, no matter what Fernaud said. Besides, it wasn't like he had filed a lawsuit. He had been right not to trust Bastien.

"Well, go ahead," he responded to Bastien. "Report me to the Law Society. See how far it gets you."

Marking didn't want to be reported to the Law Society again. Those bloody fools never had to get their hands dirty with clients like Pasquale Bastien. Besides, how did Bastien know about the Law Society? Had he been speaking to some other solicitor? Marking wouldn't put it past him.

"Mr. Bastien, you do have the right to change solicitors whenever you wish." He tapped the cigar viciously against the edge of the ashtray. Disturbed smoke eddied upwards. "But you should know I intend to file a lien with any other solicitor you choose and compel compliance with our agreement for the work I've done. I've already advised you orally of my extensive research concerning your claim." No need to tell him his research consisted entirely of speaking to Jean-Claude Fernaud. He brushed at the smoke.

"I advise you that you should disclose our agreement to any other solicitor you approach. No solicitor may be willing to take your case under the circumstances." Probably not true, knowing what he knew of his comrades at the bar.

"And until we resolve this," Marking said, "I will not be able to proceed. You've cast doubt on our relationship. I will send you a letter so that we will be quite clear on that. But I should tell you that I believe time is of the essence with respect to your claim." Maybe he could push him.

It never hurt to put pressure on a recalcitrant client, in Marking's experience. He ground out his cigar with a stabbing, twisting motion. The wet end added to the brown stain on his fingers.

"I've told you what information I need from you to proceed," Marking concluded. "If you want to go forward on the basis of our agreement, please advise me. Until then, I will do nothing further. Goodbye, Mr. Bastien."

Marking banged down the receiver. "Greedy little bastard," Marking said out loud.

Eleven

Lunch with Simon Aaron was always a matter of extremes. Sometimes a palatial feast, often a quick hot dog grabbed on the run. Today was Côte Basque, one of the best restaurants in New York, and the food was subtle and savory. Jonathan had flown in that morning from Boston and was reveling in his old haunts. The gray skies and the wispy rain were somehow comforting.

Simon was picking at his crab terrine. He was as grumpy as an old bear. A rather pudgy, aggressive, but very well dressed old bear in his soft gray Saville Row suit. For a man who stood only 5 feet 4 inches, Simon was a presence that filled up a room. He was known up and down Wall Street for the sheer energy generated wherever he moved. There was nothing subtle about Simon. He was a force to be contained or reckoned with. And there was no containing him today.

Simon regarded investment bankers as a necessary evil, but not one to be borne stoically. "Jonathan, I don't trust these guys. And I'm only going to get one chance to make this happen," Simon growled. They attracted glares from the nearby table. Simon studiously ignored them. The patrons looked as starched as the tablecloths.

They had taken a table with no one sitting on either side, although the restaurant was full and several people were waiting at the front, beseeching the maitre d'. It was a measure of Simon's power or a very substantial tip. Probably both. Jonathan had been musing on that for the last minute or so, but now he had to respond.

"You know Henry Kent is going be about as happy to see me as finding dog shit on the soles of his John Lobb shoes," Jonathan said, his fork poised halfway to his mouth. He was eating wonderfully tangy chicken piccata.

"Actually, that's the one thing I'm looking forward to. I may need those guys to raise capital for Witten's, but I don't like them." Simon gave Jonathan a grim little smile. "You've never been shy, have you?" He wiped at the corner of his mouth with his crisp white napkin. "Damn, though, I wish we didn't need them."

Aspen & Leach was an *arriveste* investment banking firm with a very old name. The result of a hundred years, three mergers, a liquidation, an acquisition and a name change. They were adept at finding money and grabbing little fistfuls of it as it was pushed across the table. Aspen & Leach had become a new power on Wall Street. It attracted very young, very smart, aggressive, money-hungry young turks. And Henry Kent fit the bill to perfection.

There were a lot of deals that Kent had proposed to Simon through the years that caused him to wonder whether they were meant to make money for him or for Aspen & Leach. Actually, he was pretty sure of the answer, and it didn't endear the firm to him.

Aspen & Leach occupied seven floors in a high-rise building on Park Avenue. The walk from Côte Basque was short and brisk. The rain had stopped for the moment. There was a clean, sharp smell in the air. Little puddles rainbowed on the pavement. Jonathan walked carefully so as not to splash his cuffs.

A secretary was waiting at the guard's desk in the lobby to usher Simon through security and direct him to the proper conference room. Henry Kent and his people were already there, dressed in the best of English style, white-collared and -cuffed, Asprey cufflinks, Hermes tie and braces. Standard issue investment banker uniforms. Kent had been the head of mergers and acquisitions for three years, since he was 38. He had a self-regard some thought exaggerated. Jonathan counted himself firmly among the some.

"Simon, it's good to see you again," Kent said, rising from his chair and striding forward. Jonathan noticed how well his hair was cut, accentuating the touches of gray at the temples. Kent extended a manicured hand to Simon.

"It's been a while," Kent said. "You certainly look fit. London must agree with you." He made a gesture back towards the conference table. "I asked Larry Sims and Marty Fischer to sit in. I think they can add something to our discussions. We've given this situation a lot of thought, and I think you're going to like our strategy. I'm really glad that we'll have this chance to work together."

Jonathan had ceased to exist upon entering the conference room. Now Simon turned toward him. "Henry, you remember Jonathan Franklin. I asked Jonathan to help me with this problem."

"Oh, sure. Franklin, didn't we do the Wright deal together? That was a while ago. You retire or something? By the way, nice tweed jacket." Kent kept a straight face with just the hint of a smirk tugging at the corners of his mouth. Jonathan saw a smile pass over Larry Sims' lips before he turned away.

"Actually, Henry, we did three or four deals together. Great fun, as I recall," Jonathan said.

Henry Kent had already turned his attention back to Simon Aaron. "Well, Simon, why don't we get started? Here's how we figure it."

The wind-driven rain had started to beat at the windows when Kent presented his first chart. On the 73rd floor of a high-rise building, a storm becomes almost personal, and the light seemed to play into the atmosphere of the room.

It had taken an hour. The charts were beautiful. Kent's presentation was forceful and commanding. His ideas were typical. To the questions Jonathan asked, the responses were not as nice as one could hope for in polite company. On the other hand, this wasn't polite company.

In any case, Jonathan thought it was time to start moving the meeting on to where he wanted it to go. He needed Aspen & Leach's information, its resources and its name. He had his own plans.

Jonathan picked up his coffee cup and stood. "Those are terrific ideas, Henry." He gestured with his coffee cup. "But would you mind if we explored some other possibilities?" He began walking around the conference table towards the front of the room.

Kent's face froze. A vein in the side of his temple started pulsing. "Look, Franklin, this is my meeting and my deal. What the hell do you think you're doing?"

"Actually, Henry, I was going to ask you to sit down and let me explore some alternatives."

"You were what?" The question ended on a high note.

Simon Aaron leaned slightly forward in his chair and spoke in a quiet voice. It was all the more pointed for its softness. You could barely hear him over the sound of the rain.

"Henry, I hear you. You know I respect you and your people. Your ideas are always creative. And I know how much of a pain in the ass Franklin can be." Simon turned to Jonathan and smiled his Cheshire cat smile. "Believe me, I know. But I asked Franklin to help me out here, and when he speaks, he speaks for me."

Jonathan thought that Henry Kent looked as though he were about to have a stroke.

"You know, the funny thing is," Simon said, "Franklin was the one who insisted upon engaging you." Which was an outright lie. "But, if you don't feel like you can work with him, I would understand."

He paused and gazed out at the rain for a moment. His eyes were distant. The silence hung in the air. No one moved.

"I suppose we can use Aubrey's again." Jonathan admired the slight undertone of resignation in Simon's voice. A virtuoso performance. "But you know, they've been doing so much of my investment banking business that I've been getting a little uncomfortable. And when Franklin wanted to hire you, it seemed like a pretty good idea to me."

Bravo! It all came back. Why Simon was so good in negotiation. A sensitivity to people and a sense of the dramatic. Jonathan couldn't contain the trace of a smile. He struggled to suppress it. He turned sideways, bent his head and casually covered his mouth as if to stifle a cough. It was a good thing he was standing behind Kent.

Every investment banker on Wall Street knew Simon Aaron's companies had accounted for a total of $116 million in investment banking fees in 1997. They knew it as well as they knew the names of their own children. The emotions that played across Henry Kent's face were a panorama of anger, greed, calculation and capitulation. Then his face broke out into his most ingratiating smile.

"Actually, Simon, I've always enjoyed working with Jonathan. I don't know where you got that idea." He sat down.

Jonathan shrugged off his jacket, pulled down his tie and unbuttoned his collar. He was completely focused as he picked up the felt-tipped marker and adjusted the whiteboard to eliminate the glare from the ceiling lights.

"The key here is to neutralize United Worldwide. Witten's stock is depressed and trading way below its intrinsic value, based on my reading of its financial statements." Simon Aaron nodded.

Kent sat stiffly, watching him. Jonathan could see the muscles working in his face where his jaw was clenched. Mr. Kent wasn't a happy camper. Jonathan liked that. Maybe his competitive instincts weren't so rusty after all.

"I need your people to confirm this, Henry, but when I pulled United Worldwide's loan agreement and compared it to its balance sheet and cash flow statement in the latest 10-Q, I think they're up against their loan covenants." Kent motioned to Marty Fisher to make a note. "They don't have a lot of cash on hand. Which means that they'd have to get an amendment to their loan agreement to float more debt to make a run at Witten's with cash." Jonathan paused to let that sink in.

"They won't be selling stock either." His mind bubbled with the exposition, placing brick on top of brick, careful and straight. "I think the SEC would have a field day. From what I read," Jonathan said, "United Worldwide is using some pretty aggressive accounting. It's not the first time for Vincent Rollins. And that's starting to affect its stock price." The rain increased outside, the drops blurring the windows, cocooning them in the conference room.

"Its agent bank must be getting a little bit nervous, and I'm sure the syndicate banks are giving it an earful. Citibank's the agent. We can confirm with them." Everyone in the room understood that major corporate loans, often in the hundreds of millions of dollars, are negotiated and documented by one of the major money center banks, like Citibank, and parceled out among a group of banks to spread the risk.

"Simon, I showed you the list of syndicate banks," Jonathan said. "You have a strong relationship with two or three of them, don't you? You think you can lean on them to make them understand that an amendment to United Worldwide's loan agreement wouldn't be good for them or for you?"

Simon nodded again, but didn't say anything. He was focused on the ideas, and his face was set with concentration.

"United doesn't have the time to negotiate a new loan or the money to try to buy out some of the syndicate banks. That means that if Rollins wants to make a run at Witten's, he'll have to do it with stock. Simon, you still own twenty-one percent of Witten's' stock."

"A little more."

Jonathan had a strange sensation. He was flying again, the tingle in his face, the rush of air. It made him feel alive. He realized how much he had missed doing deals. And how afraid he had become that his skills had withered while he was in his little office in the law school, safe behind a wall of old journals. How insidious the fear was that had quietly poisoned him. His voice felt strong as he continued.

"Good. That gives us an edge. They need a majority to take control. And you have a poison pill in place. We did it for you a few years ago when I was still at Whiting & Pierce. It was pretty plain vanilla, as I recall. The automatic distribution of preferred stock if a raider acquires more than fifteen percent of the stock without the board's approval. That should make it prohibitive for Rollins to tender for your shares." Man, he was on a roll. Like old times.

"If they try to come at us with a pure stock deal, I don't think they can get enough support to put pressure on the board to withdraw the poison pill. In any case, last year the Securities and Exchange Commission rapped Vincent Rollins across the knuckles pretty hard for some shenanigans on one of his deals, and that won't go down very well with Witten's shareholders, particularly the Brits."

That drew an amused grunt from Simon. He sipped on his Diet Coke. Larry Sims went to the back of the room for another pecan tart. His third. It was starting to show around his middle. Sims slipped back into his chair.

"Now," continued Jonathan, "I think Rollins is pretty smart."

Kent's manicured fingers were tapping on the bright surface of the mahogany conference room table. "But I don't think we . . ." he said.

"Hold it, Henry." Jonathan held up his hand. "Let me finish. Then pick it apart." That felt good.

"When Rollins sees where he is, I think he'll back off until he can figure out a way to make a run at Witten's for cash," Jonathan said. "Simon, that should give us the time we need to restructure your debt and get the money to pay off your bonds. Thoughts?"

It was quiet for a moment, with only the sound of the rain on the conference room windows. Then, before anyone else could speak, Simon Aaron said, "I like it."

The taxi ride back to the Carlyle was longer than usual. Jonathan had taken a room at the hotel instead of staying with Simon in his apartment there. He still wanted to keep his distance.

The heavy rain had stopped and the clouds were breaking up. A little drizzle still dampened the windshield of the cab, and the cabby had his lights on.

"I really appreciated how you handled Henry Kent today," Simon said. "I like your strategy. It should work." He turned his head towards Jonathan. "You may be almost as good as you think you are." His lips creased in a small smile.

Jonathan chuckled. "Coming from you, Simon, it's a great compliment. But tomorrow I think we need to divide up the effort and create an action plan. Kent and his people should start the discussion with your lenders on restructuring your loan, and they should review the indenture agreement for the subordinated debt." The blast of a horn beside them interrupted them momentarily.

"You should figure out the best way to get to Rollins' banks. The less obvious, the better. As for me, I need to get over to London. My lecture at the LSE is on Saturday. Can you set me up next Monday at Witten's?"

"Sure, I'll have Lauren make the arrangements." Lauren Lucier was Simon's executive assistant. Tall, attractive, with long legs, china blue eyes and prematurely gray hair, she ran Simon's administrative apparatus with an iron hand. As far as Jonathan could tell, she was the only person Simon was truly fond of and about the only person he listened to. And Simon had made her rich with options in his deals.

"Touch base with Nicole DeSant first thing. You can rely on her. She knows Witten's inside and out."

Simon lapsed into silence, his back against the seat, content to watch the shoppers in the drizzle still bustling along 5th Avenue, beside Central Park, clutching umbrellas over their heads.

Jonathan was still restless, working off his suppressed energy from the meeting at Aspen & Leach. He touched Simon on the arm. "Here's the way I see this playing out. I..."

Simon leaned forward, turned to Jonathan. He put his hand on his arm to silence him. His look stopped Jonathan in mid-sentence. "I was just thinking about how much joy I get from owning Witten's," he said, ignoring Jonathan's statement. "It's not about the money, you know. It really is a whole other world. It's strange. Look at me. A poor Jewish boy from New York. I love the world of art, and the sort of people I meet through Witten's," he said, a wistful smile crossing his face. "And the respect it brings me. I've never felt so troubled or indecisive in my life. I need Witten's." Jonathan felt as if he was eavesdropping.

"That's really why I called you." Simon's eyes were unfocused as he leaned back against the seat, his mind slipping back in time.

Twelve

His thoughts drifted as the cab edged its torturous way back to the Carlyle. A smile threaded Simon Aaron's lips as he recalled his father.

"Simon, how could you do this to your mother?"

He had never seen his father's ears turn red, and it would have been interesting if he hadn't been afraid that his father was going to have a stroke. He'd been what then? Maybe 20.

"For this we sent you to a fancy college? For this we scrimped and saved? When she heard about this, she broke into tears."

Simon's family wasn't rich. They'd migrated to New York from Poland in 1938 to settle in another Jewish ghetto. But they weren't exactly poor either. He had never lacked for anything essential. There was the nice enough two-story house in a decent neighborhood and a used Cadillac.

Simon wondered how much of this scrimping and saving business was pure bunk. And Simon didn't think City College was so fancy anyway. What had brought all this emotion on was that Simon had just announced that after graduation, he was taking a job with a small chain of funeral homes in upstate New York.

"This is my luck. I work for 20 years, day and night—for this. An undertaker. I should have a son who's an undertaker. Shame on you, Simon."

Not an undertaker, really—the administrator in the back office. But Simon had learned not to try to make such fine distinctions when his father was in this kind of mood.

"Other fathers have sons who are lawyers and doctors. I have my son, the undertaker."

Simon's family had survived the Polish pogroms and been lucky enough to get out before the war. The first few years had been tough. The Depression was still in full sway, but Simon's father pushed desperately to make enough money to scrape out a bare living. It was hard and scary when you didn't speak English.

His mother saved every cent. When the war came, Simon's father finally got a job in a factory and things got easier for a while, until he was drafted. Simon was two when his father left. It got much harder, but they made it through until the war ended. In the '50s and '60s they had prospered a little.

But from Simon's father's point of view, things had gone downhill after he was demobilized and finally came home. At least with his boy. Simon was a continuing disappointment, particularly when he was old enough to show an independent streak. His father was a proud, strong-willed, domineering man. To his consternation, his son was strong-willed too.

The cab braked hard, throwing Simon forward and breaking his concentration for a moment. Jonathan growled at the driver. Simon drifted away again.

He dropped out of Hebrew class because it was boring. Simon discovered bacon from his high school friends. His family was outraged. He stopped going to temple with his father on Saturday mornings as soon as he thought he could get away with it. "That boy, that boy," his father muttered. "He's going to give me a stroke."

Simon wasn't mean-spirited. He was simply self-centered. He loved his parents in the hazy kind of way any young man does. It was just that he had a mind of his own.

He concluded during his many all-nighters in college that the "garbage collection" theory of business held the most promise. As Simon figured it, a short, fat Jewish boy without any money needed an edge. Why go into accounting with all the other smart Jewish boys?

He believed in himself, but he always wanted that edge if he could get it. And as he reasoned, if you were willing to do things others weren't, you could get that edge. That was where a bright young man might find a way to make some real money.

What he was looking for was an industry of mom-and-pop businesses where everyone made a living no matter how inefficient they were. There was steady demand in the funeral home business, and what easier way to make a lot of money than when the clients were grieving and distracted? Or dead. It was hard to shop around.

Simon Aaron was a big man in a lot of ways, although height wasn't one of them. Simon had been, to use the politically correct term, vertically challenged since he was a child. But once he found out about business, he rarely came up short.

After four years, he bought out the chain of three funeral homes that he had gone to work for. When the owner died, he gave the family all the money he could borrow from his reluctant father, all of his own savings and a promissory note. Two years later, he acquired his fourth and fifth funeral homes in neighboring towns.

His concepts of cost control and marketing improved cash flow. With a few small bank loans, he continued to build the company until he had 30 funeral homes. He worked seven days a week and had his finger on every part of the business. Well, not quite every one. He didn't like blood. But no detail was too small for his attention.

In 1970, when he was 30, he took his company public and used his stock as currency to buy up more funeral homes. The company kept growing.

Simon knew of that fellow Steve Ross down in New York City who had used his funeral home company to buy up a motion picture studio out in Los Angeles, Warner-7 Arts or something like that? But that was never Simon's ambition. He started buying cemeteries in 1973. Vertical integration, or perhaps horizontal, depending on how you looked at it.

In 1986, a big company out of Canada offered to buy him out. Simon came away with $92 million in cash. In 1986 that was big money.

Simon and his wife Miriam went to Europe for two months on the first real vacation they had had since their honeymoon. It took just three weeks after they got back for Simon to start prowling the house like a caged bear. "For God's sake," Mimi said, not wholly in jest, "get a job." As it happened, that's when he got a call from William Long.

Bid 'Em Up Bill Long was a disciple of the investment banker Michael Milken, the junk-bond king. Milken had revolutionized the merger and acquisition world and American industry in the early '80s. He didn't create junk bonds (or high-yield bonds, which was a more polite Wall Street term), but he figured out that the yields were far higher than was justified by the risk and if the yields were high enough, he could tempt insurance companies, savings and loans and mutual funds to buy enough bonds to make a market. A very deep market.

Milken was a predator. That market created the financing that allowed entrepreneurs to bid for old-line industrial companies, with their wonderful assets and dozy management. If a company wasn't using its assets to produce a good enough return, a raider would buy them using Milken's junk bonds. Then he could sell off part of the assets, kind of like buying a cow with its own milk. Share prices skyrocketed in old-line companies as they became targets. Stockholders loved it. Management felt decidedly otherwise.

Simon was flattered by Long's call and by Long's interest. "Mimi," he told his wife, "this guy's famous. He's in *The Wall Street Journal* every day. And he called me. He wants to have lunch."

Long wanted more than lunch. He had a great company that was ripe for a takeover, and it would be a perfect vehicle for Simon. Furniture manufacturing.

"Don't worry," Long told Simon over an elegant meal. "Management's in place. When you get rid of the deadwood, no problem. You're a great manager. A great entrepreneur. It's all the same skill set." It wasn't, but that wasn't important to Bill Long.

"Look, I believe in you," Long said. "And I'm prepared to put my money where my mouth is." What he meant was other people's money. "I think we can get this company for $200 million." Long used the term "we" loosely. He meant "you."

"You put up 20% for the equity," he told Simon. "My firm will sell high-yield debt for the part of the purchase price we can't finance with bank debt. I'll get the firm to issue a 'highly confident' letter so you can make your tender offer right now. The shareholders know we can raise the money if we say so. It's like cash to them."

Simon was intrigued. The furniture company had a brand name and a good market share. He bit. He bid. He won.

Only the company cost him $250 million, not $200 million. The board held out for more money. Other bidders came nosing around. And Bill Long blind-sided him.

Bill Long had earned the name "Bid 'Em Up" on Wall Street, where he was renowned for his ability to prove, beyond any doubt, that any price that had to be paid for a target company was fair, based on his projections, which were in turn based on his assumptions. Bill Long had never met a takeover candidate he didn't like. It didn't hurt that the higher the price, the higher his fees. Nor was his reputation tarnished by the failure of any of his deals. At least not after he closed them.

But Simon had spent over $2 million on the deal by then. He wanted to close. He had to close. And unfortunately, the furniture manufacturing industry was just about to enter a bad patch. The company was sound once Simon had sorted it out. But it was cyclical, and cash flow was declining rapidly. With $200 million in new, expensive debt, on top of the other debt the company was carrying when Simon bought it, he was in a real jam.

The first call Simon made was to Bill Long. "Bill, this is Simon Aaron. Yes, I hope you're well too. Look, I've got a problem here. We're bleeding cash. I think we should look at refinancing the debt."

"Simon, I'm glad you called," Long said. "But man, this is a real rough market. And people aren't crazy about the furniture business right now. I think you'll have a tough time refinancing."

Simon noticed it was now "you," not "we." "Bill, I don't think you understand. If we don't do something, the company may have to file bankruptcy."

"Simon, I hear you. I wish I could help."

"Look, Bill, you told me you'd be there for me when I got into this deal. And it would be a terrible thing if the company fails." Particularly since Simon had $52 million invested in it. "A lot of people will be hurt, including your investors." Simon was almost pleading. "Isn't there anything you can do? Maybe a bridge loan from the firm? I would give up a big piece of the company if it would pull us through."

"I don't think the firm would be interested, but I'll ask. Look, Simon, I have to take this other call. I'll get back to you."

Of course he never did.

Simon's advisers told him to walk away. Mimi told him to walk away. But that wasn't in Simon's makeup. He put in another $50 million more of his own money, almost everything he had left, to buy some time. He sold off subsidiaries, he sold plants. He disposed of any assets that were not nailed down. He lost 20 pounds worrying. He got an ulcer.

But after two years, the industry started to come back. Simon saved the company, and himself in the bargain, but it had been a hard lesson. From then on, Simon was shadowed by a fear of failure and a savage determination for control. He swore off high leverage and junk bonds forever.

Or so he thought.

Thirteen

Jonathan's transatlantic flight was uneventful, except for the few odd looks he drew when he got up every hour to do calisthenics in the aisle. He spent most of the flight thinking about his presentation at the London School of Economics, although his thoughts drifted occasionally to Witten's and his Monday meeting with Nicole DeSant.

He unscrewed the plastic bottle of water the stewardess—flight attendant—had brought him and lifted it to his lips. Hydration was important on these long flights.

It was perfect. The teaching he loved and the business challenge he craved. He felt good. More alive than he had felt in a whole year. Besides, he'd make a lot of money. Not all bad. He smiled to himself, then leaned again over his lecture notes. No, not bad at all.

The weather in London was overcast and wet. But the city always seemed to have an inner life and a spirit of its own. He loved its theatre, its cab drivers, the very smell of the place. Jonathan was surprised to see Roberts, Simon Aaron's driver, waiting for him outside customs.

"Roberts, nice to see you again. How have you been? The kid still growing up?"

"Mr. Franklin, just this way please," Roberts said, ignoring his questions without appearing rude. Still the proper British retainer.

"I have the Jaguar. Let me take your bags. I understand we will be staying at Claridge's on this trip."

Claridge's is one of the great hotels of London, a large brick pile set on a leafy street in Mayfair. It clings to the old ways and caters to the upper class European and American visitors—the essence of English refinement at a very steep price. The day manager, in morning coat and striped trousers, rose and stepped forward as Jonathan entered.

"Mr. Franklin, so good to see you again. It has been some time since you were last with us. We have reserved your usual suite. I hope that is to your satisfaction."

Jonathan was amazed. It had been five years.

The next two days were a blur to Jonathan, between seeing Lawrence Mattson, the professor of international political economies who was making the arrangements at the LSE, dining with the bald and bespectacled poobahs of the faculty at a club Jonathan could never have located again, and the final preparation of his speech notes.

The old wood-paneled lecture hall was gratifyingly full on Saturday, and no one fell asleep during his speech. Or at least no one he noticed. Mostly young men and women, but a professor or barrister here and there. More than he had expected. The question period was spirited, and the students and faculty seemed genuinely interested.

A final dinner with Mattson—"Tour de force, old man," "Splendid," "Top-notch"—then finally, gratefully, home to Claridge's and bed.

Jonathan awoke late on Sunday, feeling more or less normal. He was surprised how weary he had become. A combination of jet lag and the nervous energy that had bled away with his lecture. He had needed a good night's sleep. Now he felt impatient to get out and walk London's streets.

Fortified with a true English breakfast of fried eggs, thick bacon and broiled tomatoes, Jonathan grabbed a hotel umbrella and briskly exited the paneled lobby into an overcast winter's day. He had to remember to buy an umbrella. The breeze ruffled his hair, and he pulled his muffler up around his neck. He wandered the narrow back streets and dead ends of London, poking into shops and watching the people.

These were streets that Ben Franklin had walked in his time. And it seemed as if little had really changed. He fingered Ben Franklin's small silver snuffbox in his pocket as he walked. His father had given it to him, and he had taken to carrying it since his father's death.

That moment came back, real and vivid, the 17-year-old gangling boy and his bigger-than-life father, having lunch at the country club on the day before he left for Harvard College. How uncomfortable his father had seemed, shifting in his seat.

"Jonathan, I'm proud of you."

That came as a surprise.

"You know, it's hard for me to believe that you're going off to college already. I envy you that."

Funny, Jonathan didn't. He was simultaneously terrified and excited. He felt awkward and ungainly.

"My dad gave this to me when I went off to the war, and I thought you might like it."

His father passed across a small silver snuffbox.

"We are, uh—how do I say this without making it sound stuffy? Well, let me put it another way. You know that Ben Franklin was our ancestor," he said, pointing to the little antique piece. "We've had that box in our family for over 200 years. Turn it over and look at the inscription on the back."

It read, "To Benjamin Franklin from your friends at the Philadelphia Library Society." And below, "1768."

"I hope you'll treasure it as I have," his father continued. "It brought me luck."

His father sat quietly for a while, looking at Jonathan with an odd expression Jonathan had not seen before and could not interpret. Then he started again.

"Well, I'm not very good at these farewell things, but I love you," his father's voice caught, "and I'll always be there if you need me."

Jonathan had been embarrassed. He remembered looking down at his plate, racked by feelings he couldn't acknowledge, much less understand.

"I do have one small piece of advice for you," his father said. He wiped at his lips with the white starched napkin. As Jonathan waited, his father looked deeply into his eyes. It felt eerie. "Maybe it will save you some time." His father paused. "Success is easy. I believe men are shaped by their failures and how they deal with them. Every one of us has his failures. Many, many failures."

That was the real surprise. His father was the most successful person Jonathan knew. Jonathan thought there was a tear in his father's eye.

He recalled the feel of his father's hand on his across the table. Again, he felt a twinge of regret at not spending more time with him.

A brief visit to Turnbull & Asser in Jermyn Street to pick up some bow ties to complement his tweed jackets on more formal occasions, then a brisk walk back to the hotel to prepare for the theatre. Tomorrow was going to be a busy day.

He forgot to buy an umbrella.

Fourteen

She was beautiful. About 28, blond, tall and willowy. She wore a trench coat with fox collar and cuffs open to show her figure. Her heels tapped the marble floor. A well-dressed man walking out of the hotel nodded admiringly, his eyes following her. She ignored him.

She walked up to Simon Aaron on this quiet Sunday morning, as he spoke to the concierge in the lobby of the Carlyle Hotel. He had his back turned. She touched his arm.

"Excuse me," she interrupted. "Aren't you Simon Aaron? The chairman of Witten's?"

Simon turned and took in the full view of who was asking the question. He smiled. He hadn't known his reputation had spread so far. "Why yes, actually, I am," he said, his smile broadening to his eyes. "How can I help you?"

She gave him a radiant look and handed him an envelope. "You already have," she said. "You're served." She turned on her heel and strode out, her graceful hips swinging demurely beneath the swaying coat.

It took two beats for Simon to respond. A flush of red stained his neck. "Shit."

He drew stares.

"Why the hell is someone serving a summons on me? What do I pay you for, damn it?" Simon demanded of Robert Kahan, head of litigation at Whiting & Pierce. "Why did they serve me in the lobby of the Carlyle Hotel?"

Simon was holding his office telephone in a death grip and shouting into it. He was staring at the luminous Picasso painting on the wall twenty-five feet away without seeing it. The thumb of his left hand rubbed the arm of his leather chair in a stress reflex that had worn a spot on the rich brown leather.

"This is a pissant lawsuit. They're only asking for $400,000. Are these people idiots?"

"Simon," Kahan said. "Calm down. I haven't even seen the complaint." He ignored the ensuing tirade that poured from the telephone.

Kahan turned in his chair and pulled a yellow pad out of the birds-eye maple credenza behind his desk. He had hand selected the credenza and desk when he made partner 18 years ago, and its lustrous grains pleased him even now. He took a Mont Blanc fountain pen from his shirt pocket, carefully unscrewed the top and laid it exactly parallel to the pad.

Robert Kahan was known throughout the New York bar for his sangfroid. It served him well. He was equally liked and feared in New York litigation circles by those who knew him. Those that didn't tended to underestimate him. It was a tendency that he nurtured.

"Everyone knows we represent Witten's," Kahan said. His voice was soft and careful. "Any reputable lawyer would call us to accept service. That is, anyone normally would have called us. So it seems like someone wanted to make a point."

"They did. And, damn it, I don't like it. Do something."

Kahan made a small backhand motion to the young associate sitting across from him. They had been discussing another litigation matter when Simon called. "See you later," he mouthed, pointing to the telephone.

Into the phone he said, "I'll be in a better position to talk to you after I can look at the summons and complaint." He had known Simon a long time and dealt with many emotional outbursts, for which Simon was famous around the firm.

"Why don't you have your assistant fax it over here while we're on the phone? You have my direct fax number. Out of curiosity, who's the lawyer for the plaintiff? It's at the top of the first page of the complaint."

Simon read him the name of the lawyer and the name of the firm. At the same time, he buzzed his secretary and handed her the document with the fax number scribbled in the upper corner.

"I know Mary Lee Winters," Kahan said, writing down the lawyer's name on his pad. "She's a trial lawyer. Really something to look at. But she's a ball-buster. She'll do any high profile case she can get her hands on. She loves the publicity. Hold on for a second." Kahan turned away from the phone and spoke to someone in his office.

"Sorry, Simon. My secretary just brought me in the fax of the summons and complaint. Let me look through it."

There was a pause for a minute or two. Then Kahan came back on the line.

"It looks like the plaintiff is claiming that a picture he bought through Witten's is a forgery. He wants his money back plus interest. He identifies the painting as an American Impressionist work done in pastel on paper, and he says he purchased it about six months ago. That ring any bells?"

"No," Simon responded. "That's not a big item for us. Three hundred thousand dollars plus maybe."

"Well, not to worry, Simon. Witten's has a lot of defenses. We've been through this before."

"Yeah." Simon wasn't pleased to be reminded.

"Witten's isn't responsible for the authenticity of a picture unless it was negligent. You didn't own the painting, after all. You just sold it." Kahan enjoyed his erudition. There was the streak of the pedant in him. But a streak he kept carefully in check in front of a jury.

"Besides, proving negligence is difficult," he said. "First they have to prove the picture was a forgery, then that Witten's was negligent in not discovering it. Then there are our contract defenses. That's obviously why this lawyer's trying to embarrass you. Our Ms. Winters wants to put on the pressure so we'll settle."

Simon cut in. "We don't want any publicity. Every guy with buyer's remorse will sue us." Simon struggled to control himself. He added almost off-handedly, "Besides, I'm trying to do some financing."

"Right. First thing we need to do is get an expert to look at the picture. Do you want to use Jean-Claude Fernaud again? He did a bang-up job for us last time. Great witness. Wonderful bearing on the stand."

"Sure. I'll call him. But why the blazes are they suing us anyway? Why not the seller?"

Kahan flipped back to the third page of the complaint.

"It says they looked for the seller but couldn't find him. Probably didn't look very hard. Witten's has deep pockets. Besides, it puts pressure on us to find him and get him served."

Simon cut Kahan off again. He wasn't noted for his patience. "I'll ask Fernaud to get in touch with you so you can coordinate his getting the picture to look at. He's coming to New York in the next week or so on business. Try to get him everything he needs so we can all sit down together. Look, I don't want this in the newspapers. Witten's has enough trouble right now. So put a muzzle on this lawyer and let's see if we can get this case settled. Okay?"

"Of course, Simon."

Simon dialed Jean-Claude Fernaud's telephone number. While the phone rang he looked out his office window. The day was gray and heavy. The phallic boastfulness of the Manhattan skyline strutted its stuff unseen. Fernaud's voice brought him back.

"Monsieur Fernaud. This is Simon Aaron. I'm glad I caught you in. We've got another little problem. I'm going to need your help."

Fifteen

"Nicole, it is Henri." He had reached her at Witten's. It was still early in the day. She hadn't slept well again. A cup of breakfast tea steamed on her desk. A lump of sugar dissolved in the bottom, making little bubbles. People bustled by in the corridor.

"Let me close my door. *Un moment.*" This wasn't like Henri. He rarely called. Never at the office. She picked up the phone again. "Henri, *bonjour. Ça va?*"

"I am fine." He spoke quickly. "Please forgive me for calling you at your office, but I have an urgency."

"Of course. What is wrong?" She braced herself.

"Last night, while I was at the opera, I received a call from Vincent Rollins. I do not know how he obtained my private number."

"Ah. Have you spoken to him?" She stirred the tea with her manicured little finger and raised the cup to her lips to sip. Her lipstick left a red imprint on the edge of the delicate china cup.

"No. I wished to speak to you first. Do you know why he is calling me? We have never been on cordial terms."

"I believe I may. He understands we are accumulating Witten's shares. He called me several days ago. He seeks our co-operation." She took another sip of tea and replaced the cup in its saucer. "As you are aware, he is also interested in Witten's. I listened, but put him off. He seems to be under pressure. Perhaps he feels you would be more receptive."

"That is possible. How did he learn of what we are doing?"

"I do not know. It surprised me. Perhaps he has someone in the brokerage firms."

"You did not mention him when we last spoke."

"I did not think of it then. He called once more after you hung up. I did not take the call. Perhaps that upset him." She yawned and raised her small hand to cover her mouth. "How is our investment proceeding?"

"We have accumulated more shares. And both I and your father have bought subordinated debentures, as you suggested. We will continue. I believe we shall be well placed to move when we decide to do so. Do you think that Vincent Rollins may interfere with our plans?"

"I do not know. But perhaps we should take precautions. When do you believe we will be ready?" This wasn't making her feel better. And that lawyer Simon had asked her to meet was due to arrive soon.

"It will be some time. It is difficult to accumulate the shares without disrupting the market. The debentures as well. There is not a great trading volume. We must be careful. And I do not like the idea that someone knows what we are doing. I will, of course, change our brokers."

"Will you speak to Vincent Rollins?"

"Certainly. If only to assure myself that he will not disturb our plans. And perhaps he may be of use. I will call you after I speak with him. *Au revoir, cherie.*"

What might it all mean to her? She raised her teacup and sipped at it again as she waited.

Sixteen

Monday dawned bright, but clouds were starting to move in from the west. Jonathan set out on a brisk walk to his appointment with Nicole DeSant. The wind played at his thinning hair. Piccadilly bustled with businessmen grasping their furled umbrellas. It reminded him that he needed to pick one up.

A nip was in the air. He walked along with his hand in his pocket, rubbing the little Franklin snuffbox his father had given him. An involuntary smile brightened him. He was back in the game.

It was almost eleven when he arrived outside Witten's, off St. James's Street. He paused at the entrance and ran his hand through his hair to smooth it. Might as well make a good impression. He straightened his tie and walked in.

Malcolm Witten had acquired the town home of the Duke of Sheffield in 1808, at the time of the troubles with Napoleon, when the London real estate market was a shambles and the property was cheap. The Duke of Sheffield was in financial ruin, having gambled away his fortune at Boodle's gaming tables. Witten opened his auction house later that year, and it had operated since that date in the same imposing location, becoming, along with Sotheby's and Christie's, the visible commercial pulse of the art world.

A liveried commissionaire opened the door for Jonathan. The signs pointing toward the exhibition rooms were tasteful, and the great entry hall was already bustling with all sorts of people—dignified men in dark suits with colorful handkerchiefs in their breast pockets, casually dressed Americans with cameras around their necks, tradesman carrying tables and pictures being delivered for exhibition or taken away. Jonathan made his way to a small stand-up desk in the far corner.

"The administrative offices? All the way to the back, sir, then left through the last door."

Jonathan found himself in a cluttered warren of quiet offices in an atmosphere of worn elegance.

"May I help you, sir?" asked the polite young lady just inside the door.

"Please. I have an appointment with Ms. DeSant. Nicole De-Sant. Can you tell her that Jonathan Franklin is here?"

"Of course, sir. A moment, please. May I have tea brought to you while you are waiting?"

Jonathan refused, wondering how long he would have to wait if there was time for tea. Not long at all, as it turned out. A well-dressed, dark-haired young woman of perhaps 33 approached him and held out her hand in the reserved way women do.

"Hello, Professor Franklin. I am Nicole DeSant. I shall be pleased to provide you with whatever assistance you require," she said, looking directly at him. But something in the way she stood suggested that she was tense.

She about as tall as he was in her high heels, and he couldn't help but admire her trim figure as she led him back towards the rear of the wing of offices. He was habituated to the subconscious appraisal of women—not beautiful, glasses, gray eyes, well turned out, nice dark hair, good cut, a 7.5, maybe an 8—when he almost ran into her as she stopped and opened the door of a small win-dowless office. As it was, he stopped uncomfortably close to her. He caught her scent of expensive perfume. He took a step back and then entered.

The office was a shambles, but in a patrician sort of way. Per-haps because of the colorful art catalogs lying everywhere. A lot prettier than the stacks of old law reviews he seemed to collect.

Probably a lot more interesting too. Sometimes he questioned his commitment to academia.

"Please forgive the confusion," she said, her hand sweeping the small room. "We have an auction on for this coming weekend, and there are a thousand small things that are always awry. Please have a seat."

She sat down behind her small desk and cupped her hands on the desktop, leaning forward. She looked stiff. "It is part of my job to be sure everything comes off properly. Now, Professor Franklin, how can I be of help to you?"

"First, please call me Jonathan. Professor Franklin is much too formal, and besides, it makes me feel old."

"If you do not mind, Professor Franklin, that makes me uncomfortable. I would prefer not to."

Her manner wasn't unfriendly, but there was a decided lack of warmth. Jonathan was surprised and a little put off.

"May I offer you tea?" she asked.

"Coffee, if you have it. Did Simon explain to you why I'm here and what's happening?"

Nicole raised her index finger and picked up the telephone. She said a few words into it. Then she looked up.

"Mr. Aaron asked me to be completely open with you. I will do what I can. I have been with him since he acquired Witten's some eight or nine years ago. I think he trusts me, or at least he is more open with me than with the others here. But he has recently been more reserved."

Her light gray eyes were fixed on him as if to glean some response. She remained unnaturally still. "I know that there is some financial stress and that Mr. Aaron has asked you to assist him in resolving the problem. That is a compliment. He is not an easy man to please." Jonathan again felt a coolness in Nicole DeSant.

"Look, Ms. DeSant, maybe you can start by telling me what you do here and how Witten's works. I just want to get a feel for the business." He looked around the room. "I was in London for four weeks when we were doing this deal years ago, but things were so intense that I never got down to actually seeing Witten's. I mean, seeing its business." He made a vague gesture with his hand as if to take in the entire building.

"We were having a bidding war with Vincent Rollins, and the Witten's Board was not entirely sure that Simon was their cup of tea. They only seemed to know Rollins was not. We weren't sure until the last day if the board would find an English suitor. God knows, they tried. I don't think I slept the entire four weeks." He ventured a smile. Wasted.

They were interrupted by an assistant bringing in a teacart set with an antique silver tea service. The silver pieces were polished to a high sheen that glistened in the light. Nicole got up to pour his coffee and returned to her seat.

"Thank you." He lifted the cup to his lips and sipped carefully. "Ouch. Hot." He fanned at his lips. Then he blew on the surface of the coffee and took another sip. Nicole DeSant watched impassively.

He was starting to feel claustrophobic in the small space. Besides, the coffee was awful.

"Yes, I remember that it was a difficult period," Nicole DeSant finally said. It was almost as if she had waited deliberately to let him flounder. "Mr. Aaron was very concerned. We were working together more closely then." She looked at the thin gold watch on her wrist. "However, Professor Franklin, this is a busy moment for me, so perhaps we should continue."

There was that tension again. Why?

Seventeen

She was all business. "Professor Franklin, to understand the auction houses, you must first understand their relationship with the art dealers." She picked up a pencil from her desk. "My cousin has been an art dealer for many years. Let me ask, do you know the name Henri DeSant?"

"No, I don't think so. I'm sorry." He leaned back and crossed his legs, gripping his knee. He felt an uncomfortable pinch at his stomach. He uncrossed his legs.

"He is perhaps the leading art dealer in the world in Impressionist art. He has galleries in New York, London and Paris and deals in the finest pieces." She tapped the pencil against her lower lip and leaned back. Her gray eyes never left him. "He is well known in the art world. Mr. Aaron was his client for years before he acquired Witten's."

"I guess my art education isn't up to snuff," said Jonathan.

"Do not be embarrassed." She said it coolly, meaning quite the opposite. "If you are not in the art world, there would be no reason for you to know. In any case, the relationship between the dealers and the auction houses is very uncomfortable." She leaned forward again and started to put the pencil down. She noticed a smudge of lipstick on it and rubbed it between her fingers.

"They are both symbiotic and competitive, you see, which explains the peculiar way in which they treat each other. Dealers often represent important collectors at the major auctions. They even buy for themselves if they anticipate being able to resell the picture at a profit to a client like Mr. Aaron. Or if they want the piece to hold. Major houses also pay the dealers a commission for introductions."

He found he was distracted by his thoughts. He had been thinking about why she was so cool toward him. "I see," he said. He didn't. He hadn't been listening.

"On the other hand, dealers can no longer expect to be asked to sell a major collection. Collectors and trustees now come to us directly, or to be more precise, the major auction houses know all of the major collectors and maintain a close relationship with them as both buyers and sellers. That, in fact, is my job."

"Okay." Jonathan nodded. He leaned forward in the chair. He needed to focus. He needed to understand what was going on.

"However, some major changes in the mid-1970s greatly troubled the dealers. First, the auction houses became advisers to major purchasers. The dealers were furious. I still remember some of the discussions that took place at table when my cousin Henri came to visit us. I was only a little girl then, but I can remember how red his face became. I thought it was funny."

A personal tidbit. Maybe he was breaking through. Did he care? Dammit, why was he even asking himself the question? He took off his glasses and started to polish them with his knit cotton tie. Her look stopped him. How unsophisticated. He dropped the tie.

"But the worst thing that the auction houses did to the dealers was to adopt the buyer's premium, actually a percentage surcharge on the purchase price the buyer pays for a piece of art."

Jonathan interrupted. "Sorry, I didn't quite get that. The buyer pays the auction house to buy a piece of art?" He put his glasses back on and adjusted them by the earpieces. "I thought the seller paid. That's a neat trick."

"Correct. The London houses only charged a commission to the sellers until then. Christie's introduced the idea around 1974, and all of the other houses followed. The art market was very troubled. But the dealers believed that the auction houses were taking money directly from their pockets. The London Art Dealers Association sued. That was unheard of here."

There was a knock at the door. As Nicole looked up, a tall, distinguished older man with a mane of silver white hair, wearing a beautifully cut blue pinstriped suit, opened the door without waiting for a response. Jonathan noticed a small red rosette in his buttonhole. The man held himself erect, giving Jonathan the impression of an aloof, disciplined manner. His hands looked misshapen.

"*Bonjour*, Nicole," he said. "I am sorry to interrupt."

Nicole stood. "Jean-Claude, may I present Professor Jonathan Franklin. Professor Franklin is assisting Mr. Aaron with a business matter. He was a partner at Whiting & Pierce and was one of Mr. Aaron's attorneys."

Jonathan struggled to his feet. He had gotten stiff without noticing. That was the problem with getting older. You got stiff in all the wrong places.

"He is now the Weinberger Distinguished Professor of Law at the Harvard Law School in the United States," Nicole said. "He has just made a very well-received presentation at the London School of Economics. Professor Franklin, this is Jean-Claude Fernaud, the head of our Impressionist art department."

"A pleasure, Professor Franklin," Fernaud said, holding out his hand with a slight bow. "If I can be of service to you, please do not hesitate to call upon me." His handshake was careful.

"And a pleasure for me, Mr. Fernaud," Jonathan replied.

Fernaud turned to Nicole DeSant and they exchanged a few brief sentences in French. Jonathan thought Fernaud's tone was cross, although his high school French failed him in his attempt to translate. Fernaud left in an unsettled state.

"Ms. DeSant, you speak beautiful French. I have no ear for languages. My friends tell me I can hardly speak English." Nicole DeSant gave a small laugh. Another score.

"Thank you, Professor Franklin. But you hardly need be impressed." She shook her head, making her dark hair dance, reflecting the light. "My family is French, and while they moved to New York after World War II, I grew up speaking French at home. But, of course, I had to speak English to my classmates, though they teased me terribly because of my accent. I do remember how cruel they could be. I also speak fluent Italian and German and just a bit of Japanese."

"Wow."

"Language skills are an important attribute of my job. But, Professor Franklin, let me continue with what we were discussing." She glanced at her small gold watch. "I am a little pressed for time." Her manner again was cool and businesslike.

"We try to hold down the seller's commission as much as possible, of course, because it is very competitive and it is important to be chosen to sell the major collections. Major collections have become an essential part of our marketing." She stopped. "But surely you know all this from your work when Mr. Aaron acquired Witten's?" she asked quizzically.

"No, actually not. My concern was the deal and the financing. I looked over the financial statements, but I didn't have time to go any further. That was really the job of the investment bankers."

She paused again, apparently having lost her train of thought. She looked at her watch again. "Would you please forgive me? I am distracted. I must get Monsieur Fernaud some information he needs immediately for the auction this weekend. Would you mind if we continued our discussions tomorrow? Can you meet me here at four?"

"Of course."

Jonathan spent a few minutes wandering through the exhibition rooms of Witten's, looking over the art works, his mind elsewhere. Nicole DeSant was a self-assured woman. He was left with a sense of her presence and a vague sense of unease. He was not used to being received coolly.

Women liked him. Men liked him too. He worked at it. He preferred a cordial atmosphere. He felt confused.

This woman was classy, smart and sophisticated. Pretty too, kind of, in her own way. And something about her being foreign was intriguing. The way she spoke in such careful English.

But her manner suggested that she disliked him. He rubbed at the little silver box in his pocket. What could he have done? He had never even met the woman.

And he wasn't sure what she wanted. Did she want to get ahead with Simon? Or was there something else? For that matter, what was her relationship with Simon? Whatever it was, judging by her remarks, it wasn't simple.

All this was still going around in his head later as he stepped into the shower just before dinnertime. He found himself anticipating tomorrow's meeting, and, of all things, a little nervous. And it occurred to him he still hadn't bought an umbrella.

Eighteen

"I thought museums only acquired art," Jonathan said. "I didn't realize they sold it."

Jonathan had arrived at four. He tapped on the door and then opened it. Nicole DeSant had been in her cramped office on a call with a museum director. She hadn't heard the tapping. Nicole paused on her call and stared at him for a moment, suppressing a frown. This man was intrusive. She didn't like the idea of him overhearing her phone calls and then blithely asking such a question. How long had he been listening?

Jonathan was oblivious. He was assessing Nicole. He admired her well-cut dark suit and cream silk blouse. But she had on different glasses. Today they were oval-shaped with a red cross-piece holding the clear lenses. They had red ear pieces.

It wasn't that they looked bad. They looked great. They matched her bright red nails. But did women have different glasses for different outfits? Had he missed something? Was he ever going to understand women's fashion? Or women, for that matter?

Nicole had been discussing a sale of some of the museum's paintings. She had motioned him to a chair as she hung up the phone.

"Professor Franklin, in fact, museums are some of our best clients. They do it so regularly that they have a name for it. It is called deacquisitioning. A museum may own as many as 100,000 art pieces."

There was that coolness again. What had he done?

"I had no idea," he said. He spread his hands and tried a smile. It faded on his face.

"It is certainly true of major museums like the Museum of Modern Art in New York," Nicole said. "Two thirds of the art that most museums own is always in storage. They simply do not have room to show it. Of course, they try to rotate the art on display, but still. . ."

"Ms. DeSant, aren't museums prohibited from selling donated art?"

Why was this man continuing this ridiculous conversation? Did he have no art background? "Professor Franklin," she shifted in her seat and struggled to keep her voice level, "you tell me. If there is no restriction on a gift, and the proceeds are used to acquire other art or to support the museum, why could they not sell anything they own? They do want to be discreet about it. Usually they will wait until a donor has passed away. Otherwise, you understand, it would not be good for business."

Jonathan smiled again, a little uneasily. She certainly had a stilted way of speaking. The careful enunciation of someone fluent but more comfortable in another language. Well, at least he was asking intelligent questions. That should impress her. He was aware of her gray eyes, even behind her glasses. He crossed his legs and smoothed the front of his trousers.

"Collectors love to buy works that a museum has owned," she said. "It gives the work . . . what word am I looking for . . . ah, panache. If I recall correctly, last year MOMA raised over $70 million in this fashion."

"Wow. They must sell the good stuff." Live and learn.

"Yes, the good stuff, as you say." She was having trouble keeping her temper. She reminded herself that wouldn't do. "But not the best stuff. A museum may feel that it has too many pictures by an artist, say Monet. Last year, MOMA sold one of the Water Lilies to a man from Las Vegas for $9.2 million. We handled the sale. They felt that the other eleven paintings in the Water Lilies series that they owned were sufficient." How much more information did he want? He just sat there.

Jonathan nodded attentively.

"You see, museums are in business too. They have many of the same problems as other businesses, but we do not think of them in that way."

He sat silently for a moment. He didn't know what to say. He improvised. "How long have you been with Witten's?"

"It has been almost four years."

"Is that when you got to know Simon?"

"No, Professor Franklin, as I mentioned to you yesterday, I have been with him since he acquired Witten's."

"Of course, sorry, you did say that." Why did she make him nervous? "I don't think we met when I did the acquisition."

"Oh, but we did. Mr. Aaron brought me to the closing dinner in London, but you and I met only in passing. You were so much more important." In her experience, men liked to be flattered. She wasn't wrong, at least with Jonathan.

"Forgive me. I didn't recall." He hadn't missed the innuendo. Simon had brought her to London. "You must have been in your mid-20s then. How did you meet Simon?"

She frowned, as if it were a painful subject. Or perhaps an impertinent question. He couldn't be sure with this woman. He couldn't read her yet.

"Actually, I was just 25, and I set out to meet Mr. Aaron. I asked my cousin Henri to introduce me. I felt that I could be useful to him." *Or vice versa*, Jonathan thought. *This woman gets what she wants.* "I knew that he was acquiring Witten's, and I was interested." Her voice was firm without being aggressive. Pretty self-assured. Surprisingly so.

"I had taken my graduate degree in art at the Sorbonne. I was working in the contemporary art department at Christie's. Witten's had fallen on bad times, it was very backward, but it had a wonderful reputation." The phone rang and she paused for a second to murmur a few words.

"Excuse me. Now where was I?"

"Mr. Aaron."

"Yes. I worked in Mr. Aaron's organization in New York for some years, coordinating his art activities. He suggested that I take over this position, and I agreed to come to London." She stopped and pursed her lips. The overhead light flashed on her glasses as she moved her head. "But perhaps, Professor Franklin, we should continue to discuss Witten's and not me."

Nicole DeSant had stiffened slightly. Her speech was noticeably more formal.

"Sure. Sorry."

"You met Jean-Claude Fernaud yesterday. He is someone with whom you should speak." She folded her hands in front of her on the desk. "He has played an important role with Witten's for nearly 50 years. He will be able to give you much more of the technical background than I can. He understands the business as no one else does. Perhaps that would be something you wish to do? If so, I shall try to arrange it."

"Yes, I'd like to do that very much. Fernaud does seem like an interesting man," Jonathan said. "Was that the Legion of Honor he was wearing in his lapel?"

"Professor Franklin, I am impressed." Her voice softened a little. "Most Americans would not be aware of the rosette at all. But, yes. Jean-Claude was made a *Chevalier* three years ago. As you know, it honors his contribution to France. He has spent years tracing art that was plundered by the Nazis and seeing to its return. He has been responsible for some amazing discoveries."

"Stolen Nazi art? The war's been over, what, more than 50 years now. I thought that was all finished in the 1950s."

"You must know that there were hundreds of thousands of art works looted by the Nazis. Thousands upon thousands of freight cars filled with art. It is still turning up almost every month." She reached for a pencil on her desk and started to tap with it. Was he boring her?

"Just last week," she continued, "I saw an article on more pictures that were recovered, and last month there was a major international conference in the United States on plundered art. The ownership of the art is one of the great legal questions in the art world today. So many records were destroyed during the war, including those of Witten's. And for years, dealers and collectors have looked the other way."

"Amazing." He glanced at his watch. It was already six o'clock. "You know, Ms. DeSant, I do find this fascinating." Actually, he found her interesting and a little mysterious. She was bothering him. "I would love to continue this discussion, and I am here alone. Would you think it rude if I asked you to dinner?"

Nicole started to shake her head, then hesitated for a moment. Her gray eyes delicately assessed his usefulness. She made a decision. "Perhaps Witten's can take you to dinner, Professor Franklin. It is only appropriate that we entertain an important advisor to Mr. Aaron who is here alone in the city. Shall we say 8:30 this evening at Mistral?"

The weather had turned clear. A good thing, because he still hadn't gotten around to getting an umbrella. The doorman hailed a cab for Jonathan, and Jonathan gave the driver the name of the restaurant. God knows where it was. It was one of the new French bistros that had found their way to London. From what he had heard, it had great food and a better wine list.

Jonathan enjoyed his wine, and one reason he never liked to have someone buy him dinner was because he wanted to make sure the wine was first-class. Too many rich clients hadn't the slightest taste, and Jonathan had had some dreadful wines. Well, you learned to smile then too if you wanted to keep the client.

But he still thought life was too short to drink bad wine. And he usually didn't have to, although he wasn't any too sure about

Nicole DeSant's taste in wine. Or her other tastes, when it came to that.

As the cab pulled away from Claridge's, he turned his attention to the driver. Jonathan loved the lumpy black cabs and the lumpy good-natured London cabbies.

"And how are we this evening?" the cabbie said, his voice brimming with good humor. "A lovely night you got, sir." He pronounced it "sur."

For Jonathan, the cabbies were part of what made London great. These were true professionals. He had actually seen them, grown men, studying for their license, pedaling their bicycles around London, learning their routes. London's maze of streets and alleys were mystifying. He had been told it took three years to qualify. Most of them owned their own cabs. It was a profession.

In Boston, you were lucky if your cab driver could find a historic monument. In New York, you were lucky if he could understand the name.

Nineteen

He arrived at Mistral just at 8:30 and walked into the lovely, understated room. Jonathan was aware of the gentle tinkling of glassware and the murmur of engaged voices. The lighting was subdued, and candlelight flickered on the pale yellow walls.

Nicole was already at the table, a waiter hovering over her attentively. Apparently she was well known here. She raised her head as he came in. He shed his Burberry and muffler to the waiting attendant, and with a *"Monsieur,* please," the maitre d', with a gesture of his hand, led him across to the table.

"Professor Franklin, good evening," Nicole said. "I hope you will enjoy Mistral. I find it just the right combination of atmosphere and fine food." She held out her right hand. The antique gold ring she was wearing seemed to be configured with a crest. He shook hands and sat.

"Would you like to start with an aperitif?" she asked.

The only things he saw were her startling, pale grey eyes. He hadn't been as aware of them behind the glasses she wore at work. She looked different, more elegant.

She still had on what seemed to be the same dark suit she had worn at the office, but she had added a vividly patterned silk scarf draped over her shoulder. And her jewelry was striking.

"Actually, not an aperitif, but I would enjoy some white wine. Perhaps we could order a bottle now. I can order it, if you'd like."

She looked at him quizzically and held up a delicate manicured hand to signal the waiter, ignoring his offer. Her red fingernails appeared more vivid in the dim light. The waiter appeared as if magically. "Jacques, may we see the wine list?"

The wine list was encouraging. As big as a telephone book, with page after page of fine wines. Nicole was intent on the investigation of white Burgundies.

He read along with her upside down, a useful skill left over from his lawyering days. It was helpful to be able to read your opposite's notes across the table. You had to be subtle. You also learned to hide your own notes. Or write like a doctor. He had adopted the latter strategy.

She seemed to have reached a decision, and she turned her face up to him with her mouth pursed. "The Batard Montrachet is pleasant. Do you like it? I suggest the '89. The '92 perhaps will be as good, but it is still not quite ready, I think."

"Wonderful." He couldn't help the smile that bloomed on his face, although she might not approve. "Where did you learn so much about wines?"

She actually smiled back at him and laughed. Well, darn. Her laughter was light and musical, and she leaned forward a little. "You must not forget that I am French. I started drinking wine when I was six years old."

After the beautifully chilled wine was brought, a small amount of the golden wine poured into Nicole's delicate crystal glass, flickering in the candlelight, the little tasting ceremony performed, and the wine approved and poured, the blossoming wine started to do its work. They relaxed a little, sitting quietly, enjoying the ambiance.

Jonathan broke the silence. "You know, there's something that puzzled me this afternoon when you introduced me to Mr. Fernaud."

"Excuse me, Professor Franklin," she interrupted. "He prefers to be called '*Monsieur*' Fernaud. He is very French."

"I'll remember that. But when you introduced me to him, I hadn't told you all those things about myself."

She raised an eyebrow. He liked the eyebrow thing a lot. "Professor Franklin, in the art world we understand that provenance is important. History, you understand. And I did not get to where I am without learning to do my homework." *Quite thoroughly*, he thought. It would be useful to remember.

The '82 Pichon Lalande she selected to go with the beef bourguignonne was, if anything, better than the Batard Montrachet. The red wine glowed in the dim light. They ate in pleasant silence. A mellowness encouraged him to speak.

"Ms. DeSant, I want to clear the air," he ventured.

She raised her head and looked at him. Her eyes didn't seem to hold a challenge, as before.

"Maybe I'm wrong, but I sense you're uncomfortable with what I'm doing here. I'd really like your help. I need it."

She was quiet for a moment. She stared down at the tablecloth. Her fingers worked a crease in the starched white linen. Then it seemed to Jonathan as if some spring inside her released. She sighed.

"Of course, Professor Franklin, I apologize. It is not you. I have been under a great deal of strain in the last few weeks. You have done nothing at all. The auction preparations for this weekend have been difficult."

She went on with a subtle hesitation. "And Simon, Mr. Aaron, is important to me, and in some way, it upset me that he turned to you. He has always been most open with me until recently."

He nodded and smiled at her. "Look, as far as I'm concerned, we're in this together. Simon told me that he had complete confidence in you." He was exaggerating. "I'm sure you're reading something into the last few weeks that isn't there. Simon has also been under enormous stress. You know, he's scared of losing Witten's. He's really not himself. He's less certain and far less aggressive than I've ever seen him. He's emotionally involved, and it clouds his judgment and his actions."

"Thank you for that."

"No, I mean it."

Nicole smiled. She had lovely eyes. "Perhaps then, we can start again."

"Look, Ms. DeSant, is there any chance I can get you to call me Jonathan? Professor Franklin seems so formal."

She leaned back. "I think that would now be possible. And please, call me Nicole."

"Good. I'd like to be friends. You seem to have had an extraordinary career. I'd like to know something about you, if you're okay with that." His tone was diffident. "I seem to remember the name DeSant in banking from some of my international transactions. Is that your family?"

"They are in banking, yes. And some other businesses now." She seemed a little uncomfortable again. She was picking at her food. "I am not close to them, except for my cousin Henri. We in the family seem to have little to say to each other."

"I remember your saying you were born in New York, right? Do your parents still live there?" They paused while the waiter refilled their wine glasses.

"I grew up very French. We only spoke French at home, and I attended a French boarding school for several years, until Maman died. She died when I was 16. It was very sudden." Nicole was momentarily pensive, thinking back, and continued slowly.

"She was very beautiful. I loved the way she looked and how she laughed. I missed her very much. My father was wonderful to me after she died. I had no brothers and sisters. But he seemed somehow remote."

"So your father still lives in New York?"

"Oh, yes. We still have our apartment there. But I think he is lonely since I moved away. He does not have many friends. You remind me. I really must call him tomorrow. And you, Professor . . . excuse me, Jonathan," she asked, changing the subject, "are you by chance related to your famous American statesman, Benjamin Franklin?"

"Well." He drew it out. He felt a bit embarrassed. "Actually, my family is, but I never paid too much attention to it," he understated, sipping his wine. He thought of the little silver snuffbox in his pocket. He resisted touching it. "I know that he was a great man, and I admire everything I ever read about him. A genius. And he had such a wonderful *joie de vivre*."

The corners of her mouth turned up, showing a mischievous side to her personality that Jonathan found fetching. "Oh, yes. I have heard of him dandling the French ladies on his knee when he was 75 years old. You know, one of those ladies could have been my ancestor. My family was the banker to Louis and Tallyrand. And terrible social climbers, I fear. Your ancestor," she added, her light laugh tinkling, "might have courted mine. Who can know? We might be cousins."

"Well, I, for one, am glad we're not," he said, putting on a mock stern face. He tried to raise one eyebrow but only succeeded in looking quizzical. It drew a raised eyebrow and a smile in return. Jonathan found himself playing. He enjoyed it.

"Seriously," she said, "you must feel proud to be related to such a great man. He seems so human."

"Oh, I am. It makes me feel like I'm a part of our history. And I always wanted to be like him, even as a little boy." His embarrassment had fled. "I used to fantasize about it. But it's not that simple."

The waiter approached and picked up the bottle of Lalande. He refilled Jonathan's glass. Nicole's was still half full. She placed her hand above it. She waited for the waiter to depart.

"Why?" she asked.

"I don't know. I guess my parents were afraid it would go to my head. My mother always felt like the family was too full of itself. My mother was Jewish, and I don't think the family ever really accepted her. So I've always been ambivalent."

"Why did you quit the law to teach? I understood that you were very successful."

He leaned back in his chair, threw his head back with a half laugh and looked back at her. Her expression was puzzled. "Boy, that's a big question. Are you sure you want to hear all this?" He wiped his mouth with his napkin and put it beside his plate.

Nicole nodded.

"You really have no idea what it was like. A guy like Simon could tear your heart out if he didn't get the result he wanted. And he wasn't the only one. Successful? I succeeded in working twelve hours a day, seven days a week for the last five years I was with the law firm."

"Was there nothing enjoyable?"

"A lot of things. I loved the mental stimulation. I have a competitive streak, and I like to win. But I had no personal life. I not only carried a cell phone in my pocket, I even had a telephone in my bathroom, like in some hotel. Deals are living things. You have to press up against them. You have to feel them in your whole body to do them well. But they feed on you."

She nodded again. This man loved to talk. Good. If only she could steer him to the right subjects.

"I ran my deals like a general. That was my job. On some of my deals, I would have lawyers on three continents working day and night. But with the time differences, so was I."

They both sat back while the dinner plates were cleared and the waiter removed the crumbs from the tablecloth with a little silver scraper. The captain presented the dessert menu. They ordered.

"Please go on," she said, watching him as he fiddled with his glasses. It seemed like a nervous habit.

"Well, while lawyers were working all over the world, I sat in the war room and made sure the deal happened. Solving the next problem became the great joy of my life, but when the deal was done, everyone went away. And I still had to take out the garbage."

"I beg your pardon?" She was shocked.

He waved a hand. "It's my way of saying I got depressed coming off a high. I had to do ordinary things again. It was kind of like a woman after she has a child, you know."

"Ah." What a peculiar way he had of expressing himself.

"Then Harvard came along, and I collected my few assets and opted to get a life. It scared the hell out of me. I think it's the bravest thing I've ever done." That stopped him. He hadn't verbalized that before. He hadn't really been conscious of it. "Excuse me while I break my arm patting myself on the back," he said a little sheepishly.

Nicole smiled thoughtfully. Men were so transparent.

Jonathan liked the way she was looking at him. There was something in her eyes. What? Maybe she liked him.

Dessert arrived. A beautiful presentation of *tarte tartin*, the brown, sweetened apples on the delicate flake pastry set off by the white *crème fraîche*, garnished with perfect red raspberries.

"But look at this," she said as they finished dessert, "we have had our entire dinner and we have not even discussed our business at all. I would like to continue our discussions. Could I offer you an after-dinner drink? We will be more comfortable at my flat, and it will be more private."

Intriguing. He called for the check, which Nicole took from his hand with a shake of her head. "*Non.* It is our pleasure."

"I am reminded," she said as they entered the cab, "Monsieur Fernaud told me today he is leaving on a trip immediately after the auction on Saturday. If you will come in tomorrow morning, he has agreed to spend some time with you. He would not usually do so on the week of an auction. He is a dear man, but he reacts badly to stressful situations. He can be short tempered. Monsieur Fernaud fought in the Resistance during the war, and I understand the Germans tortured him. He was in the hospital for over a year after the war ended."

The taxi ride was short. He was surprised that her flat was on a beautiful little park in one of the most exclusive neighborhoods of Belgravia.

As he exited the cab first, he turned and extended his hand to help her out. He smiled down at her. "I'm glad you asked me over. I have a business interest in assuring you are safe and sound, you know." He looked around at the shrouded green park enclosed by a locked iron fence, surrounded on all four sides by elegant old townhouses.

"Of course you do," she said, arching an eyebrow but taking the extended hand.

"You live in a beautiful neighborhood."

"My cousin Henri and his family have owned this flat forever. I am just a tenant at sufferance. They can throw me out on the street tomorrow," she said.

The apartment occupied three floors and was impeccably fitted out with expensive antique furniture. Nicole pointed to a couch in the living room.

"Please, make yourself comfortable. May I get you a port or perhaps some sauterne?"

"Port would be delightful. Need some help?" He placed his hand on her arm. She smiled and shook her head. The light glinted on her dark hair.

She produced a decanter and two small crystal glasses and sat down beside him.

"Let us toast," she said. "To Witten's."

They clinked glasses and drank a bit of the deep ruby red liquid.

"Delicious," Jonathan said.

"Yes, '55 Taylor's. I thought you might enjoy it." She held up her glass again. "And to our collaboration."

It was 11:30. She had a decision to make.

Twenty

Getting him into bed had been easy enough. Men were simple. Innocent, really. The real romantics. Women were much more practical. Those thoughts brought a thin smile to her lips.

Rain feathered the windows in her bedroom, shredding the gray light. She stretched luxuriantly. Jonathan stirred but didn't awaken. He turned over, scrunched his pillow and started breathing deeply again.

It had been the right decision. She felt better. Back in control. Time wasn't so important now. She could get the information she needed over breakfast. Or lunch or dinner, for that matter.

She was lying with her hands behind her head. The counterpane she had kicked off exposed her small, firm breasts. The chill of the morning air stiffened her pink nipples.

She was proud of her body. She worked hard to keep in shape. It had always served her well. Just because she thought like a man, she saw no reason she shouldn't use every advantage she had. Besides, there was nothing wrong with sex. She enjoyed it, at least on her terms. And no one had ever objected. She smiled, more broadly this time.

The rain was coming down even heavier now, slapping at the windows. Beside her Jonathan still slept, snoring softly. She looked over at him. Breathing easily, his face open and relaxed. He seemed like a nice enough man. She brushed the thought aside. He knew what was going on. That was all that was important. Besides, you cannot trust men. She knew that. Not Simon. Not even her father, that dear man.

Her father had never had any idea who she really was. She had been raised strictly. Her mother didn't believe in vanity. How many times had she heard her say to someone, "Do not tell her she is pretty. We do not want to turn her head."

After her mother died, her father had tried hard. He had brought her back from boarding school. He had enrolled her in an upscale private school nearby. Not French. He said he wanted her to be part of his world.

But he always seemed sad. So vulnerable. She wanted to comfort him. She would never have thought of causing him more pain. She readjusted the pillow under her head.

Maybe it was easier for other girls. Maybe they could talk to their mother or their girl friends. She never made friends easily. She found her own way. It was difficult for her to express her feelings. She had gotten very good at performing. She smiled again, ruefully, lost in the past.

"Why the smile?"

She jumped.

"Sorry. I didn't mean to scare you."

"No. It is not a problem. I was just thinking about some things. Did you sleep well?"

"Pretty well. Strange bed and all. It was a lovely night. You're a surprising woman." He turned his head and kissed her lightly under her right breast. It was a practiced gesture. His lips tasted the salty tang of her body.

"And why is that?" she asked, turning to him, a smile around her eyes.

Jonathan was patting around on the bedstand for his glasses. "I'm blind as a bat," he muttered. His hand touched the metal frames and he slipped them on. "Ah, there you are."

"Yes, *monsieur*. Here I am. Unknowable." She raised an eyebrow.

"I don't seem to be able to figure out what you're going to do next."

"Is that bad?"

"Not at all. Just... well... surprising."

Her laugh was mellow against the rain.

He rolled over further and kissed her, grazing her stiff nipple lightly with his finger. "Perhaps you should call me Jonathan."

"Yes, perhaps I should," she said with a playful cry, snatching away the covers and rolling over on top of him.

It was an hour later before they made their way out of bed. He was trying to straighten out his glasses where she had knocked them askew in their play. Knocked them off, actually. He was the first to speak.

"I really love rain," he said, turning in the bed to glance out the window. "But we've had more than enough of it the last few days, even for me. I've been trying to buy an umbrella. . ." He left it hanging and rolled back towards her. "Want to brave it anyway and go out to breakfast?"

She paused to think, then shook her head. "No, I would rather make breakfast here so we can talk. I would like to understand more of what is happening at Witten's and what Simon is planning."

He was impressed by the businesslike way this woman thought. "Great. I make a mean omelet. Can I help?"

"That would be useful." She rolled out of bed and slipped into a yellow silk robe with lace at the sleeves and neck. She tied the silk pull at the waist. "Perhaps you would not mind getting started while I shower and dress. I must be in my office early."

"Not at all."

She turned around, smiling to herself.

Twenty-one

Jonathan returned to his hotel to shower and change before his appointment at Witten's. Nicole had departed in a rush after breakfast and left him to lock up, leaving him annoyed and somewhat perplexed. This wasn't following any pattern he was familiar with. He saw the red message light blinking at him as he opened the door to his room.

"Jonathan, this is Simon," the voice on the answering machine said, gruffly. "I just flew in. We need to meet with the investment bankers and the lawyers in New York next Wednesday. I want you to come with me on the plane Monday." Simon paused for a moment, and then in a more accommodating tone, as if catching himself, continued, "If that's convenient, of course." Maybe Simon was learning.

"I have to go to Frankfurt tomorrow for a Sanford's board meeting," he continued. "Can we have breakfast before I leave? I had some interesting discussions with a few of the key guys at Rollins' lead bank over the last few days. You'd be surprised what those bastards wanted... well, maybe you wouldn't be so surprised." Jonathan yawned and covered his mouth. He was tired.

"I'd like to be a fly on the wall if Rollins asks for an amendment to his loan covenants," the disembodied voice continued relentlessly. "In any case, we should talk. I'll come to you. Nine tomorrow at your hotel, if that's okay. Call me. Oh, and thanks."

He liked this new Simon. He wondered how long it would last.

* * *

It was 11 a.m. before he finally got to Nicole's office. She had the phone cradled between her shoulder and her ear, and her mouth was set in a hard line when Jonathan poked his head around the door of her office. She gave him a rueful smile and waved him in. One small hand fidgeted with a pencil. Her fingernails were plum colored today. And she had on matching glasses. He wondered if her toenails were the same color. When the heck did she have time to do them? Women were strange creatures.

He sat listening for a few moments to Nicole's terse responses, broken up by apparently long and unsatisfying explanations on the other end of the phone. She looked up at him and shrugged. She pantomimed "long call" with her hands, still holding the pencil, then motioned over her shoulder down the hall, toward Fernaud's office. She mouthed, "See you later." She pressed a button on the phone console.

An assistant arrived to show Jonathan the way. She knocked and opened the door slightly. "Monsieur Fernaud, Ms. DeSant asks if you have time now to see Professor Franklin?"

Fernaud sat behind a sophisticated computer setup. The motion of his misshapen fingers on the keys was unusual, but he seemed to have mastered the movements. He looked up, his hands poised over the keyboard.

The tall, elegant old man placed his hands on his knees and stood with a small grimace of pain. He came around his beautiful antique desk. There was a slight arthritic limp.

His office was larger than Nicole's and had three large windows that flooded the room with light. It was cluttered with paintings, reference books and catalogs of past and present Impressionist sales at Witten's and its competitors. But the clutter seemed surprisingly well ordered when Jonathan looked more closely.

"Ah, Professor Franklin," he said, holding out an elegantly manicured hand, "welcome. I hoped you would stop by." His hand was soft. Jonathan noticed the watery blue eyes that still held the sharp look of an eager mind. His face was still handsome despite the coxcomb of loose skin at the neck. "I would enjoy a few minutes respite from my work." He motioned Jonathan to a chair and resumed his seat behind his desk.

"The auction Saturday includes only a few Impressionist works," he said, fingering a catalogue on his desk, "but we are also auctioning the Klyberg collection in three months, and it is causing me a great deal of concern. The Klyberg collection of Impressionist art is among the finest to come on the market in years. It is very prestigious for Witten's to have been chosen above Sotheby's and Christie's, but I am afraid we granted the family quite favorable terms."

"Oh?"

"Yes. We made a very large guarantee."

That got Jonathan's attention. He leaned forward. "Monsieur Fernaud, are you saying that Witten's has promised to pay at least a minimum price for the collection? Why would you do that?"

"It is a matter of competition." Fernaud made an open-handed gesture. "Alas, to secure the most prestigious collections, all of the auction houses compete very keenly. You see, such a collection can provide the foundation for an entire sale. Indeed, even an entire season." He took some papers from the printer as he spoke and tapped them into order. He put them on the corner of the desk. "And recently, it has become necessary to make financial guarantees. Witten's guaranteed the Klyberg family a minimum of $100 million from the sale. Christie's actually offered to buy the entire collection outright from the estate for $110 million."

Jonathan jerked upright, responding to the magnitude of the amount.

"And yes, we are at risk," Fernaud continued. "Mr. Aaron has spoken to me personally about how important it is to Witten's that this auction be successful. We are certainly doing everything possible to make it so. I am leaving for New York on Sunday to see to some of the arrangements myself. But please, I digress. How may I help you?"

"I'm trying to get a grasp on the auction business," Jonathan said. "I understand that you came to work at Witten's shortly after the end of the last world war."

"Yes, this is a wonderful employment for one like me, who is an artist at heart. It is a joy to work among beautiful paintings and passionate people." Fernaud looked down at the colorful auction catalogues strewn on his desk. His hands remained motionless, resting on his desk. "Witten's is like a family to us here, although perhaps a poor one from the standpoint of our compensation."

Jonathan thought he detected a touch of bitterness.

"And, of course, there is a certain sadness in handling such beautiful pictures, even pictures of surpassing beauty on occasion, and knowing that we will never be able to possess one. But then, how many people can?" He accompanied the remark with a Gaelic shrug that only the French can muster. "Most of us here would not trade this for the world, although when one reaches my age, one does look at things somewhat differently. But I ramble on. You must have some particular curiosities."

Jonathan adjusted himself in his chair to avoid a glare from the windows.

"Is the light bothering you, Professor Franklin? Shall I draw the blinds?"

"No. I'm fine," Jonathan said, settling himself. "Can you give me some idea of how all this works? Obviously, I'm aware of what I read in the newspapers about the art market and the fabulous prices that some of these paintings bring, particularly your Impressionists, but there must be a good deal more to it than that." It was warm in Fernaud's office. Jonathan was sweating. He disliked the way the English always overheated their homes and offices, as if they were afraid of a chill.

Fernaud gave a dry chuckle and spread his hands. Jonathan noticed the angry knuckles and the blackened nails that a careful manicure couldn't quite cover. He hastily suppressed that curiosity.

"The auction itself is very glamorous, but really, it is just the small tip of the mountain of work that we must do," Fernaud said. "As Mademoiselle DeSant may have told you, a significant part of her position is to maintain a relationship with people who are important to us. She may have dinner with important collectors from time to time, and correspond with them, much as a museum director might do." Fernaud started to lift a delicate china cup to his lips and stopped. "Goodness, please forgive me. Can I get you tea or coffee? I completely forgot. I am so easily distracted these days."

"No, thanks. I just finished breakfast. But please go on." Jonathan remembered how awful the coffee tasted, and he had never developed a taste for tea. Fernaud gave a small nod and replaced his teacup in its saucer. It gave a small, satisfying clink, the clink you get from fine china.

"Perhaps Mademoiselle DeSant did not mention that we keep very close records on all the major collectors throughout the world. Witten's employs socially prominent representatives in many major cities. People whose names you would know, often the wives of major business executives. They receive significant entertainment allowances as well as a small salary. We know who has which pictures, we know about their families. Our representatives keep track of any public mention of their financial situation and, I blush to say, any gossip about their circumstances." It caused a smile to flicker on Fernaud's lips. Jonathan found himself smiling too.

"No kidding. Gossip?"

"In fact, we even have a service that reads the obituaries in the daily newspapers of all the major cities. That seems perhaps morbid, but it is an important element of our business."

"Excuse me, Monsieur," a sallow-faced young man dressed in a coat and tie interrupted, tapping at the open door. "I didn't know you were with someone. There's a piece at the front counter that I think you may want to have a look at."

"Professor Franklin, this is Mr. Vetch, one of my assistants." Fernaud's voice was dismissive. "Perhaps you would like to come with me. This may be interesting to you in your quest for knowledge."

The small group made its way through the narrow back halls, now bustling with people preparing for Saturday's auction, and out into the front of the Grand Hall, where a nicely groomed young man stood behind a small desk accessible to the front entry. It was cooler out here, thank goodness.

The young man was holding a picture that had obviously been handed to him by a rather nervous-looking woman in a faded, flowered dress. The woman was past middle age and plump. Her hands were rough and red in patches. Jonathan noticed there was a button missing from her coat. Her purse, which she held in both hands, shielded her.

"Monsieur Fernaud," the young clerk said, turning as they approached, "this is Mrs. Peterson. She brought in this picture," he said, handing the small work to the older man.

"Mrs. Peterson." Fernaud smiled and nodded at the nervous woman. "We are delighted that you have thought to bring your picture in to us. Can I ask you how you acquired it?" Jonathan was aware of how Fernaud's voice had changed, deeper and more melodious. His manner was almost courtly.

Fernaud's courtesy seemed to ease the woman's anxiety. Her worn face relaxed, and she didn't seem to hold her purse so tightly to her.

"Oh, yes sir. It has been in me family for now on fifty years. Me Mum, God rest her soul, made sure that I should have it, 'cause she knew how I used to moon over it. I thought it looked real nice. But times being what they are with us, and my Donald being made redundant, I thought I'd bring it in and see if it was worth somethin'."

Fernaud picked up the picture and studied it carefully, then turned it over and examined the back with equal attention. He then took a jeweler's loupe out of his pocket and again looked closely at the front of the picture. Finally he looked up.

"Yes, Mrs. Peterson. I think it is a very beautiful picture you have here. It appears to me that it may be a sketch by Manet for one of his early paintings. If you will leave it with us for a few days, we will give you a more thorough view, but if I am correct, we would be happy to help you with it. It could be quite valuable." He handed the drawing to Vetch. "If you would like, Mr. Vetch will be happy to tell you what we require and give you a receipt for it."

"Oh, sir, thank you, but we ain't got no money." She eyed the picture nervously.

"Of course, there will be no charge to you," Fernaud said.

As the group dispersed, Jonathan turned to Fernaud.

"That was fascinating. Do many pictures just come in over the transom like that?"

"Oh, yes, Professor Franklin. You would be surprised at the many ways we get works of art. Indeed, sometimes important works of art. Let me show you something back in my office that I found at a farmhouse the last time I was in France. Quite an interesting Van Gogh oil study for one of his cypresses paintings. Small, but I think, very beautiful."

Twenty-two

The picture was indeed small, but stunning. All the power of Van Gogh's brush strokes, the moodiness of his swirls and the intensity of his feelings, perhaps of his madness, vibrated in the deep blues and vivid yellows of this very small oil.

Jonathan held the picture carefully. The office had become very quiet for Jonathan, even though Fernaud had left the door open. He turned it to catch the light and shook his head. "Monsieur Fernaud, I am amazed. I had no idea that such art works could just come out of nowhere."

Fernaud stood behind Jonathan, looking at the picture over his shoulder. He was easily six inches taller. Jonathan could feel his breath on the back of his neck. It was uncomfortable. Jonathan took a half step away and turned slightly toward him as Fernaud spoke.

"Yes, this is an important small work. We had all thought it lost during the war. You know, of course, that many works were destroyed and many others stolen and dispersed." He sighed. "We are still seeking to trace this art."

"Nicole told me about your efforts to recover art stolen from France during the war. I think it's a fine thing to do," Jonathan said.

"Thank you, but I do it because I want this beauty returned to the people of France."

Fernaud held his hand out for the Van Gogh study and looked at it admiringly in the sunlight that streamed into his office. He smiled a little wistfully. "I found this in a small farmhouse in Perigord, to which I had been led by some inquiries I made through friends, after a good deal of research," he mused, almost to himself. "I was looking for a more important Van Gogh that had been lost during the war, but as it happened, this turned up in the possession of a French family who had no idea of its value. I persuaded them to allow us to sell it on their behalf."

He tapped his finger on the frame. "While it is not an important piece within the usual national concerns, it is important historically as well as being an exquisite work of art. To think, it might have been so easily destroyed."

Jonathan gestured towards the windows. "Don't you keep something so valuable in a vault or somewhere secure? You seem to have several valuable paintings right here in your office."

"While it is not at all obvious, Witten's is as secure, and its security systems are as modern, as any museum. These pictures are as safe in my office as in a bank vault, I assure you. But I do have these pictures here for a reason," Fernaud said. "Have you ever read the front of a sales catalog? No? Let me show you one." Jonathan hadn't expected that.

Fernaud shuffled through a stack of papers, pulled out an auction catalog and opened it. He passed it over to Jonathan.

"See here," he said, pointing over Jonathan's shoulder to a lot of small type on a page just inside the cover. "The auction house makes a very limited warranty of authenticity, particularly of older works. On the other hand, we deal with a very select group of people who are able to spend millions of dollars on a painting. That is why we have our own experts, and that is why I have these pictures here in my office."

Jonathan looked confused.

Fernaud moved to his desk and replaced the catalog. Then he turned back to Jonathan. He seemed to stand more erect. "We cannot very well tell one of our important buyers that we have no responsibility for an artwork that we may sell him for millions of dollars, notwithstanding what our catalog says. Our reputation is perhaps the most critical asset that we possess. We... I... spend a great deal of my life assuring Witten's that its reputation will be secure. And if I am wrong, it could be devastating for us."

"Yes, that makes sense," Jonathan said, adjusting his glasses on his nose. They always seemed to be askew.

Fernaud sat down at his desk, slid his chair back and crossed his long legs. The creases in his trousers were razor sharp. He motioned for Jonathan to sit down. Then he tented his damaged fingers under his chin.

"You saw what happened downstairs," Fernaud said. "That Manet sketch will join the pictures up here in my office in a few days. There are, of course, all manner of technical tests that can be done on a painting, all of which may be more or less conclusive. But the tests do not identify the artist, you know, only the time when a painting was executed. So, a painting done in Rembrandt's time by one of his students would pass any such test, but it would not be a Rembrandt."

"Of course."

"Also, a good forger can use old materials as well. The most important thing for me is for the picture to look right. So I live for a while with these pictures that come to us in an unusual way." A suppressed excitement edged his voice. "I can almost sense if something is amiss. In some cases, artists have peculiarities with certain colors. In others, the colors may not be quite right. Our new concern for the environment has changed the makeup of the paints that are available."

Fernaud unfolded himself and rose. He went over to a bookcase beside his desk, ran his finger along the titles and pulled out a book. He came around the desk to stand beside Jonathan, who had also risen.

"Professor," Fernaud said as he flipped through the pages, "let me show you something here in this book, one, by the way, to which I contributed and helped to research." He stopped on a page and ran his finger down it.

He pointed to a paragraph as he handed the book to Jonathan. "Ah, you see, there is a reference to a Van Gogh study done for one of the Cypresses, and you see here, it speaks of it being lost during the war, likely destroyed. This research, if you will, is important in authenticating a work that has an unusual history. I will do such research on the Manet sketch as well."

"Have you written many books?" Jonathan asked.

"No. Sadly, I have not had the time. My work is very demanding." He took the book from Jonathan and returned it to the bookcase. "But I am deeply involved in research as part of my duties, and so I have contributed to many books on Impressionist art. This one," he tapped the spine of the book he had just reshelved, "was published only last year."

Fernaud again picked up the small painting from his desk. "But here, look again at the Van Gogh." He came around the desk and handed it carefully to Jonathan. "Now, turn it over. You see on the back. That stenciled number?" He pointed. "Yes—and now look up further on the right and you will see another stenciled number." His finger moved. "Yes. There."

"They look exactly the same to me."

"They are. It is our peculiar style. The Manet that we saw downstairs will first be taken to our pictures group. It is part of my department." There was an inflection in his voice when he said "my." Possessive. "Each department of Witten's has its own arrangements for controlling the art that it is to sell. There, a number will be stenciled on the frame and entered in our records with an appropriate description."

Fernaud paused to clear his throat. "Excuse me." Then he continued. "In this way we can keep track of all of the very valuable pieces that we hold. But it is also useful, because if a picture comes to us more than once, it helps us trace the picture's lineage, which we call its provenance. All auction houses do this in a distinct way. As do many galleries. So you can see, the Van Gogh passed through our hands many years ago."

"When was this Van Gogh sold?"

"It appears that we sold it originally around 1931. Many pictures passed through our hands during those difficult years. Unfortunately, we cannot tell exactly, because all of our records before 1943 were destroyed in the Blitz." He sighed. "That was one of the great losses Witten's suffered during the war."

"So, Monsieur Fernaud, you've done your research, you've lived with the picture." He handed the picture back to Fernaud, who put it on his desk. "What then?"

A squabble of pigeons erupted on the ledge outside Fernaud's window, breaking his mood. "Those birds. They are such a trial to me," Fernaud said. Jonathan had difficulty suppressing a smile. "I have done everything. But yet. . ."

He strode across and jerked up the window, scattering the birds in a cloud of coos. A gust of wind disturbed the papers littering his desk, and he hastily pulled the window back down. "Dirty birds," he said with a vehemence that surprised Jonathan. Then Fernaud shrugged and turned back to the picture.

"In the case of the Van Gogh," he faltered a little, trying to regain his concentration, "it will be taken to others within my department, where it will also be examined. However, I must say," Fernaud added with emphasis, "no one has ever questioned my judgment on these matters." There was pride and steel in his voice.

"Then it will be cataloged and sold, we contemplate in the same auction with the Klyberg collection. Which, of course, will be one of the most important auction events of the last several years due to the exposure that it will receive. It is necessary in order to realize the best price. We estimate that this Van Gogh oil, in that auction," he made an in-and-out motion with his right hand, "should bring between $6 million and $8 million."

Jonathan silently thanked God he hadn't dropped the thing.

"Yes," said Nicole, taking them both a bit by surprise, "the Klyberg paintings are causing a great deal of excitement among the major collectors. Sixteen excellent paintings, including a major Monet and a first-rate Van Gogh." Nicole's glasses were down near the tip of her nose, as if she'd been reading. Quite fetching, Jonathan thought.

Fernaud looked pleased.

"Part of my responsibility," she said, "is to get as much publicity as possible in the major art publications, and they will require a history of the Klybergs and photographs of the pieces, as well as background information on each of the paintings. Then, of course, we must take the collection, along with other pieces intended for the auction, on tour. I will spend three weeks taking the pictures for exhibition to our galleries in New York, Los Angeles, Buenos Aires, Tokyo and Geneva."

"How peculiar," Jonathan observed. "Why Buenos Aires?"

Nicole pushed her glasses up with her index finger. "Well, as Monsieur Fernaud can tell you better than I, that is the art world in a nutshell." She shifted on her feet and placed one hand on her hip. She tilted her head, causing her dark hair to sway.

"As the Japanese have become less accommodating buyers, the Latin Americans seem to have taken their place as important collectors. Of course, the colonies," she said, "are still our primary market." Her gray eyes flashed with humor.

Nicole placed a hand on Jonathan's arm. "But really, I came to steal you away from Monsieur Fernaud. Witten's will undoubtedly collapse if he does not attend to it properly. Besides, I am starving and you promised me lunch. Perhaps I can help you with anything else you need to know. And, Jean-Claude, thank you for taking the time to see Professor Franklin."

"So," she asked as they walked towards her office, "did you learn what you needed to know? And how did you like our Monsieur Fernaud?"

"This has been a very productive day, Nicole. He's obviously a knowledgeable man. Quite interesting. Are you ready for lunch?"

"Jonathan," she said, kissing him quickly on the cheek and giving him a gentle push, "I said that to get you out of Jean-Claude's office. I am far too busy to even consider lunch." She placed her hand on his arm again. He stopped and turned towards her.

"Oh, and the auction Saturday night starts at 7:30. You should come. You will find it interesting."

"I'd like that."

"I have a seat reserved for you at the end of the first row. But come stand with me to the side during the first part of the auction. I may be able to point out some things to you that you otherwise might not notice. Is there anything else you want to see now? I will set it up for you." They started walking again towards the door of the administrative offices.

"No. I want to think about what Fernaud told me. He certainly understands Witten's. By the way," Jonathan said, turning his face to her as they walked, "Simon sends his regards. He's flown off to Frankfurt, and he probably won't get to say hello on this trip. He and I need to return to New York in a week. In any case, since you won't have lunch with me, let me get out of your way for the moment. Do you have time for a quick dinner tonight? Just a few questions."

"Not tonight, Jonathan. Perhaps tomorrow. But please, a very brief one. At seven?"

Twenty-three

"Just how big is Witten's now?" He wanted to get her talking.

Nicole and Jonathan were at a small restaurant on a quiet side street, several blocks from the noise and crowds of Piccadilly Circus. More comfortable than fashionable. The candlelight reflected off glasses and cutlery and made flickering shadows on the wall.

"Witten's has grown since Simon acquired it." There was a subdued quality in her voice. He noticed that she was now referring to Simon in the familiar. "We now have 94 offices and 14 sales rooms in 38 countries. Witten's employs over a thousand people."

"It has grown." He was surprised at how much.

They were interrupted by the waiter with their coq au vin. It smelled delicious. Wine, mushrooms and a hint of garlic. They sat and ate quietly for a few moments. The room was full of murmuring dinner sounds. Cutlery clinked. Somewhere in the back a plate broke on the floor. Jonathan paused to take a sip of wine and then dabbed at his mouth with his napkin. He hesitated. He didn't want to sound stupid. But he had always wanted to ask the question.

"I've wondered," he said, "why a Van Gogh is worth $75 million and some other picture's worth $2 million? Not that I could afford either one."

"Actually, there are two answers." She seemed to perk up a bit. She raised her head and favored him with a smile. Maybe it was the stupid question. It wouldn't be his first.

"It is a matter of fancy. Impressionist art, particularly what we call pretty art, has become very much the fashion. There is a madness to collecting, with its own rules. People live and breathe it. You cannot imagine the intrigue among them." She cut a tiny bite of chicken and put it in her mouth. She chewed for a bit and swallowed. She didn't want to make him seem foolish for asking so silly a question, and she needed to control her voice.

"They can be far more devious than in a business matter. It is a passion. The strange thing is that it is either intense or completely absent." He recalled what had attracted him to the way she spoke. Perfect English, but just a little stilted. And the cadence was different.

"Second, Jonathan, there are many rich people in the world and very few great Impressionist paintings. To be able to live with beauty and perhaps have a good investment as well, it is indeed rare."

"Oh, so what you're really telling me is that it's a matter of supply and demand," he said. "Got it. Now how do I know what's becoming popular?"

"You become an art expert and then you guess." She paused deliberately. "Probably wrong." She seemed to be enjoying herself now.

He grinned. "What's a circle bid? I read about that somewhere."

"Ah, so you are an expert on the auction business, Professor. You have been holding back on me," Nicole said. Her gray eyes had a twinkle. "A circle bid is illegal. And, of course, therefore, could never happen. *N'est-ce pas?*"

"Oh, sure. Absolutely not. Not in my experience." A couple bustled by on their way out, chatting loudly. Americans.

"A circle bid," she said more seriously, "is where a circle of dealers agrees not to bid against each other. They designate one of their group to bid and set a maximum price. If there are few other bidders, they get the piece cheaply, if the seller has not set an adequate reserve. Then they re-auction the piece among themselves, their circle, and split the profits."

"A reserve?" Jonathan picked up his wine glass.

"Ah, a reserve is a minimum price that the seller sets with the auction house. Sometimes on a single piece, and sometimes on a group of works in the same auction. We are careful when we accept a reserve." She paused and moistened her lips with the tip of her tongue. "It greatly complicates the auction for the auctioneer, since he must keep track of all the reserves. If a reserve is accepted, but the bidding does not reach the reserve, the auction house buys the piece in a house name and returns it to the client."

"The things you know. Now I'm definitely impressed," he said.

The waiter cleared the dishes, and they ordered coffee.

Nicole was having a good time too. It surprised her. It had been a long time. But she cautioned herself to be careful. She had another agenda.

"Well," she said, "if you are so impressed, let me add that I know of cases, particularly in contemporary art, where a dealer who owns 30 pieces by an artist will put up a piece for auction and have someone bid it up to, say, $25,000. Then the dealer will use the publicity of a new record sale price to increase the price of his remaining paintings. And a dealer might bid up any piece, even against his own client, if he thinks the piece will be sold too cheaply, and he has other pieces by that artist for which he has paid more."

Jonathan set down his coffee cup. "Boy, am I a babe in the woods."

A mental nod flashed through Nicole. It was endearing somehow. "You will see all this at the auction on Saturday. I am sure you will enjoy it."

"I've never been to an art auction before."

"Good, then it is settled. Now I wonder if perhaps we might go. I would like to walk for a bit and then return home. There is still a great deal I must do tomorrow."

Jonathan signed his credit card slip and rose. He helped her slip into her raincoat and got into his own. He extended his arm and she folded her arm into his. It felt good.

The rain was falling in a fine, light mist, just enough to give the street lights a glow. Still no umbrella. Oh, well. He took off his glasses and put them in his pocket. They strolled in companionable silence along the path inside the park beside Piccadilly. Tiny rain drops sparkled on her hair. She didn't seem to mind.

The traffic made a gentle hissing sound on the damp street off to their right. The mist seemed to enclose them in their own space. No one else was walking in the park. Finally, at a word from her, they left the path and he hailed a cab.

He walked her to the door of her flat. She turned and gave him a light kiss and squeezed his hand.

"Thank you again for a lovely evening." She placed a hand against his chest as he leaned towards her. "I had a splendid time. Good night. Do not forget the auction on Saturday."

He watched her until the door closed. Then he let out his breath. He returned to the cab with a warmth inside him, as well as a deep sense of frustration. What the hell was going on?

Twenty-four

Jonathan reached Witten's at 7:15 the next evening. It had been a struggle.

An expectant bustle was evident as well-dressed people were already flowing up the graceful stairway to the great, high-ceilinged octagonal auction room. He spotted Nicole standing by a far corner at the front of the large room and made his way through the chattering crowd.

He raised his voice to be heard. "Nicole, sorry I'm late. The traffic's awful."

"I am glad you are here." She leaned towards him, making her dark hair fall across the side of her face, and spoke close to his ear. He caught a subtle wafting of expensive perfume. A diamond stud flashed. "Your seat is right over there," she whispered, pointing toward an empty seat in the first row. "But stand here with me for a moment."

She straightened, turned her head and nodded toward the rear of the room. "Look towards the back. The man just coming into the room. The one with the yellow pocket handkerchief. He is Eli Lurien, a major American collector. The man with him is Richard Adam, his dealer and advisor." She shifted her glance to a man who had walked away from Lurien.

"The man who just said goodbye to them and sat down in the last row, the one in the pink shirt, he is a major London dealer, Richard Petree. I believe they are interested in the same piece. Mr. Petree has taken a seat in the last row so he can watch Mr. Lurien and any other bidders. However, I know that Mr. Lurien does not want to be seen bidding on any piece." She was leaning so close to his ear he could feel her breath tickle.

"The auctioneer must watch him closely. He has instructed us that he is bidding on a piece so long as he is fingering the knot in his tie. The auctioneer may have several such bidding instructions to observe. And if I am not mistaken, Mr. Lurien also has instructed Mr. Adam, his advisor, to bid openly for the same piece in which he is interested, and then to drop out." She placed her hand on Jonathan's arm as she made her point.

"It is all a very clever little game of ploy and counter-ploy. The major players all know each other, you see." She turned toward Jonathan, her hand still on his arm. Her subtle perfume surrounded him. "Now," she continued, "you see at the front of the room, the screen to the side of the auctioneer's podium. That is where a picture of the artwork is projected." She raised a manicured finger to point. Her nails were pale, iridescent green.

Another young woman came over and whispered something to her. "Leave it with me. Thank you," she said and turned back to Jonathan. "I'm sorry about that. These evenings are quite hectic." Jonathan nodded as she pointed again at the front of the room.

"The actual piece, if it is small enough, is on that rotating stand on the other side of his desk. Larger pieces are hanging on the walls." She turned and gestured toward a large painting, then looked back toward the front.

"There above the desk—I suppose you might call it a numbers board. The bids are instantly displayed there in several currencies, starting with English pounds, then dollars, then yen and so on, so everyone can understand the bid. I will be over there on the telephone," she said, nodding her head to the side and pointing to the side of the room where a table held a bank of telephones, "taking bids from those who have arranged to bid in that manner. We should start in a few moments." Light flashed on her antique gold ring, the one with the crest he had noticed before.

"How can you possibly keep up with the bidding?" he asked.

"It is difficult," she admitted. "We are trained to listen and speak at the same time. We must understand the bid, whether the current bid is for or against our bidder, and communicate all of this information on a continuing basis to him, while following his instructions without error."

"That sounds hard."

"It is. It takes a long time to do it well."

"But what if I want to bid on a piece? How do I know when to stop?"

"You should not do that." She started. Her voice was emphatic. "A bidder must do his homework, due diligence, I think you called it. And you have not. In the auction business, you cannot rely upon anyone, even the most trustworthy people." There was a rising sense of anticipation among the people in the room as latecomers shuffled towards their seats, murmuring apologies.

"Witten's and the other major auction houses try to be fair in the estimates of value we put on each piece in our catalogs. The estimates are always in a range of what we believe the piece to be worth." She stopped for a moment as if to consider her words. She continued carefully. "But it is a matter of judgment. And there are things that can affect our judgment. Where the auction house has a guarantee, or if the market is in transition, it may make an estimate—how should I say it—less exact."

There was a stirring as the auctioneer, Neal Maslan, entered the room. She shooed Jonathan to his seat. He could feel the tension mounting towards the first bid. It was almost palpable.

"Good evening," Maslan murmured with a small smile. Everyone hushed. Neal Maslan was a great auctioneer. He was a superb combination of judge, showman, salesman and humorist with his Oxbridge accent. His voice was perfectly modulated, with just the right touch of world weariness in it. He held his audience rapt.

Jonathan loved it, half business and half entertainment, as Maslan ran through the items, coaxing bidders, smiling, pointing, pausing for what must have seemed interminable seconds to the high bidder before gaveling down a piece with the tap of his little brass weight and a "Sold to the gentleman in the third row." You could almost hear the high bidder exhale his held breath. Two hours passed in a moment.

"Well, I have to say, you were absolutely right. That was fascinating."

They had adjourned to Merriam's, an elegant little restaurant around the corner from Witten's, for drinks. "I never knew an auction was so much fun. Why, I almost bid on one of the pieces myself. It was only my iron discipline that prevented it." He smiled broadly. "And oh, the $250,000 opening bid."

Nicole was obviously exhausted, but she managed a wan smile in return. "And I was interested in you because I thought you were a rich man," she said.

"Ah ha!" he said. "I knew you were interested in me."

She brushed him away with a tired grin. "It is not fair to try and take advantage of a lady when she can hardly stay awake."

"All kidding aside . . ." Jonathan said, but was interrupted by the entrance of Jean-Claude Fernaud with an elegant older woman on his arm. The woman was tall and slim. Her gray hair was elegantly done. She was strikingly handsome.

Nicole saw him, smiled and nodded as he was shown to a table across the room. He acknowledged them with a small bow in their direction. A man at the far table stood and shook Fernaud's hand enthusiastically. The seated woman smiled up at him and acknowledged his companion. They were engaged in conversation even as the maitre d' held out her chair and seated them.

"It appears," observed Jonathan, "that your Monsieur Fernaud has remarkable stamina. And excellent taste in women, as well."

"Oh, yes," Nicole responded, "Monsieur Fernaud lives well, as he deserves. He collects fine wine and he is a gourmet cook. He is also a wonderful artist. And he does still adore beautiful women."

"He certainly lives the good life. How does he afford it? He implied to me that the salaries at Witten's aren't large."

"Witten's is very generous with Jean-Claude. He has a large expense allowance for entertaining clients and prospective clients. It is important to us that Jean-Claude be seen in a certain way. And he is also fortunate. He has spoken of several successful investments."

They sat a while, quietly sipping their champagne. Rather good for champagne by the glass, he mused. That was new since he was last in London. Perhaps there was hope yet for the Brits.

"Jonathan." Nicole broke the silence. "Please forgive me. I am not very good company tonight. I am exhausted. Perhaps we can make this an early evening."

"Of course. Let me call a cab."

As he held the door open for her, she put her hands on the front of his shirt and tiptoed up to kiss him lightly on both cheeks, in the European manner. The street light caught the luster of her dark hair as she turned her head.

"I do like you," she said softly. "But let us have dinner tomorrow. I would look forward to seeing you then."

Twenty-five

Jonathan awoke early on Sunday to an overcast and chilly day, threatening rain. The weather reflected his mood. He grunted as he did his eighteenth crunch lying on the floor with his knees up. Too much rich food and good wine had driven him unwillingly to it.

He had tried pushups, but after three his shoulders hurt. He wasn't a willing subject. He grunted again on his 20th rep, then rolled over and pushed himself to his knees. His muscles ached and he was muttering under his breath. He swore to himself to watch it from now on.

He spent the rest of the morning reading fitfully, and in the early afternoon he finally gave up and headed out through Shepherd Market to Hyde Park, his hands buried in his topcoat, rubbing his little silver snuffbox, with his chin hunched down into his muffler against the chilly wind. A light rain started to spatter around him, but he trudged on, hardly aware, his mind turned inward, lost in an inner dialogue.

This relationship's driving me nuts. What relationship? I don't even have her telephone number. Why would I want a relationship anyway, for God's sake? The woman lives in London. Besides, I don't have time for this. I'm seeing two women already. Damn.

He was attracted to her. Okay. It had happened before. But he kept thinking about her. He could even remember how she smelled. He felt off balance. He didn't feel he could get his arms around this woman, either literally or figuratively. What did she want?

And why wouldn't she sleep with him again? She seemed to like him. "Is there something wrong with me?" he murmured. He nearly ran into an old man walking along the path who gave him a strange look. He hadn't even seen him.

"Excuse me. Sorry," he said, taking a few shuffling steps sideways. The man stared at him like he was an idiot. Maybe he was. He wound out of Shepherd Market and headed up Piccadilly toward Hyde Park. He passed the Athenaeum Hotel. He almost bumped into a couple who burst out toward a waiting cab.

He was still lost in his thoughts.

Why am I pushing this? This is sophomoric. At my age, you'd think I'd know what I want. Well, okay, what do I want? His mind was a blank. "I don't know, damn it!" he said aloud.

He had walked more than a mile on the Serpentine and the rain was starting to come down hard. The rain had soaked through his coat, and he suddenly felt cold. He made his way out to Knightsbridge Road and hailed a cab. He shivered as he entered the car. He hoped he wasn't catching cold. It would serve him right.

The phone was ringing as he unlocked the door to his hotel room. He grabbed for it.

"Jonathan, it is Nicole."

"Nicole, hold on for a minute."

Jonathan shrugged off his wet coat into a heap on the floor and stepped into the bathroom to grab a towel to dry his hair.

He grabbed the phone off the bed as he rubbed at his hair briskly. "Nicole, I'm back. Sorry."

"I am still very tired from last night," Nicole said. "Please understand. Would you mind if we had an early dinner? The auction wore me out."

He sneezed.

"Bless you," Nicole said.

An early dinner sounded like a good idea. "Of course. Why don't I come by and pick you up at seven? I promise to get you home no later than nine. Let's do something casual so we don't have to get dressed up." Maybe even undressed, he hoped. "Something close to you. You choose. By the way, I don't have your telephone number."

They were ensconced in a small neighborhood Italian restaurant by 7:20. Very downscale, but cheerful, checkered tablecloths and all. Apparently it was one of Nicole's favorite local spots.

The restaurant was filled with the quiet noise of people coming down after a hard day. The waiter came by to light the candle on the table. It was romantic in the flickering light. The murmur of soft conversation filled the candlelit room.

A basket of warm, crusty bread was on the table. Jonathan could smell it. Golden olive oil swam in a small plate. He had done his best to ignore them. But he loved warm bread. He gave up and took a piece. He broke it apart and dipped it in the olive oil. He popped it into his mouth. It was delicious. So much for the exercise.

As he chewed the bread, Nicole spoke. "Jonathan, I am sorry that you must return to New York so soon. When do you expect to be back in London?"

He swallowed his bread and cleared his throat. "I'm not really sure. It depends on how Simon's situation shapes up." He waited as the waiter filled their glasses with sparkling water. "I also have classes starting again in the first week in January," he said. "I may not be able to make it back right away."

The waiter hovered. He ordered a bottle of Chianti Classico Reserve. The good stuff.

"I am disappointed," she said. She really was. It surprised her. "But I will be in New York soon. I must visit *Art News* and *Art and Auctions* about articles on the Klyberg collection. I also must see my father. Perhaps we can see each other. I will have more time then." She still needed to keep up on what was happening.

"I'd like that, but can I be straightforward with you?"

"Of course." She looked into his eyes.

"I don't have any idea what you want from me. Or where this is going. Are you seeing me because Simon told you to? Help me, I'm lost."

"Where do you want this to go?" She actually wanted an answer.

Jonathan blushed. "I don't know."

"Then Jonathan, how can I?" She gave a little shrug. "May I ask, have you been married?"

The waiter returned with the Chianti and poured it into two short, thick glasses. "Shall I come back in a few minutes?" he asked. A nod.

"*Salut.*" They clicked thick glasses. A satisfyingly dull thunk. Candlelight flickered through the deep red wine. Jonathan sneezed.

"I hope you are not becoming sick," Nicole said.

"This will help," he said, holding up his glass. He took a long sip. "If I can raise my blood alcohol level high enough, it will kill all the germs."

Nicole suppressed a smile. "Married?" she prompted him.

"Right. Uh-huh." He gritted his teeth. It wasn't where he wanted to be. "This is uncomfortable." He took another sip and started reluctantly. "I was married, once, a long time ago. Can't you tell? I still have the scars. Do they show?"

"You sound bitter. Was it not a happy marriage?"

"No, it wasn't unhappy. We married after law school. But Barbara wanted a career in investment banking. She was good. Actually, she was very good. Between her being on the road half the time and me working night and day, I guess we just never got our marriage going. No, I'd say the marriage was neither happy nor unhappy. We just loved our jobs more than we loved each other."

"*Quel dommage.*" She folded her hands in front of her on the table. He noted the grace in her movement. Her fingernails were clear tonight, with translucent white tips.

"But the divorce was really nasty," he said. "I was shocked at how angry and sad we both were. Live and learn."

"Then you will understand how I feel. I have never wanted a relationship. It would interfere with my career. I love what I do. And I am very good at it also. I was not even interested in seeing anyone until you came to Witten's."

She brushed aside a twinge of guilt. And a twinge of something else she wasn't so quick to identify.

"And to answer your other question, Simon would never intrude on my personal life, nor would I let him. You are an interesting man, Jonathan." He actually was. "You are bright and you have a sense of humor. Humor is a wonderful quality in a man. And I like older men, the way your hair is graying at the temples."

Jonathan grimaced.

"But a relationship for me right now will have to go slowly. I would enjoy seeing you and spending some time together. No obligations. Let us see, shall we?"

Twenty-six

The letter came in an oversized envelope, deeply engraved with a seal and crest over the words "Department of French National Museums." Theodore Marking hadn't spoken to Pasquale Bastien in almost three weeks. On the other hand, he hadn't received any communication from the Law Society either. Better yet, there was no scuttlebutt around about a new solicitor, and no one had requested his files.

Marking was sucking on a paper cut and cursing around the finger in his mouth as he tore open the envelope the rest of the way. He unfolded the hand-laid, watermarked stationery and picked up his cigar. He took a puff as he began to read, spilling ash on the paper. He brushed it away. A spiral of blue smoke hazed the air.

> We have received the notice of claim on behalf of your client, Pasquale Bastien, and have forwarded it to the appropriate departments in France and Germany. Based upon our investigation, we are compelled to advise you that we must deny your client's claim. We enclose a copy of a bill of sale from a Monsieur Emil Rosenberg, properly executed and witnessed, transferring the referenced painting.
>
> While the Government of France does not accept the title of Nazi war criminals to works of art transferred during the War, it is the position of the Department of French National Museums that the painting was properly sold by Monsieur Rosenberg and upon repatriation it will become the property of the Republic of France.

"Damn," Marking shouted out loud. He swatted cigar smoke away from his eyes. Now at best he was going to have to find a barrister to handle the lawsuit. Where was he going to get one of those arrogant bastards to do it on a contingency? They would all raise that nonsense about it not being proper under the law rules. Bollixed up anything they got their hands on. They thought they knew everything.

He thumped his chest with his fist. Heartburn. He shouldn't have had the pickles.

And even if he found a barrister, he would have to split his fee. Assuming he still had a client. He hadn't bargained on this. What was the smart thing to do?

Marking tossed the letter on his desk and shook his head. Then he had a thought. Maybe he could use this to his advantage. He picked up the telephone and dialed.

"Monsieur Fernaud, please."

There was a pause and a woman's voice came on the line.

"Hello, I am Monsieur Fernaud's personal assistant. I am sorry, but Monsieur Fernaud has gone abroad. We do not expect him back for several weeks. No. I am not at liberty to disclose Monsieur Fernaud's hotel. I will take a message if you like. Or you can seek to reach him through Witten's offices in New York."

Marking was shouting into the telephone.

"I do realize that it is important, Mr. Marking. You need not raise your voice to me. I will get your message to him promptly. Yes," she said, "if you will send me a copy of your letter by telefacsimile, I will also forward that to Monsieur Fernaud."

"Bloody bitch," Marking said, banging down the phone. "I need to talk to him about this bill of sale thing before I can get Bastien properly sorted out."

Twenty-seven

Harrods had been a full morning. He went there on every trip. At least he had avoided a cold. He drew in a deep breath through his nose. He felt better.

Now the packing was done for the trip home. Jonathan rang for room service and ordered a turkey sandwich and a Diet Coke. He'd been running so hard he had forgotten to eat. He settled into a chair.

Now that he had a few minutes, he called his house in Concord to check for messages. After the beep, he dutifully entered his number code. There were two messages.

The sun attempted to breach the barricade of clouds but fell short and crept back in. Growing light changed again to mottled shadows. He reached over and switched on the table light.

"Jonathan, this is Benjamin Cohen," the voice on his answering machine said.

Jonathan was a little taken aback. Why was the dean of the Harvard Law School calling during the school holidays?

"Look, I need you to call me. I just had a discussion with the dean of the B-School, and she has some issues with the proposed joint MBA/JD course that you want to teach. Get back to me as soon as you can. Thanks."

The next message was from Valerie, the young red-headed model. "I miss you. Will you be back soon? Can I see you? I'm lonely. Call me." Her voice was a purr.

The vision of Valerie's firm, naked body came into his mind. He thrust it away. That was unlike him. What was he doing? He hit himself on the knee. Better call Ben Cohen. He certainly wasn't going to call Valerie.

As he dialed the law school, he ruminated on what Ben Cohen wanted. It couldn't be good.

"Thanks for getting back to me so quickly," Ben Cohen said, in his usually cheerful voice. "Sorry to bother you, but Elsbeth Warren over at the B-school doesn't think your course proposal will fly. She thinks we're behind the times over here."

What she meant was, Jonathan was behind the times.

"She says unless you can update your business transactions proposal with some new economy deals, she doesn't think any of her B-School people will sign up. After all, this is 1998. All the rules have changed. The valuation matrix has to be completely re-worked, and the transaction timing has to be streamlined. Other-wise, there is no way her students will buy into this, according to her."

Jonathan flopped down on his back onto the bed. What bull-shit. He stuffed a pillow under his head.

"Warren also thought that you should include a session or two on going public," Ben Cohen said, "and she asked if maybe you could get Mel Kleiner to come up and give a guest lecture." Kleiner was the reigning king of technology investment banking on Wall Street. An amazingly nice guy for an investment banker. He would actually say hello. And sound like he meant it.

"I would love to meet him too," Cohen said. "Anyway, I told her I would talk it over with you and get back to her next week. Any thoughts?"

The phone went quiet. Jonathan lay on the bed and rubbed his head. His eyes were closed.

"Jonathan, are you there?"

He took off his glasses and threw them on the bed beside him. His eyes remained closed. "Ben, are these people out of their minds? Maybe I'm the one who's over the hill. Look, first of all, on a practical level, it's damn near impossible to sort out several good new case studies on Internet and technology deals in the next few weeks. I have to be sure there are some that fit before I can start preparing the course material. Second, I'm not sure that I buy into all this 'new valuation matrix' crap." Jonathan rubbed the bridge of his nose. "I can't get my mind around the fact that Amazon.com is worth more than General Motors. Anyway, how do you go about buying a company without knowing what you're buying? Do these people have any practical experience?"

"Uh, Jonathan, Elly Warren is on the board of three technology start-ups and co-founded an e-commerce company to provide free product coupons that they sold to Epion.com this year for $4 billion in stock." There was something hushed in Ben Cohen's voice, almost reverence, as he said the numbers.

"I think her share was around $172 million. That was before the stock doubled and she cashed out. She seems to know what she's doing. I'm surprised she has time to run the B-School, she has so many meetings with venture capitalists."

There was a knock on the door. "Hold on a minute, Ben. I need to get the door. Room service."

The waiter set the tray down on the table to which Jonathan had pointed. The waiter removed the silver dome from the turkey sandwich and presented the bill. He looked at it. It was a good thing he wasn't paying. Jonathan understood the silver dome. He signed off. The waiter smiled and departed.

He picked up the glass of Diet Coke. "Sorry about that, Ben," he said, lifting the receiver and sitting down again on the side of the bed. He took a sip before returning to his thoughts. He put the glass of Diet Coke down on the nightstand.

"You know, Ben, I think that you and I are in the wrong business." He swung his legs over the side of the bed and lay down. He gave his hair a vigorous rubbing, leaving it sticking out at weird angles. "Maybe this lady is right about me. I just don't understand this new paradigm, I guess. Let me do some research and think about it. I'll call you in the next couple of days and let you know if I can get it done."

"Oh, Jonathan, one other thing," Cohen said. "Warren told me to buy some shares of Relationship Software in the initial public offering. She's sure it's going to pop. She can get me a 'Friends and Family' allocation from the company. She sits on their board. She asked me to mention it to you too. Should we put down a few dollars?"

"Sure, why not," Jonathan said. When people around you are making lots of money being dumb, being smart isn't an asset.

Roberts, Simon Aaron's driver, was waiting in the lobby at ten that evening. It was misting. Jonathan smiled. He still hadn't gotten around to buying an umbrella. Now he wouldn't need one.

Traffic in London was agonizingly slow, and it took almost an hour to reach Midlands Airport, where Simon hangared his plane. Simon was waiting at the executive aviation terminal. They immediately boarded Simon's new G-5 and were in the air within ten minutes. Looking at the sleek new $30 million jet, Jonathan knew that Ben Franklin had been right. Older boys have their toys too. The difference is just the price.

"Jonathan," Simon leaned forward, shifting in his leather seat to look directly at him, "did you get to see what you wanted at Witten's? It's really quite a place, isn't it?"

"Yeah, Simon, thanks. I got the Cooke's Tour. Nicole was very helpful. I also spent some time with Jean-Claude Fernaud. He gave me a lot of insights. I had no idea that the auction business was so complex."

"Good. Nicole's a terrific lady. Quite extraordinary in her way. You should get to know her."

What the hell did that mean?

"Fernaud is almost a fixture at Witten's," Simon continued. "We're going to hate to lose him."

"Lose him?" echoed Jonathan.

"Yeah, didn't you know? He's retiring in March. I'm surprised no one mentioned it to you. His knowledge of Impressionist art is incredible, but he's in his late seventies now. The Klyberg auction will be the last one he participates in. I'm glad he's staying on for it. We guaranteed the estate a $100 million from the sale. It has to go well. It kind of surprised me that he agreed so readily to help with the sale. He actually suggested it."

"Why did it surprise you?"

The attendant brought Simon a scotch and soda. "Can I get anything for you, sir?" she said, turning to Jonathan.

"I'd love a glass of Chardonnay."

"You'll like this wine," Simon said. "It's a Zager Reserve. I own part of the winery."

"They make great Pinot," Jonathan said. The attendant interrupted to deliver the wine. Jonathan sniffed at the glass, then took a sip. He rolled the wine on his tongue, making a slurping sound. Then he swallowed and savored the lingering finish at the back of his palate. "Delicious," he pronounced.

"Yeah, anyway," Simon said. He was clearly unimpressed. "As to Fernaud, to be honest, his retirement wasn't entirely voluntary. He wanted to stay on as head. He was quite insistent, really, but we felt like we needed a younger man to carry on. Of course, we took care of him. He'll continue to get his full salary. But it was apparently quite a blow to him to lose all the prestige, not to mention his expense allowance. Jean-Claude's developed a taste for the good life."

Jonathan raised his glass and took another sip of wine before speaking. He spoke over the rim of the glass. "Fernaud mentioned the guarantee to me. Why in heaven's name would you go out on a limb like that?"

Simon gave a grimace. "Witten's needs this auction. Business has been awful. Last season Christie's got the Ganz collection. Being the seller of these world-class collections has become the key to the success of each of the major houses. Any of us would kill for one, but hopefully not ourselves. We're going to spend several hundred thousand dollars promoting the sale."

Jonathan whistled.

"Apart from the auction catalog, we had to promise the Klyberg estate that we would produce a coffee-table book of the collection to sell for the benefit of the Klyberg Foundation." Simon settled back into the deep leather seat. "This business is getting nuts. If you think that you've seen elaborate road shows for a securities offering, you should see the world tour and receptions we'll do for the Klyberg collection."

"Can you make money with those kinds of costs?"

"I'm hoping we can break even. Maybe, God willing, make a few bucks. But the sale will attract buyers from all over the world, and that will also attract sellers who want to sell their paintings in the same auction, under the most advantageous circumstances. Having a major collection like this creates a lot of buzz and a lot of other business for us."

"I hope so." Jonathan glanced at his watch. "Not to completely change the subject, but we've got to get from there to here, so maybe we better talk about what we're going to say to the investment bankers on Wednesday. Where do you want to take this financing?"

Jonathan and Simon spent the better part of the next two hours discussing subordinated loans, convertible debentures, rights offerings and a myriad other financial alternatives, the pros and cons of each approach, timing, the stability of the financial markets and what Vincent Rollins might have in mind to stick a pole in their spokes.

At 41,000 ft., the Gulfstream G-5 cruises at 500 knots, and it reached New York, allowing for the time change, about an hour after it left London. If you weren't there for the ten minutes it was parked at the Signature Air terminal, it had never been there, but Jonathan and Simon were in New York, not London. They were settled in at the Carlyle in the small hours of the morning. It was raining.

Jonathan looked troubled as he and Simon sat down to a late breakfast the next morning. He hadn't slept well. They were waiting for their coffee.

Jonathan scratched his cheek. "Simon, there's something I just don't understand. The art market is booming, right?" A grunt. Simon wasn't a morning person. "Witten's has a great market position, right? How can it have such a liquidity crunch?"

"Yeah, all that's true," acknowledged Simon, "but the business has changed in the last couple of years. Competition has gotten cutthroat among the three major auction houses. We have to put up a letter of credit to collectors if we make a sale guarantee. Major buyers sometimes need financing that we have to provide. Sure, we take the pictures we sell as collateral, but it all eats into our working capital. And, as I told you, marketing has gotten out of hand, what with the major commitments we're making."

"So?"

The coffee arrived, and Jonathan poured a cup of the life-giving fluid and sipped. He closed his eyes. "Ahh." He held his cup in front of him in both hands.

"It's starting to turn around now," Simon interrupted. Jonathan opened his eyes and put down his cup. "We've reorganized and cut costs to the bone. Give it a year and Witten's will be making money again, hand over fist. That's why Rollins is sniffing around."

"What you really need here, then," Jonathan mused aloud, looking towards the ceiling and pulling down on his tie, "is some short-term money, with a little time cushion." He looked back at Simon. "Well, let me work on it. I may have some ideas by the time we get downtown tomorrow. I think my mind is still in London, along with my stomach. But I seem to remember something interesting that may fit in here somehow."

129

Twenty-eight

Jean-Claude Fernaud arose early. Dull yellow light spilled under the drawn shades and pooled on the floor. The large, dark room was cool. He sighed as he rolled back the covers, pushed aside his goose down pillow and slipped into his house slippers. His eyes slowly adjusted to the light as he cinched his green silk robe around his waist. He stretched his long frame and yawned.

I love coming to New York, he thought. Even in his quiet retreat he could sense the tempo of the city. So much more vibrant than London. He settled into one of the deep chairs. *And they do attend to me so well here.*

Fernaud's hotel was a small luxury hotel on a side street in the Upper East Side, where you couldn't get a reservation unless they knew you. There were 18 suites. Each suite was individually appointed with antiques and the finest accessories. The finishes were expensive and tasteful.

Every suite faced onto a spare interior Japanese garden. The pathways glistened in the light rain. Each suite commanded the price of a suite in the finest hotels in the city, of which it considered itself one, although no one would know its name. Nor did it want its name known. It catered to an elite European clientele who knew it and were, in turn, known. It was unthinkable that any member of the staff would not address Monsieur Fernaud by name, with, of course, great deference. The standards were European; the expectation was perfection. Fernaud had been staying there for years. He was comfortable. It suited him.

He stood up and walked into the bathroom. A deep, lacquered, black lotus-shaped bowl sat by the wash basin. The lustrous green undertones spoke of its age. It was always in his room when he arrived. He ran hot water into the bowl and slipped his hands into the water. He sighed. The pain was almost his constant companion now, growing worse particularly in the colder months.

He balled his fists in the water and released them. The movement relieved the pain in his fingers a little. His thoughts drifted back to the dark room where the Nazi interrogator had held the hammer over his smashed knuckle and smiled. He recalled the gold tooth grinning at him through the red haze of pain. Then the Nazi broke another knuckle.

A quiet tap on the door broke into his thoughts. He shook off his hands and dried them on the small towel he had set next to the bowl. Then he went to the door.

Breakfast was quickly and elegantly served at his table in the living room. There were no checks to sign. And certainly, no money changed hands. All that would be handled genteelly on the final bill.

How nice, Fernaud thought as he settled back into his chair with his third cup of coffee. He carefully placed the cup on the table. The movement caused him a twinge of pain through his fingers. He ignored it, looking out into the garden.

I shall miss this once Witten's no longer pays for such things, he thought, then soothed himself with the vision of the upcoming sale. *Yes, that will be good*, he mused, smiling to himself.

But today I must do several things to assure that the result is satisfactory. So much effort has been made. Art and Auctions *magazine will be particularly important. I must prepare my notes this morning for the interview. There must be proper attention to the auction. I also need to call the baroness and remind her of the time I will pick her up for the reception at the Levines' tonight.*

Ah, the baroness. It will be good to see her again. A woman who knows how to be a woman. So unlike the dreadful women of today.

He picked up a pencil and made a note on a hotel notepad. *And I shall need to arrange for the car. I also must call George DeSant and make an appointment to see him tomorrow. Yes, that is essential,* he thought, his mouth tightening. He absently tapped the point of the pencil on the pad, making little dots.

Putting down the pencil, Fernaud picked up the telephone and dialed the Carlyle. "Simon Aaron, please." The line went silent for a moment.

"Ah, Mr. Aaron, this is Jean-Claude Fernaud. Good morning. Yes, I am fine. I am also here in New York, and I believe that I will see you at the reception this evening. I am escorting the Baroness DeHart. Yes, she is excited to see you again, also. I will give her your best wishes. I am looking forward to it as well." Fernaud picked up his coffee cup and brought it tremulously to his lips. He sipped and returned the cup to the saucer on the table.

"I wanted to assure myself that you received the report I prepared on the American Impressionist pastel," he said, "and that the lawyers were satisfied. No, Mr. Aaron, it is genuine. I believe there is no question. Yes, that is satisfactory. I will be pleased to meet with the lawyers to prepare my testimony while I am here, if it is required." He changed the receiver to the other side and stretched his hand.

"I also hope it settles quickly, Mr. Aaron. I would not like to have anything interfere with the Klyberg sale. Until tonight then. Goodbye."

Fernaud put down the phone and thought about Simon Aaron. *How little he knows of art. Certainly compared to me. How strange that I should be working for a Jew. And yet, how appropriate.*

He glanced out the window and took another sip of coffee. He wondered if the rain would interfere with his plans.

There was another quiet tap at the door. He crossed the room and opened it to a bellman holding a large envelope. "Please forgive the interruption, Monsieur Fernaud, but a fax has arrived for you marked 'urgent delivery.'"

He closed the door with a nod and opened the envelope.

"Ah," he murmured, returning to his chair, "a note from that fool, Marking." It amused him that the note was handwritten. *He seems to be quite agitated by a letter from the Department of National Museums*, he thought as he attempted to decipher the handwriting. He moved his shoulders slightly so the table lamp illuminated the paper more directly.

He turned the page to a copy of the letter and read it to himself. The letter brought a smile to his lips. He chuckled at the convoluted reasoning of his countrymen. How shrewd of them to recognize the validity of Emil Rosenberg's bill of sale but to deny title to Herr Goering in order to claim the Matisse for themselves. And how absurd.

But how should he deal with Marking? He could of course tell him that the Nazis often extracted a bill of sale for pictures they extorted from Jewish families. It must have been some quirk in the German character, some desire for order. He could also lead him to cases and international agreements ignoring coerced bills of sale. But should he? Was it best to keep him interested, or to attempt to further delay him? Marking had already ignored his advice, obviously, and filed a claim with the French. How best to keep Marking in hand?

As he pondered the question, he idly turned the page to look at the bill of sale. His hand froze and the amusement died on his lips as he looked down at the page in front of him. There in a neat, copperplate handwriting was the signature of Georges DeSant. The witness to the bill of sale.

How long could it be before even a fool like Marking asked who this Georges DeSant was? And how long from asking that question to finding DeSant? My God, it was a direct link between the Matisse, Emil Rosenberg and Georges DeSant that was staring him in the face.

And how long would it be after they found Georges DeSant before they also found Jean-Claude Fernaud?

Twenty-nine

The breeze snatched away the sound of the window groaning in its track as it came up unevenly. The old man tipped over the windowsill. As he fell, his head hit the small ledge that encircled the fifth floor of the building, deflecting his fall so that he just missed the mother and her little boy walking down Central Park West towards the entrance to the park.

The little boy cried out and turned toward his mother to grasp her skirt. She scooped him up in her arms and rushed away from the crumpled, frail body lying face up on the sidewalk in the pool of spreading blood.

A crowd of gawkers gathered within moments. The doorman of the building rushed out to find out what was going on. An old woman was pointing upwards, jabbering excitedly to the man next to her. The man nodded, his lips pressed into a line.

One man had the presence of mind to call 911 on his cell phone. The first policeman appeared within minutes. After a hasty glance, he called his precinct.

Lt. Julian Wayne arrived in front of George DeSant's building a half hour later, hunched into his worn topcoat against the chill of a late fall afternoon. At least the rain had stopped. Wayne glanced at the plastic name badge above the uniformed officer's shirt pocket. "He got any I.D. on him, Tyler?"

"Don't know, sir. I didn't want to touch the body 'til you got here. But he seemed to be holding this." The officer handed Wayne what appeared to be an article clipped from a newspaper. There was blood staining the corner. "It was near his hand. I was afraid it would blow away."

"Okay, bag that. We'll look at it later. Let's see who this old guy was."

Wayne stepped toward the body, careful not to get blood on his shoes. Then he drew back George DeSant's coat with a pencil and took a wallet from the inside pocket, using his handkerchief. He opened it.

"Guy's name seems t'be DeSant. Lives here. 16th floor. Get me the doorman. Then call off the ambulance and tell the coroner to get over here. He's got another one."

The young officer came back with a Latino-looking man wearing what appeared to be the coat and hat of a rear admiral. "Lieutenant, this is Luis Almarez. He's the doorman here." Almarez was small. A head shorter than Wayne, who was no giant himself. A thin face the color of worn copper, and a wiry build. The coat was too big.

Wayne turned to Tyler. "Move this crowd along. I need to talk to Luis here."

Almarez looked uneasy, shifting from foot to foot. "Man, I don't want no trouble with 'a cops. Why do you wanna talk to me?"

"Luis," Wayne smiled, at least if tigers smile, "is that any way to do your civic duty? Why're you acting so upset? Didn't have anything to do with this, did you?" Wayne's smile broadened to show a mouth full of yellowed teeth.

Alvarez blanched.

"Luis, do you know that guy?" Wayne said, nodding toward the body. "Name's DeSant, maybe."

Alvarez glanced towards the body, then looked hastily away. His face seemed to lose color. "No man, I know the name, but I never seen him. I'm just here temporary. Regular doorman got sick. I don't know none of these people."

"Well now, Luis, that's real unfortunate like. Makes it a lot tougher for me. What do you know?" The emphasis was on "do."

"I don't know nothin', man." Almarez kept his eyes down. He shuffled his feet.

"Tch, tch, tch," Wayne made a clicking sound. "Sure you do, Luis. You just don't know it. Let me help you." A predatory smile flitted across Wayne's face. "Did anyone come to see DeSant today?"

"Lotsa people come in and go out. I don't remember 'em all."

"Well, think about it, Luis. Maybe in the last few hours. You ask their names and call up to the owner to make sure they're expected, don't you?"

Pigeon shit plopped onto the ground by Wayne's foot, speckling his shoe. He looked up. "God damned pigeons," he muttered. "Mayor said he was going to do something about them."

He took hold of Almarez's arm and took a step away from the building. He let go of his arm and leaned down into his face. "Well, Luis, do you ask their names?"

"Yeah, they said I should do that."

"Do you write down the names?"

"Nah. Nobody tol' me." Almarez's voice rose with some combination of fear and bravado. Wayne's voice hardened.

"Okay, did anyone ask for DeSant?"

"Maybe, man, I'm not sure."

"What do you mean, maybe? When?"

"Hey, I tol' you I'm not sure. A couple hours ago. Might a been an hour."

Frustration suffused Wayne's voice. "What was the guy's name? You asked him, didn't you?"

"Man, I got no idea."

"What did he look like?"

"I don' remember."

"Yeah, great. Was he tall or short? Do you remember how he was dressed?"

The doorman shrugged his shoulders and shook his head. He seemed to shrink under Wayne's interrogation.

"Did you see him leave?"

"I only watch 'em come in. I don't see none of 'em leave."

"Look, Luis, do you have a key to DeSant's apartment?"

"No one give me no keys to nothin', man."

Wayne made a weary gesture. He hated this kind of case. Nobody ever knew anything. He reached inside his jacket and withdrew a card. "Okay, Luis." He handed the card to him. "Call me if you think of anything else." Almarez took the card reluctantly.

Wayne motioned over the young officer. "First call forensics and get 'em down here. Then get hold of the regular doorman and check out this guy's story." He gestured at Almarez. "And find out if DeSant lives with anyone."

Wayne paused a moment to organize his thoughts. He realized that Luis Almarez was still there. "Get outta here," he growled. Almarez retreated hurriedly.

Then he turned back to the uniformed policeman. "Find out who has a key to his apartment. I want you to have a good hard look around. Don't touch anything. Tell forensics it may be a suicide. Maybe not. Have 'em go through the place. And you better see if you can dig up the next of kin. We got nothin' down here. I want your report on my desk in the mornin'."

Thirty

The trip downtown to Whiting & Pierce was dreadful. The cars were bumper to bumper, each jostling for the slightest advantage. The driver slammed on his brakes as a yellow cab darted in front of him. The car lurched. Jonathan caught the window strap to steady himself. The driver muttered a muted curse. The shrill complaint of horns spattered the car.

Simon stared out the window, ignoring it all. He kept shifting in his seat. He seemed distracted.

Whiting & Pierce still maintained its offices in a glass and steel tower on Wall Street, with a view out over the harbor to the Statue of Liberty. Many of the big Wall Street law firms and most of the investment banks had fled to Midtown years ago. But Whiting & Pierce stuck with its old ways. And the rent declined, which didn't hurt.

The table across the far wall of the conference room was filled with pastries and sliced honeydew, kiwi and golden raspberries. Coffee was served in china cups made with Whiting & Pierce's own pattern. Bagels were the law firm's nod to modernity.

Harvey Champlin, one of Jonathan's former protégés, was the lead partner. "You look great, buddy," Champlin said, holding Jonathan's hand in a warm handshake. Champlin smiled broadly and patted his other arm gregariously. "Teaching must agree with you. We miss you around here." Well, at least there wouldn't be any trouble executing the game plan once they'd agreed on one.

Larry Sims and Marty Fischer, two of the three investment bankers from Aspen & Leach, arrived within minutes.

"Where's Kent?" Simon demanded.

Larry Sims was the senior investment banker on the ground. He looked uneasy. "Simon, Henry asked me to apologize profusely," Sims said. It carried all the sincerity he could manage. It wasn't much. "He was called out of town suddenly. But he wanted me to assure you that he'll be available on his cell phone at a moment's notice."

"Asshole!" Simon snarled.

"Well, let's get down to it," Jonathan interceded to head off an explosion. Actually, Jonathan was pleased. As far as he was concerned, Kent hadn't had an original idea in years. And he was a turf player. Besides, Jonathan wanted the field to himself. It seemed he was something of a turf player too, at least in this situation. It surprised him.

Jonathan shed his tweed jacket and pulled down his tie. He got up to get a Diet Coke. He buttered a raisin bagel and put some honeydew melon on a pretty ceramic plate. It was something he missed. Endless food with no one counting. Even if the honeydew did taste like cardboard. Besides, if you ate standing up there were no calories. It was Franklin's First General Law. He had chewed on it a long time, and it was starting to show.

They spent an hour canvassing the alternatives. Witten's lending banks were being difficult. They weren't prepared to extend the due date on the loan, or permit payment of the subordinated debentures. If the subordinated debentures were not paid, it would put the senior debt—the bank debt—in default. That would result in a cross default of all of Witten's debt and could lead to a bankruptcy. Rollins would pounce. It was the Gordian knot Witten's was tied up in. The seemingly insoluble challenge. Jonathan loved it. This was almost fun.

Simon couldn't seem to sit still. He paced over to the buffet table, looked and came back. Then he got up and walked over to the window. His face was frozen. Was he bored? Scared? Was he even listening? Was Simon having second thoughts about bringing Jonathan in? Jonathan found it a little disconcerting. But they had to get on with it.

A public offering of more subordinated debt or any other security was out of the question. The disclosure required by the Securities and Exchange Commission rules would be devastating. Besides, it would take two or three months before the securities could be sold. Too long.

Marty Fischer floated the idea of a private placement of equity. "No," everyone concurred. With the stock price depressed, and taking into account the 30% discount a buyer would demand because it couldn't sell the securities right away, the dilution could push Simon out of control.

Jonathan had been sitting quietly for the last few minutes, seemingly lost in thought. "You know," he said, almost to the ceiling, his fingers tented across his lips, "wouldn't it be interesting if we could turn this mess to our advantage."

Everyone stopped talking and turned towards him.

"What do you mean?" Simon demanded, turning from the window. He sounded aggressive.

"Simon, you told me yesterday that Witten's only needs some fairly short-term money, right? And a month or two ago I read this article about the big pension funds getting antsy about the stock market and real estate."

Simon walked back to his seat. His eyes never left Jonathan's face. His concentration was almost palpable.

"Some of them were talking about investing in fine art as a way of diversifying," Jonathan said.

"Yeah, I read that too, but Witten's doesn't own any art. We just sell it." His voice was flat. There was anger at its fringes.

Jonathan didn't back down. "I know, Simon. But tell me, when you guarantee the sales price of a collection, like you did to the Klyberg estate, what happens if you sell the collection for more than the guarantee?"

"We usually split any excess with the seller. In the case of the Klyberg estate, it gets fifty cents of each dollar over and beyond the hundred million dollar guarantee. So?"

"And if you have to pay off on the guarantee, you get the art, right?"

"Usually. Unless we choose to just eat the loss and not buy in the pictures. Sell the stuff for what we can get and pay the excess to the estate out of our pocket."

"How much available money do you need from the banks at any one time in the form of letters of credit for those guarantees?"

"Around $200 million."

"And that $200 million is part of your bank line?"

"Yeah. But I don't have any idea where you're going with this," Simon responded, asperity creeping into his voice. Simon Aaron wasn't known for his patience.

The others around the table were listening intently. Everyone was sitting still. You could hear the buzz of the fluorescent lights.

"Just one more question," Jonathan continued, unperturbed. "If you could reduce the bank's commitment by $200 million, would they let Witten's pay off the subordinated debentures when they come due?"

"Sure. The subordinated debt is only a hundred million dollars. They would loan us the money to do it."

Jonathan stood and went to the whiteboard, writing out his points as he spoke. He made a little black dot in front of each point with a sharp poke of the black marker pen.

"We go to some key pension fund players with the following proposal." Poke. He wrote out the words *$200/3yrs.* "They make available on call an aggregate of $200 million for three years. The money will be a revolving loan to Witten's, subordinated only to the bank, but it can only be used to support guarantees on art to be sold."

Poke. The little black dot glistened in the fluorescent light. *Secured*, he wrote. "The loans will be secured by Witten's interest in the art you guarantee. Since the money will be available from established pension funds, they probably won't even have to put the money in escrow, simply acknowledge that it will be available unconditionally if the guarantee is called."

"Okay," Simon said. "Why should they?"

"Now if they don't ever need to put up the money, they get 1½ percent per annum until the guarantee expires." He wrote it on the whiteboard. "If they do have to put up the money, they get the two-year Treasury bill rate, less any interest on the funds." He poked a dot and also wrote that down.

Simon interrupted. His voice was tightly wound. "That's not anywhere near enough to make it interesting for those pension fund guys." Had this guy gone soft in the head?

Jonathan ignored him. His face was relaxed and his hazel eyes were sparkling. He had a grin on his face that irritated Simon.

"Yes it is," Jonathan said, "because you're going to split any upside dollars you get from the sale with them. It becomes a venture capital deal in art, with very little downside risk to the pension funds. They have Witten's on the hook for the loan. They get their interest and their loans repaid no matter what, unless Witten's goes under. Even then they have the art. And they can make a lot of money on the upside relying on Witten's expertise in pricing the art. If you have to, you can promise them a minimum return, but I don't think you will."

Simon looked interested. He was sitting still for the first time. But his fingers worked the table.

"From the standpoint of Witten's, it's on the expensive side," Jonathan said, "since you have to give up half of your upside profit over and above the guarantee. But if you're right about the future of the business, Simon, you won't have to use the credit line after the first year. You'll also have some margin for error if it takes longer than you think to turn Witten's around, and you'll be able to pay off your subordinated debentures when they come due. There will be no dilution to your equity or control. And we can move faster than Rollins." He stopped and put down the marker. "Any thoughts?" he said.

Harv Champlin was the first to speak. He put down the glass of soda he'd been sipping. He spoke around the edges of the ice cube he'd just sucked in. It made his voice hollow. "You know, if we structure this under Rule 144A and put it in the form of a security, the pension funds could trade the paper freely among themselves. They'd like that a whole lot."

"Good idea, Harv," Jonathan said. He wrote *R 144A* on the whiteboard.

Marty Fischer, the younger investment banker, held up his hand. It flashed through Jonathan's mind that he wanted to go to the restroom. Jonathan gestured to him.

Fischer spoke nervously. "I think we can make it even better if we divide it into two tranches. One part, say 80% of the amount, can be secured on a priority basis by the art that you have to buy in on the guarantee, if that should happen. That tranche should have no downside risk at all since it will be an obligation of Witten's and secured by 100% of the value of the art."

He looked down at some notes he had scribbled before going on. "The other piece would be riskier, the 20%, since it will be subordinated to the first tranche as well as the banks, but it will have a higher return and it will still be secured. Then the pension funds can choose how they want to play. I think the combined pricing will be better for Witten's."

Jonathan was startled. *Will wonders never cease? A bright investment banker.* "Great, Fischer." He turned to Larry Sims, the senior banker. "Does Aspen & Leach think it will work? You guys are going to have to package this and sell it. And it has to be done quickly and quietly."

"You know," said Sims, "I think it just might." He pondered for a moment, smiling to himself. He murmured, "Art Market Participation Certificates. 'ARMARs.' I like that name." His eyes refocused on Jonathan. "Look, I have to talk to my syndication people. They're the ones that sell the stuff, and they know what the pension guys will pop for these days. I'll let you know tomorrow."

Jonathan turned towards Harv Champlin. "Harv, how long to do a draft private placement memorandum? We need it fast."

"Give me a couple of days," Champlin said. "I'll do the draft myself. It'll save time."

"Great," Jonathan responded. "Start now. Let's assume Aspen & Leach like the deal."

Simon clapped his hands. "Okay," he said. "Good progress. Jonathan, let's get back to the hotel. I'm beat and I have a reception at Eric Levine's tonight."

Thirty-one

It was tedious work. They sat around the conference table, half-drunk cups of cold coffee and dirty plates cluttering the surface. Each of them had an inch-high stack of papers in front of him. Jonathan yawned. They slogged on through the dreary details with the lawyers and investment bankers, putting all the deal terms in place for the Art Market Participation Certificates.

A young associate noted a typo on page A-17. "Good catch," said his counterpart. That was called exciting in the life of a young lawyer.

The conference room was far too elegant for the mundane work being done on the polished mahogany table under the elegant modern lighting. The food was too prevalent. Simon didn't have patience for this kind of legal work. Who read all that minutiae anyway?

Jonathan was beginning to suspect he no longer had the patience either. This made teaching look thrilling. Heck, it made watching grass grow look thrilling. His attention wandered all over the place. He ate too much, just to have something to do. And it made him angry. He did it anyway.

Jonathan and Simon finally made their way back to the Carlyle around six. "Breakfast tomorrow?" A nod.

"Nine?"

"Okay." And that was it.

* * *

Jonathan felt beat, but he needed to speak to Ben Cohen at the law school. Damn Elly Warren and the B-School anyway. He dialed reluctantly.

"Ben, I don't see any way to make this joint MBA/JD course work for next year." He didn't try to hide his exasperation. "Let's put it off until Spring 2000. There should be plenty of deals I can use by then, and I'll have a better feel for this 'new economy.'"

So much for that. Too bad. He was disappointed. He'd been looking forward to teaching the course. It was the part of school he enjoyed most. The kids.

He thought about giving Nicole a call as he hung up with Ben Cohen. He looked at his watch. Too late in London. How about Valerie, his little red-headed model friend in Boston? No way. Somehow he just didn't feel up to it. Maybe he was tired.

His phone rang at eight as he was finishing his rather tasteless room service dinner. The only saving grace was the bottle of white wine on which he had splurged. Or rather, on which Simon had. Nicole's voice surprised him.

"Jonathan." She sounded strange. "I have gotten a call from the New York police. My father is dead. They say he committed suicide." She started sobbing.

"My God, Nicole! I'm so sorry."

"They have asked me to come to New York right away. I do not know what to do," she said, her voice rising. "They will not tell me anything over the telephone."

He spoke quickly, but with a calm strength. "Don't worry, I'll help. Get some rest if you can. I'll pick you up at the airport tomorrow. We'll deal with everything then." She gave him her flight number and arrival time.

Jonathan rang Simon, but there was no answer. He remembered that Simon had a business dinner. He left a voicemail message to call him urgently in the morning.

"Jonathan, this is Simon." The booming voice came over the phone at 7:30 a.m. the next day. "What's wrong? Couldn't it wait for breakfast? Problems with the investment bankers?"

"Simon, I have bad news. Nicole DeSant's father is dead. Apparently he committed suicide. She's on her way here. I'm going to meet her at JFK this afternoon."

"Is she okay? Can I do anything?" Some of the anxiety had drained from his voice. Jonathan knew he cared about Nicole, but now it wasn't critical.

"Not right now. The police are involved. Look, I'm going to try and help her. Can you handle the lawyers and the investment bankers for a while?"

"No problem. Besides, we're only working until three today. It's Thanksgiving." Jonathan was startled. He had forgotten Thanksgiving. "Use my car and driver," Simon said. "What time do you need them?"

Jonathan was waiting for Flight 118 from London when it arrived at the gate. Nicole DeSant was one of the first passengers off. He could read the fatigue in her face. She looked haggard and her eyes were red and puffy. She ran up to him and took his extended hands. He drew her in to him and put his arms around her. She was trembling.

"Oh, Jonathan. Thank you for being here."

"How are you holding up?"

"The police want to talk to me. Can you come? Please."

"Sure. Where are you going to stay? Do you want to stay at the Carlyle?"

"No. I have arranged to stay at the apartment. The police said there is no problem. And somehow it means something to me."

"Well, have dinner with Simon and me. It's Thanksgiving."

"No, Jonathan." She gave a sad smile. A tear slid down her cheek. "Thank you. But I am not really hungry. And I do not feel thankful. Please, let me call you in the morning. I would like to be alone tonight."

Jonathan met Simon for an early dinner at the Post House. Over a Thanksgiving dinner of steak and a bottle of '82 Petrus, he filled Simon in. There were only six or eight people in the restaurant and a skeleton staff. It was almost quiet. That was why they'd chosen it. Not a big steak night, as Jonathan had surmised.

"Don't worry about the deal for the moment," Simon said. He put down his knife and fork and picked up his glass of red wine by the stem. He stared into the glass for a moment, watching the colors on the surface change as he gently swirled the wine. Simon knew his wines when he wanted to. It just wasn't high on his priority list.

He took an approving sip. "Exquisite," he murmured, more to himself than to Jonathan. Simon put down his glass and wiped his mouth with the huge starched napkin. Then he got back to business.

"We're okay. You just take care of Nicole. I can handle the business end for a day or so. Champlin's a good guy. He really thinks a lot of you for some reason. Oh, and Sims was there this afternoon." Jonathan looked up with anticipation. "His syndication people are excited about the idea of Art Market Participation Certificates. They think the pension plans will jump on them."

"That's good. That's really good." There was satisfaction in Jonathan's voice.

"Yeah. In fact, I get the idea they'll be pushing them on Sotheby's soon," Simon said. "I made it clear that if any word of this got out before we completed our placement, I would make sure they never did business with any of my companies again. Don't they have any ethics?" It was a rhetorical question.

Jonathan was downstairs at breakfast the next morning when he was paged to the telephone. "Jonathan, I am supposed to see a

Lieutenant Julian Wayne at 2:00," said Nicole. She sounded more rested and a little calmer. "Can you meet me at the apartment? I will have some lunch sent up and we can go from here. And thank you once more. I have never dealt with the police."

Jonathan had no problem finding the building again, one of the beautiful prewar buildings on Central Park West. The DeSant apartment occupied an entire half floor, with a beautiful view over the park and out to Fifth Avenue. It was well appointed, with a brightness and a modern taste unexpected in an older man. Yellows and bright greens. Nicole greeted him at the door and led him into the dining room, where a cold lunch had been laid out.

The room was light and airy. A small vase of flowers had been placed in the middle of the soft yellow linen tablecloth that covered the round table. It picked up the yellows in the walls. He held her chair for her.

"Jonathan," she said as she picked at her food. She looked at him with her large, serious gray eyes. He put down his fork. "I cannot believe that my father committed suicide." Jonathan was reminded of how formally she spoke English. And how much it appealed to him.

"He loved me too much to cause me the pain he knew I would have. He would not have done this to me. And so horrible a death, to jump from here. Where we lived. Where I grew up." She lowered her eyes, then raised them to look at him again. Tears made them shine. "No, no. It is not possible."

He sat quietly, not knowing what to say.

"My father had become a devout Catholic. Suicide is not acceptable, you see. And he did not seem depressed when I spoke to him last week. He was looking forward to seeing me."

"I know it must be very difficult to accept," he ventured.

"No. I am not a child," she snapped angrily, tearing up again. "You did not know him. It is not right."

"Well, let's see what comes up." He reached over to cover her hand with his.

"Forgive me," Nicole said. She dabbed at her eyes with her napkin. "My nerves are on edge. I did not mean to snap at you. You have been very good to help me." Her mouth produced the shadow of a smile.

He started to speak but she held up her hand. "I have one more favor to ask, if you do not mind. My father's lawyer, a Samuel Cunningham, called and asked me if he could make an appointment to see me. He said it was important. I suggested he come here at 4:00. Would you mind joining us?"

"No, not all. As a matter of fact, I know Sam. We served on some bar committees together. But Nicole, he may want to discuss some confidential estate matters with you. Are you sure you want me here?"

"Yes, I would appreciate your staying. You will understand these matters better than I can. And I trust you."

"Lieutenant Wayne, this is Jonathan Franklin. I asked him to come with me." Nicole and Jonathan had found their way to Wayne's nondescript office in a nondescript police precinct building in Midtown. A half-cup of cold coffee with some cigarette ash floating in it sat on the corner of a scarred government-issue desk. The walls were surplus paint green.

Wayne was wearing a crumpled tie over a stained blue shirt. Some kind of notice was thumb-tacked to the corkboard on the wall to his right.

He had a picture on his desk. It was a collie of some kind. No wife, no kids. Just the dog. He had the burr of an afternoon beard on his cheeks, but it was only two o'clock.

"Thanks for comin' down, Ms. DeSant. Sorry 'bout your father. Let me make this quick. This looks pretty open and shut. We got nothin' to show it wasn't a suicide. Apartment was clean. Neat as a pin, in fact. Contrary to what people believe, most of these jumpers are suicides. Happens a lot with these old guys. More in winter. They get depressed or somethin'. Then, bam!"

Nicole held her hands clenched tightly together in her lap. Jonathan noticed that the polish on one of her fingernails was chipped. Her face was rigid. "Lieutenant, why did you ask me here? This is a very bad time."

"Yeah. Sorry," he mouthed the words. They were perfunctory. "There was one thing."

"Oh, and what is that, Lieutenant?" she asked, her words taut.

"Your father was a French citizen?"

"Yes."

"And he fought in the war? You know, World War II, I mean."

"Well, he was not in the army. But he did fight."

"Okay. Any problems your father was havin'? Money? Health? Anything?"

"No," Nicole said carefully, "not that I know of." She leaned forward in the wooden chair on which she sat. "What are you getting at, Lieutenant?"

"Well, Ms. DeSant, when we found your father, he was clutchin' this."

Wayne passed Nicole a copy of an article from the *International Herald Tribune*, enclosed in a cellophane holder. She drew it across the desk and fumbled in her purse for a moment. She removed her glasses and slipped them on. Jonathan watched her eyes move across the page as she started to read.

He leaned over and started to read too. She adjusted the paper so he could see. The short article described four paintings that had been found in a closet in the basement of a museum in East Germany, including a Matisse and a Cezanne, that were apparently Nazi war loot. Nothing important.

Jonathan was puzzled by a slight tightening in Nicole's mouth as she progressed and a subtle straightening of her posture.

"Ms. DeSant," Wayne interrupted. "There any reason your father would be holdin' that clipping? Would that be connected here in some way?"

"No," she responded, more curtly than Jonathan would have expected, "I cannot see how this could be of concern."

"Well, thanks for comin' in, Ms. DeSant. Just tryin' to tie up loose ends. We'll contact you if there's anythin' further we wanna know."

Jonathan turned to Nicole in the car.

"Something upset you about that article. What's going on?"

She put her hand on his arm. He felt her grip. "I like you, Jonathan, I really do." Her voice was soft, but it carried a weight that surprised him. "But I do not want to talk about it." She stopped as if she didn't want to go on. "It is possible that I was wrong about my father."

Thirty-two

"Hello, Sam," Jonathan greeted Sam Cunningham with a grin. "I'll bet you didn't expect to see me here."

Nicole had brought Cunningham into the living room. Jonathan was surprised at how much older Cunningham looked. His face was puffy, and he had a ruddy complexion that looked unhealthy.

"My goodness! Jonathan Franklin." He extended his hand with a sweeping gesture to clasp Jonathan's. "It's been years. I heard you gave up your cushy job with Whiting & Pierce and went off to teach. Well, I'm glad to see you looking so well. Nice tweeds. But what are you doing here?"

Nicole answered. "Mr. Cunningham, I asked Professor Franklin to join us. He is my adviser." She spoke quickly.

That was news to Jonathan. He could still see the tension from her encounter with Lt. Wayne. There was an unaccustomed tightness around the corners of her mouth. She appeared to be straining for control.

"Well, Ms. DeSant. Can I ask if, eh, Professor Franklin is advising you in his capacity as a lawyer?" He turned aside to Jonathan. "Jonathan, you're still licensed to practice in New York, aren't you?"

Jonathan nodded. "Absolutely."

"Good. Then, Ms. DeSant, I would prefer that he act for you here in his capacity as a lawyer. In that way, we can preserve the privileged nature of our conversations. Is that acceptable?"

"If it is acceptable to Professor Franklin."

"Sure. Maybe we should sit down."

"I wanted to speak with you about your father's estate," Cunningham said to Nicole, who had taken a seat across from him on the light yellow couch. She sat with her back straight and her knees together. Her hands were clasped in her lap. "And I thought it was important that we speak as soon as possible. Do you know much about the assets of the estate, Ms. DeSant?"

"No. Very little. I never inquired, and my father never brought it up."

"Your father was the beneficiary of a trust fund that comprised by far the largest part of his estate." Cunningham put his scuffed brown leather briefcase on the coffee table The brass buttons on the bottom clicked against the glass top. He opened it, took out a sheaf of papers and looked up.

"I've been the trustee for several years. You know, Ms. DeSant, your father was a very astute investor." He leafed through the papers he had taken out. He divided the papers on the table and ran his finger down a column.

"The corpus of the trust has doubled again and again through his insights and direction of the portfolio, even after we distributed the money to him he needed to live and raise you." He put his finger on a number near the bottom. "The trust is worth somewhat more than $50 million."

"*Mon Dieu!*" said Nicole, very quietly.

Cunningham raised his eyes, and his mouth was drawn. "However, Ms. DeSant, I'm afraid I have some very disquieting news. The trust was drawn up in a most unusual manner. Perhaps you know. It was prepared and funded by your relatives in France, shortly after the war."

"Yes, I knew that. My father told me. But what is this strangeness you refer to?"

"Well, the trust contains a provision that provides that if your father commits suicide, the trust reverts to your relatives, and does not pass to you."

Nicole gasped. Her hand flew up to her lips. Then her eyes hardened.

"That is absurd, Mr. Cunningham." Anger mingled with disbelief in her voice. "Why would anyone do that? Is it legal?"

"As to why, I can't say. Perhaps the family was concerned about your father. As to its being legal, I'm afraid so. These trusts can be constructed in any way the grantor desires."

"What can we do?"

"Nothing from a legal standpoint, I'm afraid."

"You mean I cannot even contest the trust?"

"No, Ms. DeSant. This isn't a will. There are no grounds for contest under the law."

"But does the entire amount revert? Even what my father earned?"

"Ms. DeSant, I'm afraid so. The money is all part of the trust."

"It does not seem fair, Mr.Cunningham. It was our money. My father earned it. This cannot be."

She was struggling for control. This seemed to be too much for her in one day.

"I am sorry, Mr. Cunningham," she said. "May we continue this at another time? After I have had a chance to speak to Professor Franklin, perhaps we can talk again."

Cunningham rose. "Thank you for your time, Ms. DeSant. I'm sorry to be the bearer of bad tidings."

He turned to Jonathan as they walked toward the door. His voice was very quiet, almost a whisper. "Perhaps I could take you out for an early drink tonight. I want to catch up, and I have something I want to discuss with you."

"Sure, Sam. Where and when?"

"Let's say the Pierre at 6:15, shall we? See you there," he said, shaking Jonathan's hand.

* * *

"Nicole, this is getting weird."

Jonathan turned from the door and began to pace. He had his back to Nicole. He turned and stopped. "First you react in a strange way to that article the policeman showed you, and then you won't talk about it." His frustration came through clearly. "Now, this 'suicide clause' business. I've never even heard of a 'suicide clause.' " He spread his hands. "You say you want me to help. But maybe you'd better let me in on what's going on."

"Please do not be angry with me." Her eyes grew wet. She still had on her glasses. It made her look vulnerable. "This is a matter of great embarrassment to my family. We are very private. We would never speak of it. I am sorry that I got you involved."

"You don't have to tell me. If you prefer, I could just leave and forget about it." He was annoyed. "You don't owe me anything. And I don't want to cause you any more pain, God knows."

"No. Please." Her voice rose. There was a pleading quality in it. She held out her hand. "I do need your help. I do not understand what is happening. First my father's death. And now this. Perhaps it would be better if I spoke of it to someone I trust. Please, sit down. Please."

He settled reluctantly into the chair across from her again.

"You see," she started hesitantly in a thin voice, "my father was accused of collaborating with the Nazis during the war." Tears started again in her gray eyes. "Of getting art for them from the Jews. Such an awful thing. It was a terrible scandal. Our family in France is very prominent."

Her hands moved nervously in her lap. "They hushed up everything to protect the family and sent my father away to America to keep him quiet and out of the way. The family set up the trust. My father was never allowed to return to France. They forbade my father to even speak of it to them. They wanted everyone to forget."

He sat quietly, watching her face as she spoke. Shadows in the room had started to dim her features. He felt guilty about his outburst. He remembered his own father and his family. His history was important to him too. "I understand," he said softly and settled more deeply into the chair.

"I knew there was something deeply wrong," said Nicole. "I only learned what I know from my cousin Henri. My father never spoke of it to me. He was a wonderful man, but very proud."

"Go on." Jonathan kept his face neutral. He was warmed by Nicole's trust. But he was intruding into a very dark place he hadn't expected to be.

"Apparently, my father was involved in procuring for the Nazis a Matisse painting from a Jew, in return, supposedly, for my father's helping his family to escape. The family did get out of Paris, it seems. But I understand that they were killed in a bombing that destroyed the house in which they were hiding in Vichy, before they could cross the Pyrenees."

"It must have been a terrible burden for him to carry."

"Henri says that my father told him once that it was untrue, that he had tricked the Germans, but that the family would hear nothing of it. It embittered my father's life. We lacked for nothing, but we lacked for everything. That is why, except for Henri, I do not speak to my family in France."

He nodded. It was growing dark in the apartment. Neither of them stirred to turn on a light. Somehow the dimness seemed appropriate.

"As the years passed, my father seemed to get better, more free of his bitterness. It must be hard for you to understand how difficult it was for him to be cut off completely, from his heritage, from his lineage. But he laughed more in the last few years. I had hoped that he could find a little joy in what time he had left."

Jonathan thought of his own father again. How he wished he had had more time with him. Perhaps he would have understood him.

"That article that he was clutching," Nicole said, "describes a very distinctive Matisse painting. I think it is the one that my father was accused of procuring for the Nazis. I believe that he was horrified by the thought that all of his humiliation would be raised again when the painting was returned to France and its history was revealed. I do not think that he could stand it." She covered her face with her hands and shook with the muffled sobs.

It was almost dark as Jonathan made his way across Central Park, his hands thrust deep into the pockets of his topcoat. He had his silver snuffbox in his hand. He had slipped off one glove and was rubbing it, remembering his father. There was just a hint of snow in the crisp air, and the trees were dusted white. A pug ran up and sniffed at his leg. He shooed it away. He wasn't much on dogs. The pug gave a small growl and scampered back to its owner.

People walked along, brandishing their department store bags and umbrellas. A mother with two little girls chided them playfully in bursts of frosty air as they danced around her. A young couple was holding hands. He realized how much he missed the city, particularly at Christmas time.

The Pierre Hotel was almost directly across the park from the DeSant apartment, and he had decided on the spur of the moment to walk. He had half an hour before his drink with Sam Cunningham, and he wanted time to think about everything that had happened over the last two days. So much. How life changes so quickly.

Cunningham was in the bar when Jonathan got to the hotel. He half rose and extended his hand.

"Jonathan, thanks for coming."

"Sam, it's been a long time. How are things?"

"Oh, fine." His voice had a shaded tone. "You know. Law's going from bad to worse. I miss the old days when it used to be a profession and not a business."

"I agree. I think things are getting out of hand. One of the kids at school told me the other day that the big firms are starting them at $140,000. My God."

"Yeah. You know, it almost makes me laugh. When I started in '62, they paid me $6,000 a year. It's the salaries that changed everything. Hourly rates have gone through the roof. You must have been charging $500 an hour over at Whiting & Pierce."

"Actually $600. That's when I stopped talking to myself. I couldn't afford it anymore," Jonathan said, trying for irony.

"And in my shop now," said Cunningham, untouched by the humor, "it's nothing but producing billable hours and bringing in business. The management committee has really been on my back for the last year. To tell you the truth, I don't have the stamina to work 60 hours a week anymore. And I've never been a rainmaker."

"Sam, why don't you just quit? Do something else. I did."

Cunningham's quick laugh was bitter. "I envy you, Jonathan. But I got remarried a few years ago. Sandra likes our lifestyle. And I made a couple of really lousy investments."

"Tough spot, Sam. Hopefully, things will get better."

"Yeah." Cunningham deflected. "And you're happy teaching?"

"Love it." Not quite, but this didn't seem like the time to equivocate. "But I also do a few private matters. You know, the kind of spice that makes the dish."

"I was surprised to see you with Nicole DeSant," Cunningham said. There was a query in his voice.

"Don't worry." Jonathan chuckled. "Nicole's only a friend. I'm not trying to horn in on any of your legal work."

"It's the DeSant trust I wanted to talk to you about. But let's get some drinks first. I really need one."

Judging by Cunningham's face, he didn't doubt it. Cunningham caught the waiter's eye and beckoned him over.

The drinks came. Jonathan noticed Cunningham's hand shook as he raised the drink to his lips. He drank off half the glass. He put it back on the table and started to talk.

"I didn't want to say anything in front of Ms. DeSant, but I'm really troubled by the idea that Georges DeSant committed suicide. I just don't buy it."

Jonathan leaned forward in his chair. "That's a pretty serious thing to say."

"I know, but I was with Georges DeSant the day before he supposedly jumped. He was full of life. He was looking forward to seeing his daughter, and we discussed some long-term investment moves. No, it just doesn't make any sense to me."

"Sam, what about the article in the *International Herald Tribune*?"

"What article?" Cunningham straightened.

"There was an article about the recovery of some Nazi war loot in Germany. Nicole thinks it may have upset her father a lot."

Cunningham paused and seemed to reflect back for a moment. "Oh, that article." He made a dismissive gesture. "DeSant mentioned something about it. In passing. I can tell you, it didn't seem to be a big thing with him at all."

"Sam, you know how important this is. Can you hold off any determination with respect to the trust until we can get to the bottom of this?"

"Well, that could be tough, but I'll try. What are you going to do?"

"I don't know. The police sure don't seem too concerned. They think it was suicide. Maybe I can try to look into it over the next couple of weeks. I still have a few contacts, and I have to be in town anyway. I'll see what I can turn up. You work on stalling the reversion of the trust. I need to speak to Nicole."

Thirty-three

Jonathan walked with his chin down and his hands buried deep in the pockets of his raincoat. Street lights glittered on the rain-polished sidewalk. He couldn't keep this information from Nicole. But if Sam Cunningham was wrong, it would be dreadful for her.

Cunningham didn't have any real proof. The problem was, it would be just as terrible if Cunningham was right. Suicide on one hand, murder on the other. Damn!

He placed a reluctant call to Nicole when he got to his room. "I just had a drink with Sam Cunningham. Can we get together tonight? He had some things to say that we need to discuss."

"Of course, if it seems important to you. Jean-Claude Fernaud called. He just heard about my father. He asked to take me to dinner. I am sure he would not mind if you joined us."

"Look, we can meet after dinner."

"No. Actually, I would prefer it if you would come. We are meeting at Café des Artistes at 8:30. I will tell Jean-Claude you are joining us."

Café des Artistes is a small, rather elegant New York restaurant off Central Park West, famous for its murals. Jonathan was the first to arrive. Jean-Claude Fernaud arrived a moment later. Jonathan stood and extended his hand. The handshake was a careful one. He remembered Fernaud's hands.

"Monsieur Fernaud. Nice to see you again, although these are sad circumstances." Fernaud folded his long frame into a chair. The Legion of Honor was lustrous in his buttonhole.

The restaurant was dim, but not dark. The tables were set apart from each other. The dinner conversations were hushed. Fernaud leaned towards Jonathan and spoke in a quiet voice. So quiet that Jonathan had to lean forward also.

"Yes, Professor Franklin. I called Mademoiselle DeSant as soon as I heard. What a terrible thing. It is fortunate that I was here in New York. I saw her father just a few days ago."

A waiter approached the table. "Can I bring you an aperitif, or perhaps some wine?" the waiter asked.

"We're waiting for another guest," Jonathan replied, turning him aside.

He reached for his napkin. Jonathan paused as he was placing the napkin in his lap and looked up. He realized Fernaud might have seen George DeSant after Sam Cunningham. It could be important. "Monsieur Fernaud, how did you find Monsieur DeSant?"

"Well, I had not seen Georges DeSant for many years until recently. We knew each other during the war, but we lost contact. He sent me a note when I received an award from the French government a few years ago, and we renewed our acquaintance. This was one of the few times that I actually saw him." He made a small palms-up gesture with a shrug. "He seemed well."

Fernaud hesitated a moment, then spoke slowly. "Actually, he did seem troubled by something. It was just a feeling I had. I have no idea what it was. We only spent a few minutes together."

He looked over Jonathan's shoulder and rose. "*Bonjour*, Nicole," Fernaud said, as the maitre d' brought her to the table.

Jonathan stood. Fernaud kissed her on both cheeks. Jonathan got a light kiss on one cheek from Nicole. He held out a chair for her.

"I was just speaking to Professor Franklin about your father," Fernaud said. "It is most sad. I will miss him." He covered her hand with his.

The wine was good. Jonathan was taken with the precision of the waiters, like a choreographed dance to silent music. Nicole seemed to visibly relax as the evening wore on. Jonathan was pleased. It would make his revelations easier perhaps.

She folded her napkin and placed it on the table beside her half-finished dessert. "Jean-Claude, thank you for your friendship. But I am tired, and Jonathan and I still must meet to discuss some matters concerning my father's estate."

Fernaud dabbed at his mouth with his napkin. "*Bien sûr*. It has been my pleasure." They rose and exchanged brief good-byes.

"Nicole, I don't want to cause you any further distress."

Jonathan and Nicole had returned to the apartment and were sitting in the living room. Jonathan was in a chair beside the end of the couch where Nicole sat. He was leaning towards her, his hands on his knees. "But I'm no longer certain that you weren't right in doubting your father's suicide."

Her eyes opened wide. She started to say something, but Jonathan hurried on. He wanted to get it all out.

"At least, I think we need to find out more about it," he said. "Sam Cunningham feels strongly that your father could not have committed suicide. He says that your father was unaffected by the newspaper article, that he was looking forward to the future with eagerness. Monsieur Fernaud, on the other hand, sensed some underlying concern in your father."

Nicole had sat up rigidly in her chair as Jonathan spoke. Her mouth was now a straight red line. He could see the pain in her eyes.

"Jonathan, I care most about my father and how he is remembered. I do not want him to be thought of with shame, to have killed himself." Fifty million dollars registered in her mind. Her jaw tightened. "And all that money—everything my father earned—to go to my family in France . . ." She shook her head angrily. It made her dark hair move and catch the lamplight. He could see her nails bite into her palms. "No, it must not be."

He leaned across and put his hand gently on her arm. "I think what's really important here is how you remember your father. This will torment you if it isn't resolved. We owe it to him to find out what happened." He stopped. He didn't want to sound stupid or sentimental.

"I don't want to be cavalier about fifty million dollars, but right now it's your peace of mind that I'm concerned about. Cunningham had the clearest picture of your father, as far as I can tell. Maybe if I have Cunningham talk to the police, we can get them to pursue this. It's not much, but it's worth a try."

She shook her head strongly, a diamond stud flashing for an instant, her gray eyes wide. "No. Please. I do not want the police involved further in my family's affairs. I do not want more scandal. If they make an investigation, I am afraid that it will all become public again. Is there no other way?"

He paused and thought for a moment. Then he began again, hesitantly.

"Maybe. If that's how you feel, but it's going to make it a lot tougher. I know a discreet private investigating firm. Ex-FBI, CIA, Interpol and the like. We can get them involved if we need to. Let me think about it."

It was late the next day. Jonathan and Nicole again were sitting on the yellow sofa in the living room of the DeSant apartment. The clouds shadowing the sun made moving patterns of light across the floor. He turned toward her.

"I've been thinking about this whole mess," he said. "I kind of see it as a blank wall, where we have to run our fingers along it, feeling for the cracks. What your father did during the war may be important. That newspaper article is the only connection we have. As far as I can tell, there are only two ways to go. Didn't your cousin Henri mention something that your father said about the war? We need to talk to him."

Nicole nodded in agreement. "Of course."

"The only other thing I can think of that we can do is get the investigators to start digging through old records and talk to people and see if they can find out the names of the Nazis who were involved in procuring art in Paris during the occupation. Maybe they can actually find out who dealt with your father. But that's a long shot." Boy, that was an understatement. "A lot of people have died. We're going to have to get really lucky."

She shifted her position and smoothed at her skirt nervously. "This will be very expensive, will it not? Apart from the trust, I do not have a great deal of money. The trust even owns the apartment, I find." There was an echo of defeat in her voice.

"Well, yes, it may be expensive. The firm I had in mind does charge a lot. But I think this is critical if we don't want the police involved. And we may not have a lot of time. Sam Cunningham doesn't know how long he can hold off the settlement of the trust." She noticed he had used the term "we." It made her feel closer to him.

"I do not want my father to be further harmed," she said. The sadness in her voice tore at him.

"And, you know, come to think of it, this should really be an expense of the trust." Jonathan paused, then smiled at her. "Let me give Cunningham a call and see if I can get him to authorize the trust to pay the bills. He wants to do the right thing. It's Saturday, but maybe he's in the office. If he approves, I'll make the arrangements with the investigators." He rose. "Can you call your cousin? We need to sit down with him quickly. With something this important, it's my experience that this has to be done face-to-face."

.

"Henri has galleries in London, Paris and New York. He travels constantly. Let me call and find out his plans."

It was Monday morning before Sam Cunningham finally returned his call. He was having coffee in the Carlyle breakfast room.

"Sam, we're going to need to get some investigators involved. I want to use Perone, Brill & Co. I think they're the best. I want them to see if they can dig up any information on what happened to DeSant during the war, which Germans he dealt with and the like. Hang on for a second." Cunningham could hear a murmured conversation on the other end of the phone.

"Sorry, Sam, I just had to pay my bill. As to the investigators, I also may need them to pursue any information I can turn up. I think it's a trust obligation." He spoke with more authority than he felt. Years of practice. Often wrong, but never in doubt. "After all, it involves the resolution of the terms of the trust." A stretch. "We may be talking about, oh, up to $75,000, all in, maybe a little more. How do you want to handle it?"

"To tell you the truth, I hadn't thought about it, but it seems okay to me. Let me think it over and do some research. I'll get back to you in a couple of days at the latest."

Cunningham sounded like he was under a lot of pressure. Jonathan didn't want to push. "Great." He disconnected and put in a call to Nicole.

"Henri called me late last night, Jonathan. We are fortunate. He is on his way to New York. He asked if we could join him for breakfast tomorrow. He will be happy to help in any way that he can. Can you meet us at the Four Seasons Hotel at 8:30 tomorrow morning?"

After he confirmed the breakfast and hung up, he called Simon Aaron. He sure felt like he had a lot of bases to cover. And it looked like an extra innings game.

"Simon, how's it going? Have the investment bankers soft circled any of the pension funds, you know, gotten any tentative commitments?"

"Where the hell have you been?" Not exactly the answer to his question. Simon Aaron wasn't a happy camper. "The pension funds are eating up these Art Market Participation Certificates. Sims tells me his syndication people want to know if we will increase the offering by another $100 million. Champlin's doing a terrific job. He said they might have to burn out some associates working round-the-clock to grind out the documents."

Jonathan wondered when Simon would stop for breath. Not soon, apparently. He was on a tear. "I told him to burn out the whole damn firm if he had to. I made it clear that we need the final offering document no later than day after tomorrow, close of business." Simon paused. Finally. "You know, one of the few pleasures I get out of life anymore is beating up my lawyers." Simon chuckled.

Jonathan didn't. He remembered all too well.

Simon continued forcefully before Jonathan could say anything. "You have to be in the meeting tomorrow. Six p.m. at Whiting & Pierce. We need to finalize the offering. And we have a problem. One of our syndicate banks overseas is holding up the amendment to our loan agreement. The agent bank is screaming bloody murder. We can't even get the bastards on the phone," Simon groused. "Time differences, my ass. I think Rollins has a hand in this."

"Simon, what piece of the loan does that foreign bank have?"

"Maybe $30 million."

"Give some thought to asking the agent if they'll step up to buy out the overseas bank if we pay down another $30 million on the line of credit. They usually have a right to do that in their syndication agreement. You said the pension funds want to give us more money. We can expand the Participation Certificate sale."

"Good thought. Let me try them and we can talk about it tomorrow." An afterthought. "By the way, how are you doing with Nicole?"

"A lot worse than I'm doing with you," he answered ambiguously.

"Well, quit playing around and get back to work."

Simon was starting to press. There wasn't a smile in his voice. If Jonathan stepped up to the plate, who was going to cover all the bases?

Thirty-four

"*Bonjour*, Nicole. *Ça va?*" Henri DeSant rose from his table in the Four Seasons dining room and kissed Nicole on both cheeks.

"Henri, this is my friend of whom I have spoken, Professor Jonathan Franklin." Jonathan had had his cab swing across the park to pick her up.

Henri extended his hand. "A pleasure, Professor Franklin. I appreciate what you have done for Nicole."

The dining room spoke of high-ceilinged elegance with its light colors, for which the Four Seasons was famous. The maitre d', appearing at their elbow magically, handed each of them a menu. "Would you care for coffee?" he asked. At their nod, he made a small gesture to their waiter, who hurried off. "Please enjoy yourselves," he said with a small bow and departed.

"It has been too long," Henri said, looking at Nicole with affection. "You are even lovelier then I remember. The auction business must agree with you." His smile crinkled around his mouth. "Although, you know, you would be far happier in my gallery, as an art dealer."

Henri DeSant was thin and dapper, a man in his late fifties or early sixties. He had the family's gray eyes, but darker than Nicole's, almost steel gray. His accented English only added to his essential air of sophistication.

"Thank you, Henri." She smiled a little as she looked down to spread her large white napkin on her lap. The smile broadened as she looked up. "And you are as charming as always."

They were interrupted by the service of their coffee. Jonathan lifted his head at the rich smell. Each took a moment to sip.

Henri DeSant's face turned serious as he put down his cup. "Nicole, I was so sorry to hear about your father. It must have been a terrible shock to you, as it was to me. He was like my older brother."

"Thank you, Henri. I am better now." Jonathan didn't think so, but he admired her determination. "And it was about my father that we wished to speak." She brushed a strand of hair away from her eyes. "Do you recall, you told me once that my father spoke to you about the war? Can you tell us about it? It is very important." She took some time to explain.

"Well," Henri said, "perhaps we should order before we start." He signaled for a waiter. Nicole opened her purse and took her glasses from their case. She slipped them on with one hand as she picked up the large leather-bound menu. The tip of her tongue poked between her lips as her eyes ran down the page. Jonathan noticed. Was it a habit she had? He hadn't seen it before. At least he didn't remember.

A waiter appeared at their elbow. "What may I get for you?" he asked politely, looking at Nicole. She ordered and returned her glasses to her purse. Henri encouraged Jonathan to order next with a gesture of his hand.

When the waiter finally departed, Henri continued. There was a reluctance in his voice. "Nicole, I told you that I am willing to help you in any way that I can. I do not see what this can mean, and it has been a very long time." He paused, and his eyes became unfocused as he sought to recall the incident. Then he started to speak. His voice was hushed, but clear.

"As I remember, you were away at college. I tried to see your father as often as I could when I was in New York. He was a wonderful man. But he was very lonely. We had gone out to dinner. We had had a bottle of wine, but, I assure you, we were quite unaffected. Your father was, how do you say it," Henri gestured with his hands, "feeling down. Under a gray cloud, as we would say."

Jonathan was leaning forward on his elbow, his hand folded around his fist, his thumb to his lips as he listened. The waiter appeared and refilled their coffee cups. As the waiter departed, Henri continued.

"Your father started talking about how much he missed Paris, particularly at this time of year. It was spring. The cafés, the style, the very air. I asked him why he did not visit. Of course, I knew about the disturbance in the family. We all did. But I thought that it must have passed long ago. Or even so, he could come and see me and my family."

A small excitement broke out across the room as the maitre d' rushed to explain to a glaring matron why she could not bring the pug she was holding to her breast into the restaurant. It quickly subsided. Henri continued.

"He did not respond to me. But he started to speak of the war. It was a strange story, very disjointed, almost incomprehensible. He was very bitter. I was surprised. I will try to recount what he said as best I can."

"Please, Henri," Nicole said. Her voice was quiet. She put her hand on his to encourage him. But her face seemed a little drawn.

As he started to speak, a tall man approached the table. Henri rose and they shook hands warmly. Henri introduced him, and they turned away and murmured a few phrases Jonathan couldn't catch. Then the man departed and Henri resumed his seat.

"One of my clients," he said. He made a small gesture with his manicured hand. "I apologize for the interruption." Then his face fell into a frown as he resumed his dialogue. The memories were painful.

"The Nazis had occupied Paris. It was a difficult time. People were very afraid. We cannot now understand the cold fear that was part of the air. But they made a semblance of going about their lives as usual. The Nazis had allowed the DeSant Bank to remain open for their own reasons."

He lowered his voice further. "One did not dare to anger the Nazis. People had been dragged from their homes. The click of jackboots on the streets at night was a terrifying sound."

Jonathan found he was holding his breath. He felt the tension.

"The Jews were the most frightened. Our grandfather was then head of the bank. He knew many of the Jewish bankers and merchants. A few were even his friends. Those were very dark days."

They waited again as the waiter served croissants and orange juice. He poured more coffee.

"I think these are quite good," Henri said, shifting moods and lifting a croissant. "Not, of course, as good as ours in Paris." He gave a pale laugh, and Jonathan realized how taut their nerves were.

"Henri, please go on," Nicole said. She teased the story out like a snarled dark thread. It was obvious that Henri DeSant was uncomfortable. He turned back reluctantly.

"The Nazis had started seizing art works, particularly the so-called degenerate art that they were supposed to despise." Henri resumed. "Goering was particularly avid, or so your father said. He had many officers in Paris whose only purpose was to find art and seize it, by any means, for his private collection in Berlin. But Goering was insistent that no one know what he was doing. He wanted no questions." Jonathan hardly dared move. He had never been so close to darkness.

"Apparently one of these men—I do not remember the name very well, perhaps it was Kurtz or Koertzmann or some such name —somehow became aware of your father. One day he called your father to his office. Your father said he went trembling. People were called who never again reappeared."

"But what could he want with my father?" Nicole asked. Her voice betrayed her anxiety. "He must have been no more than twenty years old."

"Oh, this officer knew who your father was. And he knew of our family. He made threats. He alluded to seizing the bank and arresting our grandfather. He said the Nazis knew of the acts our grandfather had taken against the German Reich. They knew that he associated with Jews."

"That is horrible." A tear rolled down her cheek. She raised her hand to brush it away. She daubed at her cheek with her napkin. A streak of mascara remained.

"He wanted your father's assistance, his collaboration. If your father would approach a man, a family friend, Emil Rosenberg, who knew the elder DeSant, and offer to assist him in leaving Paris, Kurztmann would try to protect the DeSant family. Your father was to tell Rosenberg that there were those who wanted to help the Jew escape. But no one must know. He must not tell even our grandfather. Rosenberg, in return, must turn over his art to the Nazis. Particularly one picture. Your father was to be the messenger."

Jonathan was hardly breathing. He lifted his glass of orange juice to his lips to break the tension. He felt as if the room was closing in.

"Your father started to sob. We were in the middle of a restaurant. I was very embarrassed. He was a grown man. I felt helpless. There was nothing I could do but wait. It was most uncomfortable. He finally stopped, but as he went on, his story became less coherent and more impossible." Henri looked down and shook his head. His hand balled into a fist.

"While your father was very fearful, he was also an intelligent, even a defiant young man. It seems that over the next several days, he formed a plan, or so he said. He wanted to protect the family. He admitted to me that he was also afraid for himself. But he hated the Nazis. He hated what they had done. He could not do what this Nazi was asking him to do. He could not have lived with himself, he said. But he could not refuse. He was desperate. He had friends in the art world. Art had been his great love, you know."

Nicole sat upright, transfixed by the story. Tears rolled untouched down her cheeks. Jonathan put his hand on her arm.
"Are you okay?"

Henri paused, realizing the impact on Nicole. She nodded but
didn't look at Jonathan. She grabbed at the napkin and wiped at
her face. The white napkin was smudged with black. "Please go
on, Henri." She paused. "Please," she said pleadingly.

"He spoke to his friends." Henri's face showed the strain of
these memories. His hands made little movements on the white
tablecloth. "Was it possible to copy a picture? Could it fool the
Nazis? Could they help him? He said that he found an artist who
executed a copy of the picture. He never told me his name. Indeed, he said, it was a brilliant copy, and that he passed it along to
the Nazis."

Henri sighed and he spread his hands. "You, of course, have
to wonder whether any such thing is possible. The risk would have
been great. How much of this was the musing of a man who was
deeply troubled? Even one consumed by guilt? I do not know. I
have never heard of such a thing. In any case, this Koertzmann
was transferred soon thereafter. Your father never heard more
from him."

Nicole stared down into her half cup of cold coffee as if she
was absorbed by the little swirls of color on the surface. It felt to
Jonathan like they were there in a dark, evil place within this great,
bright, bustling dining room.

"But after the war, some record was discovered, and your
father was accused of collaboration. His story was treated as nonsense. He could not show any proof. Rosenberg had been killed
during the war. No artist ever turned up. Perhaps he was also killed,
if he ever existed. The picture, a quite famous Matisse, was never
found. But so many paintings were lost in the bombings."

"But why did our family not protect him? It must have been
awful for him," she said.

"The family was deeply ashamed. There were also important financial considerations at the time. Your father insisted, but I am told that no one believed him. Who could believe such a story? They used all of their influence to hush up the scandal and sent your father to live in the United States."

Henri sat back. His face seemed pale, almost drained. His breakfast remained in front of him, untouched. All of their food was cold and untouched.

"Well, there is the whole story. I hope it will be of some help to you. It was an unsettling evening. It is most unsettling to even speak of it now. Your father and I never spoke of it again."

Jonathan stood with Nicole outside the Four Seasons in a cold, misting rain. Jonathan drew the collar of his Burberry up and buttoned the top button. He slipped his glasses into his pocket.

"Nicole, that was a very strange story. I really don't know where to go with it. Frankly, we don't know if the story is true, or even if we have the whole story."

"I do not know what to say. My father was very brave. A patriot. I am proud of him." She clearly wanted to believe the story. "Even if the story is true, my father's pain was real. I do not see how this will help us show that he did not commit suicide."

"I don't either. You mentioned before that Fernaud was involved in finding Nazi war loot, didn't you? Maybe he can help us or add some piece to this puzzle. Or at least suggest something else to do. The only thing I can think of is to retain Perone, Brill." He glanced down at his watch, squinting without his glasses.

"Oops," he said, "speaking of that, it's ten of and I have a meeting with Perone to feel out what they can do and scope out the cost, so I can follow up with Cunningham." He took a few steps toward the curb and hailed a cab. Holding the cab door open, he turned back to Nicole. "Can you call Fernaud and see if he can see us tomorrow or the next day? I've got to spend some time on Simon's deal. He's getting grumpy. I'm tied up in a meeting with him this evening. I'll call you later."

She walked up to him and put her hand to his cheek, looking into his eyes. "Thank you, Jonathan, for everything you are doing. You are a good man." The words were so simple.

Thirty-five

"Well, well. Jonathan Franklin. My word. I didn't expect to see you again," F.X. Perone said, rising from her spare steel desk and grasping Jonathan's outstretched hand. "Man, where did you get that tweed jacket?" she inquired, a smile crinkling the corners of her light blue eyes.

Frankee Perone was firmly built and former FBI, the only woman ever to be the Special Agent in Charge of the Chicago office, and she had the respect of men twice her size. Rightfully so. She had maintained her edge well into her fifties, working out every day. And she had created a preeminent international investigating firm, in a tough business full of tough men, many of whom now worked for her. Which had made her a rich woman since the advent of globalization.

She could be subtle. She had been known to be otherwise. Her wall was adorned with a calligraphied copy of the motto that Charles Colson, the former Plumber, used to have hanging in his cubicle before he went up the river in Mr. Nixon's service: *"If you've got them by the balls, their hearts and minds will follow."* Jonathan knew from experience it wasn't just there for show.

"Jonathan, I sure enjoyed those messes you used to get me into. When I used to be able to get out of the office. You really know how to pick the bad ones." Bad meant good. "And between us, back then, I didn't mind cashing the checks." She laughed. "We could really use the money." She slapped her desk.

Perone, Brill & Co. now specialized in uncovering industrial espionage. It was a much bigger problem in the Silicon Valley than the public ever was let in on. They had also conducted some very sensitive personal investigations for Simon Aaron while Jonathan was at Whiting & Pierce.

"Let me get this straight," Frankee Perone said. Her jaw firmed. He had just finished briefing her on the background of his problem. She shook her gray head in disbelief. "You want me to find out the identity of some Nazi involved in the occupation of Paris, oh, say 50 or 60 years ago, who is probably long dead, and try to trace some painting this guy stole. Do you realize how idiotic that is?" She gave him a thin smile that showed no teeth nor any hint of warmth.

"When you put it that way, I guess I do. But I always thought you guys were pretty good. This assignment is probably just too difficult," Jonathan said. He was pulling hard on Frankee Perone's chain. He needed her, but he knew it was a risky ploy.

"Franklin," Perone growled, "you know damn well there's no one better. But you're old enough to recall," she riposted, "and maybe even young enough to remember, that we bombed those guys a little during that skirmish, and it made kind of a mess over there. Hell, there were generals we couldn't identify." At least she hadn't blown her stack.

"I can try putting some people on it and see what they can turn up," Frankee said. "It sure is helpful that you can't even give us this Nazi's name, much less the spelling."

Her voice became earnest. "Seriously, this is damn near impossible. It will take time, and it will be damned expensive. And not only are there no guarantees, I'll give you odds against. Get this straight. We get paid anyway."

"Great," said Jonathan, "the very two things I don't have a lot of—time and money. I've got to get this done before the trust reverts. What's your estimate, Frankee?"

"I would guess a month, maybe more, with a preliminary report in two weeks. Probably $60,000, at least, plus costs. We'll have to put three of our people on it to even see if it can be done. Not to beat a dead horse here, but I wouldn't give you a ten percent chance of our being able to get you anything that'll help."

"Okay, okay, Frankee." Jonathan held his hands palms out in mock protest. "I heard you the first time. Give me a few days to get my ducks in a row. Hold off on getting started on anything until I give you the go-ahead. Do you still ask for $15,000 up front?"

"Twenty-five," she said, smiling. Now her smile was a big grin. "Inflation."

"Oh, great."

"Nicole, I just got through with Frankee Perone."

He was on his cell phone, huddled just outside the door of Perone's building. It was still raining.

"It's not much better than we thought. It's going to be expensive. And she was anything but encouraging. I have to call Sam Cunningham again and see if the trust will come up with the money. Did you get to Fernaud?"

"I have not been able to reach Jean-Claude. I will continue to try."

"Okay, if anything else develops, give me a call. As I told you, I'll be tied up with Simon all day and probably tomorrow reviewing the papers on the Witten's deal and preparing for the closing. We're having dinner later if you want to join us. Right. Let me know."

He dialed Cunningham.

It was late the next morning when Sam Cunningham returned his call.

"Just a second, Sam." Jonathan put the open cell phone against his chest and turned to Simon, who was looking over an inch-thick stack of printed documents on the conference table in front of him.

They were at Whiting & Pierce again. Simon's face was set in a frown.

"Sorry, Simon. I need to take this. It'll just be a moment." It drew a glare from Simon Aaron, which he ignored. He stepped into the hallway outside the conference room.

"Sam, I met with Perone, Brill. I was about right in the numbers we discussed. It should be around $75,000. Plus costs." It was vintage Jonathan. Increase any estimate by at least 20%. You avoided a lot of problems. "I want to give Frankee Perone the go-ahead as soon as I can. She says this is going to take a while."

"To be honest, I'm not very comfortable."

Jonathan's stomach constricted. "What's up?"

"Well, it just seems to me that it's not so clear that the trust can pay for your investigation. I think I need to get a court order."

"It seems pretty clear to me, Sam. What kind of time are we talking about here?"

"Gosh, I don't know. I'm pretty busy, and I need to prepare the motion and supporting papers. It might take me a week to get it on file. Then notice to all the beneficiaries. I don't think we can have a hearing for maybe three or four weeks. And I think a lot of the beneficiaries will object." Cunningham was sounding increaseingly skittish.

"That's too long. We haven't got that much time, do we? Can't you speed it up? Isn't there some emergency procedure that can be confirmed later? We need to get into this or it'll be too late."

"Yeah." Hesitantly. "Maybe."

"Sam, I'm sure enough of this that I'll guarantee the trust repayment if the expenses aren't approved." That he didn't like. "I'm good for it. But I need you to get it moving."

"Well, let me see what I can do. I'm pretty busy right now, you know."

"You said that already. What's going on? You sound like hell."

"Nothing. Nothing's going on." He said it quickly. "I need to get back to work." Cunningham hung up the phone without even a goodbye.

"Odd," Jonathan thought. "First he's anxious for me to get into DeSant's death, and now he sounds like he's backing off. What's with the guy?"

He dialed Cunningham once more.

"Sam, it's Jonathan again. Look, have you been having second thoughts? Are you still so sure that DeSant's death wasn't a suicide?"

"I think so. . . I don't know. I'm under a lot of pressure. I just can't think straight."

"Make up your mind, Sam. A lot's riding on what you told me. And you've upset a lot of people. You better figure it out. I need you to get that motion on file within the next day or two. I'll call you tomorrow."

Sam Cunningham sat at his desk holding his head in his hands. "My God," he said aloud.

Thirty-six

It had been two days and four unanswered calls. Sam Cunningham was getting Jonathan worried. It was six p.m. when Jonathan dialed Cunningham's number for the third time that day. He was back in his hotel room sitting on his bed. His tweed jacket was tossed carelessly over the arm of a chair. It was dark and drizzly. He had on all the lights.

"Sam Cunningham."

"Sam, it's Jonathan Franklin. Why haven't you returned my calls?"

There was a pause.

"Eh, sorry. I've been pressed. Emergencies."

Cunningham sounded evasive. What now?

"Where are we? Have you thought about what you told me about George DeSant? I need to know if you've had second thoughts."

"No, I'm sure—pretty sure—about what I told you. Mr. De-Sant was full of life when I saw him. I—I've been worried about the money from the trust you asked me for. I'm really uncomfortable."

Jonathan got to his feet. Sam Cunningham was annoying him. He reached out for the silver snuffbox he had put on the desk with his keys and pocket change and started rubbing it.

"Sam, file a motion like you said. Let the court decide. Then it won't be on your back."

"No, I can't do that." Cunningham clipped his words.

"Why?" Jonathan sat down again.

"It's not right. If I don't believe the trust should pay the money, I can't do that as trustee. I have a fiduciary duty. I'm—I'm not going to let you push me into it."

Jonathan was trying to hold his temper. He still couldn't keep the anger entirely out of his voice. "For heaven's sake, Sam. I'm not trying to push you into anything. I told you I'd guarantee any advance. Nicole is a beneficiary. You damn well have a fiduciary duty to her too."

"I—"

Jonathan cut him off. "What's going on? There's an issue that has to be resolved in the trust terms. The investigation is a crucial part of that determination. It seems pretty clear to me."

"Quit pushing me." Cunningham was almost yelling. "Leave me alone."

"Sam, I respect you as a lawyer, but you're way out in left field on this one. I think you're just wrong. What I'm going to do. . ."

"Do whatever you want."

"I'm going to find Nicole a lawyer and file the motion on her behalf."

"Wait. . ."

"We'll need your declaration. I'll ask the lawyer to prepare a draft for you to review and sign, based on what you told me."

"But. . . but I can't give a declaration under penalty of perjury. I'm the trustee." Cunningham sounded terrified.

"You're a witness, Sam." Jonathan raised his voice. He put the snuffbox down on the bedstand. "You started all this. It was what you told me that raised these concerns. I can't force you to advance money from the trust or file a motion for approval of the expenses." Jonathan was gripping the phone. "But I sure as hell can ask you to stand up for what you said. And let me tell you." Jonathan's voice rose some more. He ran his free hand through his hair. "If you won't sign the declaration for any reason, I'll have you subpoenaed to testify in court. Nicole has a right to find out what happened to her father and to protect her rights in the trust."

He thought he heard Cunningham whimper as the phone cut him off. That couldn't be right. "What the hell is going on?" Jonathan said out loud as he banged down the receiver.

"Jonathan, I have to see you." Cunningham sounded distraught. "As soon as possible." It was the third day after they had butted heads on the phone.

Cunningham had caught him at breakfast with Simon, discussing the status of the financing. Simon didn't like to be interrupted. And he had become touchier in the last couple of days.

"Is there a problem?" Jonathan whispered, turning aside from his omelet and orange juice, cupping the cell phone with his other hand. He leaned away from Simon.

"I don't want to talk about it over the phone. Can we meet now?"

"I'm late for a meeting already." He had no intention of lighting Simon's fuse if he could help it. "Look, I can break free at around six. I'll come up to your office."

"No, I don't want to meet here. Meet me in the bar across from my office. The Ridge Bar. At six. Okay?"

Cunningham was in the bar when he arrived. The Ridge Bar was one of those places in Midtown that has pretensions of being chic but never quite makes it. It was empty, except for a couple of older guys at the bar who looked like regulars.

Cunningham was fidgeting, and Jonathan thought he was a little drunk. His eyes were puffy and had a dazed look. His cheeks were more flushed than Jonathan had remembered. He was leaning over a drink at a table in the back.

"Sam, what's with you?" Jonathan asked, dragging out a chair and taking a seat. "Are you going to tell me that you won't sign the declaration we sent over?" He was annoyed.

"It's not that." Cunningham's voice was so low that Jonathan could hardly hear him. He leaned forward. Cunningham was staring down at the black lacquered table. "I lied to you," he said.

"What?" Jonathan straightened. "Did you say you lied to me? About what?"

"Jonathan, I'm sorry." Cunningham lifted his eyes. "I had to. You don't understand."

"You're damn right I don't understand." Jonathan's mouth tightened. "What did you lie to me about?" He waved away the waiter with a swat of his hand.

"I didn't see Georges DeSant just before he committed suicide. I never spoke to him." The words tumbled out. He was on the verge of tears. Jonathan was glad the bar was almost empty.

"You see," Cunningham said, "I couldn't let the trust revert to the family. I'd lose my biggest client. I had to delay any finding that it was suicide. The firm was squeezing me out. I haven't got any money. I'd be ruined."

Jonathan was as near to being speechless as he had ever been. He could feel the blood surging to his face. He squeezed out his words. "Do you realize what you've done to Nicole DeSant, how you've screwed around with her head? Your client. How unethical this is?"

He paused, the anger coiling inside him. "You bastard," Jonathan said in a voice louder than he had intended. The two guys at the front of the bar turned toward them and stared.

"Jonathan, don't you think I know it?" Cunningham lifted his eyes pleadingly, his face in anguish. He licked his lips. "I saw I was getting in deeper and deeper. I was going to have to start taking money from the trust for your investigative expenses. Embezzle. Or commit perjury." He lashed back. "Damn you and your declaration!"

Then his face collapsed. He cradled it in his hands. Tears oozed between his fingers. "I couldn't do it. I'm so ashamed."

Jonathan got up from the table. He turned and walked out.

Jonathan was shaken. He needed time to think. And he didn't want to speak to Nicole until he could make sense of what had just happened. He hadn't seen her for almost two days, and for once, he was glad.

Tomorrow, he thought. It didn't help.

Tomorrow came. No answers came with it. He was sitting with Nicole in a small restaurant on Madison, over the remnants of a light lunch. It was well after one in the afternoon.

"I've known Sam Cunningham for twenty years. If it hadn't happened to me, I never would have believed it. I think he must have cracked under the pressure. But my God, Nicole, it was what he told me that started us down this path. And it was all a lie."

Jonathan played with the spoon in his coffee cup. "Now we have no access to money for the investigation, and worse, there's nothing to investigate. What a mess."

"This is very sad," she said, her large gray eyes dark with worry. "I do not know what we can do. At least I now believe that my father was not a collaborator." She reached over and placed her hand over his. "And it is a great comfort to me." She paused and looked directly at him. There was a rich warmth in her eyes. "And you are a great comfort to me."

She'd startled him. "That's wonderful," he said. Then to deflect his surprise and the emotion he was feeling but hadn't internalized, "Did you ever reach Fernaud? What do you think we should do about our meeting?"

"I did finally reach him, yes. He is in Los Angeles. He will be back on Saturday evening. I told him what Henri said. He seemed most upset. I am afraid I was also. He will see us at his hotel at two on Sunday. I think we should see him. Perhaps he will be able to help."

Thirty-seven

The taxi rolled to a stop a block from Jean-Claude Fernaud's hotel. Several black and white police cars, their light bars flashing, crowded the street. An ambulance screamed by.

Nicole and Jonathan left the cab and walked the last block. A uniformed policeman was holding back the crowd that was milling around the entrance to the small hotel. Two ambulance attendants rolled a gurney out of the hotel entrance, and the policeman parted the crowd to let them through. A sheet covered the gurney, but the outline of a body was clearly visible.

Jonathan approached the policeman. "Officer, excuse me. We have an appointment with a friend at this hotel. What's going on?"

"We got a little excitement. Seems like some French guy got himself blown away. Real mess, I hear."

Nicole collapsed into uncontrollable sobs. She held herself with both hands and swayed from side to side. Jonathan took her in his arms and held her against him, rocking her with her head against his chest, speaking softly.

Jonathan was staring at the ceiling. His hotel room was dark except for the bar of light coming in under the door. His head hurt. His back hurt. He felt his age encroaching on him. Maybe he should stop drinking so much.

He had been tossing and turning. Every time he started to drift into sleep, his mind would crank over, jerking him awake as it

187

struggled with the events of the day. Fernaud, dead. Why? Maybe he was responsible for Fernaud's death. My God!

He had gotten Nicole back to her apartment around three and spent hours with her in a futile attempt to calm her down. Finally, at around seven, she had fallen into an exhausted sleep on the couch in her living room. He'd covered her with a blanket he had found in a hall closet and quietly slipped out of the apartment. He needed to examine his own feelings.

He had found himself in a small restaurant near the Carlyle, where he sat over a bottle of red wine. For once, he wasn't exactly sure which one. He had pushed his dinner around the plate until the wine was gone, then made his way back to the hotel.

There had been yet another call from Simon, complaining about his lack of attention. He wished he could be angry, but he knew Simon was right.

What good was he doing anyway? He was responsible to Simon, he was responsible to Nicole, he was responsible to the law school. And he seemed to be doing a half-assed job for everyone. He was discouraged and more than a little tipsy.

It was two in the morning now. He lay listening to the small sounds that weave themselves into what we call silence. Then he finally gave up trying to sleep, kicked off his covers, fumbled for his glasses and turned on the light. Jonathan rummaged around in the drawers in the nightstand for a pad and pencil. A Bible offered its gilt edge in the lamplight.

He lay on his back, half-dozing, holding the pencil and pad of hotel notepaper on his chest. He waited for something to come to him. He always thought better with a pencil in his hand. Or at least, he had when he was trying to solve a legal problem. But this was different.

Or was it? The thought startled him. Someone wanted something, just like in a deal. The stakes were different, sure, and the rules certainly weren't the same. But this didn't seem like—what did they call it on TV?—a crime of passion. There was logic here, it seemed to him, albeit a logic with ferocious claws.

So why not approach it that way? What were the elements he was dealing with? It seemed to him like there were three possible drivers: the money in the trust. Those paintings mentioned in the article DeSant was clutching when he jumped. He corrected himself: "fell." He yawned. Or maybe some business deal in DeSant's life.

What else? What else? We may be able to trace this back the other way around, from Fernaud's death. He tapped his pencil stub on the pad. *Who knew we were going to see him?*

He labeled each of four pages and started listing names under each heading. Where he didn't have a name, he wrote in a generic. Where he drew a blank, he put in a question mark. Then he made columns and set down "motive," "means" and "opportunity" and started making notes. Watching all those detective shows was finally paying off.

He awoke the next morning sideways across his bed with the blankets twisted around him. Pieces of notepaper littered the bed, some crumpled under him where he had turned over. His head still hurt and his back hurt still more. In addition, his mouth tasted dry and foul.

"Another bright day," he said out loud, rolling out of bed. Much to his surprise, he felt buoyant. It was raining again.

He showered long and hard, luxuriating in the steam rising around him, breathing it in and feeling the moist warm vapors suffuse him. He went back into the bedroom, gathered together his notes and arranged them in some kind of order. Then he sat down at the desk to read over what he had written. He hoped it would make some sense in the light of day.

He was halfway through his notes when the phone rang. He glanced over at the bedside clock as he reached for the telephone. It was 6:30 in the morning.

"Jonathan, it is Nicole. Did I wake you? I am sorry to call you so early, but I had a terrible night. I want to thank you for everything you did yesterday. I was so upset. Please let me take you to breakfast. I need someone to talk to. None of this makes any sense to me. And I am frightened. I also have found something in my father's desk. I will bring it with me."

"How about in half an hour at the Plaza?" he said. "They have a decent breakfast there, and it should be quiet at this hour. I had a pretty rough night too. But I've been doing some thinking. I'd like to go over some of it with you. Maybe if there are two of us, we can make something of it."

Thirty-eight

"Nicole, $50 million is a lot of money. Even a small part of that is a lot of money to most people."

They sat in a corner of the Oak Room at the Plaza. The room was mostly empty. It was too early for the tourists. The umbrella Jonathan had borrowed from the Carlyle lay dripping in the corner. The rain had probably persuaded a lot of the locals to have breakfast at home and delay their confrontation with the city for a few more minutes.

The waiter had cleared away the remnants of a light breakfast and scraped the crumbs from the starched white tablecloth. All that was left on the table were the coffee cups, Jonathan's notes, and a large manila envelope Nicole had brought with her.

Nicole's mouth was set in a thin red line. She was shaking her head vigorously from side to side. Her dark hair swayed in anger. Diamond studs flashed as she moved her head.

"No, I will not even consider it. How could you say such a thing? I do not want to talk about it."

"Then how can we deal with this objectively?" Jonathan asked. He was drawn in by her anger to anger of his own. "We have to know who benefits. Who exactly gets the money. Who controls it. I'm not trying to indict your family, for God's sake. But that's a lot of money. Someone may be desperate. Who knows who he may go after next? Maybe even us." It was a very unpleasant thought, but Nicole seemed to ignore him.

"No! It is too horrible to even think about. It is my money. It is my father. No, Jonathan. Please. Do not do this." Her coffee lapped into its saucer as she pushed it aside.

"Okay, I think you're wrong. But as you say, it's your money. Let's go on. It may be a blind alley anyway." He had no intention of letting the issue drop, but he had to figure out another way to pursue it. Her family was suspect as far as he was concerned.

She shook her head again, more slowly this time, as if to clear it, and reached reluctantly for her coffee cup. She blotted the bottom of the cup on the tablecloth. Her hand shook a little as she raised it, dribbling coffee onto the envelope on the table. She cursed mildly in French under her breath and grabbed her napkin. She wiped at the coffee, leaving a brown stain on the envelope. Then she passed the envelope across to Jonathan.

"I found this in my father's desk. It seems to concern the trust. I did not understand all of it, but I thought it could be important." There was a remnant of anger in her voice.

He took the thick manila envelope and opened the clasp. It seemed to be an accountant's report of some kind. The velobound document had the name "Tumbler & Rose" at the top and the date November 20, 1998, with the words "Final Report." He flipped through the pages to try to get some sense of the document. Then he whistled.

"Wow, this seems to be an analysis of the Parks & Ellwood bills. And from what I can make out at first glance, it isn't very complimentary. This could be important, all right. I'll take it with me and read it more carefully." He slid the report back into the coffee-stained envelope and pushed it aside.

"Then I might have another talk with Sam Cunningham. He never mentioned anything about this. Did you find anything else? Any letters that might give us a lead? Notes on any deals? Anything that seems sort of unusual, kind of like this report?"

"No. I will look again this afternoon," she said, seeming to regain her composure a little. "But I found nothing else." She gave him a weak smile. The anger seemed to have dissipated.

He put down the report and picked up his notes from last night. He took a moment to re-sort and examine them. *Damn it*, he thought. *What is that word? I can't even read my own handwriting.* He grimaced, then looked over at Nicole.

"I need to get a look at the trust documents. We've got to understand the investments and businesses your father was involved in to see if there's anything there that could result in some kind of motive. It could be a problem. Cunningham isn't going to be too friendly after our discussion last week."

He stopped and tapped the envelope under his right hand. "And it's not going to get any better after I question him about this accountant's report. I need to figure out some way to get him to cooperate." He reached up to adjust his glasses. Then he ran his thumb over his lower lip.

"I'm not even sure we have the right to demand the records if the trust is in reversion," he said aloud, but really to himself. "Let me make a note. I need to speak to my old estate planning partner at Whiting & Pierce. Maybe he can tell me."

He looked up sheepishly. "Sorry, Nicole," he said. "Old habit, talking to myself. I think I may be getting worse. I'm starting to answer." He made a looping motion with his finger at his temple.

She smiled at him, and a little bubble of laughter sprang from inside her. It seemed to help.

"Let's go back for a second," Jonathan continued. "We still need to think about who might not want a fuss made about the Matisse your father passed on to the Germans. You know, it could be uncomfortable for some old, fat German to have his Nazi past stirred up. Maybe the timing was a problem, throwing his activities into a spotlight. Maybe a big business deal with an American company, or something like that."

Nicole interrupted. "I cannot believe that someone would kill for such a reason. It just does not seem reasonable."

"Yeah, I know, but it seems to me we need to run down every idea we can." Jonathan snapped his fingers. "I'd better give Frankee Perone a call and tell her to have her people stand down. We can't afford her without the money from the trust. Things have been moving so quickly, I completely forgot. I'll do it right after we get through here."

The waiter interrupted to refill their coffee cups, creating an uncomfortable silence. Jonathan waited for him to walk away.

"The thing that puzzles me most is, who knew we were going to see Fernaud? If we can put our finger on that, it may be the best lead we have. Did you mention it to anyone?"

"No, not that I recall," responded Nicole. "I have not been very clear these last few days, but let me think. I was talking that day with my cousin Henri and with you. Perhaps I mentioned it to Henri. He knew Fernaud, of course. But there could have been someone else. I did speak to Simon also, now that I think of it. But he only called to inquire as to how I was. We did not discuss anything else that I can remember."

Jonathan looked pensive. "I think I mentioned it to Simon myself. We were discussing timing, and I brought it up. I don't think I spoke to anyone else about it, though." He pulled the little silver snuffbox out of his pocket and started rubbing it. "Of course, they could've told someone. Or maybe we did. God knows, the last few days have been difficult. Nothing would surprise me."

Mentally, he cast Simon aside and was turning over in his mind Nicole's reference to Henri DeSant. Motive. Motive. . . Henri was someone who might benefit from the trust if it reverted and would have a lot of insight into how Fernaud might be useful to them. But the question of how to pursue that possibility was eluding him. He certainly couldn't ask Henri DeSant outright.

Maybe he could make some quiet inquiries into his finances. If anything turned up, he could decide where to go from there.

Thirty-nine

Jonathan fumbled for his cell phone. He couldn't get his hands on it, and the ringing mocked him. He was on his way out of the Plaza, and he had just opened his borrowed umbrella. The wind pulled at it as he groped inside his topcoat. He fought to suppress the umbrella's flight. The ringing stopped. He stepped back inside the portico of the Plaza and extracted the phone. One missed call. His fingers did a dance over the little keys. Simon.

He nestled the phone between his shoulder and his ear and leaned over to fold up the umbrella, which seemed about to make another run for it. He grabbed for the phone as it slipped. All the pressure was making him sweat, even in the cold. He wiped at his forehead.

Jonathan took a deep breath, then pressed the return call button. "Simon, Jonathan. Sorry I couldn't get to the phone in time."

Simon Aaron sounded bad just saying hello. He must have found out about Fernaud.

"It's true, Simon. Jean-Claude Fernaud is dead," Jonathan said.

"My God!" Simon said. His voice lifted in surprise. Jonathan missed the inflection. Then Simon said, "Shit." He was really upset now.

"I know," Jonathan said. "I can't tell you how upset I am too. Another death. It sends shivers up my spine."

"That's not what I meant. It's awful, but now we've got another problem. Look, I need to see you right away." It wasn't a request.

What the hell was this? It took him fifteen minutes to find a cab. Where did they all disappear to in the rain? Did they just melt? It was a question that had plagued him for the twenty years he had lived and worked in New York. It took another forty minutes to get through the plodding traffic to Whiting & Pierce.

"Is there a problem with the deal?" Jonathan asked as he entered the room.

Simon was ensconced in one of the larger conference rooms. He was folded into a black leather chair at a polished and inlaid mahogany conference table with his back to the door. The fluorescent lights made the outside even gloomier. Simon was staring off out the window, tapping on the table with bent fingers.

Simon jumped, turning sharply. "What!" His body relaxed. "Oh, it's you, Jonathan. Thanks for coming. No, no. The deal's fine. It's something else. Come in." He motioned Jonathan to the seat across from him.

"About a month ago," Simon said, "we got served with a complaint from one of those publicity-hungry lawyers, a woman named Winters, representing a former client of Witten's. I never told you about it. I thought we had it in hand."

"What did she want?" Jonathan had taken off his raincoat and was getting out of his tweed jacket. Leather patches on the elbows today. It was hot in the room. He pulled down his tie.

"She was claiming that a picture her client purchased was a forgery. It wasn't a very important piece. A small pastel by one of the lesser-known American Impressionists. We sold it for a few hundred thousand dollars. After we got the complaint, we had the piece brought in to us. I gave it to Fernaud to evaluate. He examined the picture closely and researched it. He concluded it was genuine. You know Bob Kahan, don't you?

"Sure. Great guy."

"Well, he's running the case. Our people think that her client had buyer's remorse. Maybe he thought he overpaid. It happens.

The problem is, this has occurred a few times over the last six or seven years. Nothing much has ever come of it, but it's starting to chip away at our reputation."

"I can see how it could be a problem."

"With all the other problems we've been having, I wanted to keep this quiet. We don't need any more questions. Kahan gave Fernaud's report to the other side."

A trickle of sweat ran down Jonathan's side. He tugged at his shirt.

"Fernaud had a big reputation as an expert witness, you know. We always encouraged that at Witten's. We were making progress towards a small settlement. But with Fernaud's death, I'm afraid the situation is going to blow up in our face."

"Why's she suing Witten's?"

"Kahan says we're the deep pocket."

Jonathan polished his glasses on his tie. "I hate those kinds of cases. It just galls me when people use litigation to extort money."

"Tell me about it."

"Anyway, Simon, I think you're on the right track, trying to settle this one. You know as well as I do, investors spook easily. Art experts are a dime a dozen, but we're going to need someone exceptional to hold this lawyer in check. I've heard about this woman, Winters. She'd like nothing better than to get a lot of press. With Fernaud dead, she'll figure we've lost our big gun."

"Yeah, we're just waiting for a call. As soon as word gets out."

"First, when she does call, we need to make it clear to her that if there's any publicity, we won't settle." Jonathan fiddled with his glasses and refitted them on his ears. "From what I hear, she likes money even more than she likes attention." Simon grunted.

"Let her know," Jonathan continued, "we're going to call in another expert. Have them tell her we need a week. That will at least give us some breathing room. Who are the top experts who might be willing to serve as an expert witness?"

"Well, there are several," Simon reflected. "Clark Miller at the Modern has done this sort of thing in the past for us. David Rintels at the Tate, maybe. Henri DeSant is quite respected, of course."

Jonathan interrupted. "I know DeSant's in town. Nicole and I had breakfast with him a few days ago. He said he would be here for a couple of weeks. He makes a striking impression."

Simon interrupted. "That's what I like about you, Jonathan. Your certainty. Rarely right but never wrong." Simon must be feeling better if he was making fun. He *was* making fun, wasn't he?

"Well, I think he would make a great witness," Jonathan said a little defensively. Perhaps a little guiltily. What he hadn't said was that he would also like to have DeSant close at hand, so he could continue his closet investigation. "Do you think DeSant will do it?"

"Well, he owes me a couple favors," said Simon. "If he has the time, I think he would be glad to help me out. Particularly for a large fee. I'll give him a call."

"Good. If he'll help, let's get him the picture right away."

Forty

"Frankee." Jonathan had finally gotten through to Frankee Perone. "Look, I'm sorry. There's a problem."

"There's always a problem when I do business with you. Now what?" Her tone was teasing. Maybe.

"Look, Frankee, I'm sorry. The trust won't fund your fees, and there's no way we can pay that kind of money out of pocket. I feel badly that I took up your time on such a hair-brained idea."

"Just my luck." Frankee Perone had an amused note in her voice. That was strange. She usually didn't react well to being stiffed. "I put a guy on it just to see if there was a way we might come up with something. And as I said, I wouldn't have given a rat's ass for your chances. Damned if he didn't hit on something on the Internet right off the bat. Some university research for a doctorate."

"You're kidding. What did it say?"

The phone went silent.

"Okay, Jonathan, I guess I owe you one for all the past business, and it looks like it's payback time, although I gotta tell you that giving it away goes against my deepest moral values."

"We're not talking sex here, Frankee."

"Don't be an asshole." He thought she said it with a smile. He hoped so. "I have three names for you. They were the key guys that Goering used in Paris. The name you gave me, Koertzmann, was close. The guy was an S.S. colonel named Eugen Kurtzmann. A real bastard, as far as I can tell. Anyway, he's dead. Died about four years ago. Good riddance."

"Are you sure he's dead? Some of those Nazis faked it and ran."

"I can't be certain, but our man confirmed the death with a call to a relative. Kurtzmann lived in a small town in Germany before he died. My guy didn't get any hint of anything wrong."

"Too bad for us. Who are the others? Are they still alive?"

"Yeah, and pretty important over there."

Jonathan felt a tingle of excitement. Talk about luck.

"One's a politician. The other's an art dealer. They were the guys who made sure Goering got what he wanted. Kurtzmann was the muscle. Do you have a fax? I'll send you what I have, together with the contact information, and some other stuff we turned up. It's pretty sketchy, and I don't know how good it still is. It's a place to start."

"Frankee, thanks. I really appreciate this. I'm touched."

"No, Franklin, I'm the one who's touched. In the head." She laughed.

"But Frankee, I need another small favor."

There was a longer silence on the other end of the line. No laugh. "You're becoming a nuisance."

Something had been nagging at him. And he couldn't put his finger on it. He felt like he had missed something. Something important. He needed to know a lot more about Fernaud's death. And he didn't know where else to turn.

"I know. And I don't want another freebie. . . well, not quite."

"Not quite's not quite what I had in mind. Come on, a girl's got to make a living here, you know."

"I'll pay." He said it reluctantly. "But I'm going to dig into my own pocket for this one, and I can't afford to pay you a big retainer." Not quite true. He could, but he wasn't about to. "What I wanted to ask is if you could do something easy for me on just an hourly basis?" He didn't have the guts to ask the hourly rate.

"The last time you asked me to do something easy, a couple of years ago. . . you remember," Frankee said, "it practically brought my whole organization to a dead stop. I had to put six of my best people on it. It's when you ask me to do something impossible, like find out the names of those German guys. Then it's easy. Exactly what is this easy thing you had in mind?" She tattooed the word "what."

"Just a couple of phone calls, nothing more." He hoped.

"Oh, and to whom are these easy phone calls going to be made?"

"Frankee, a guy was killed yesterday, a man named Jean-Claude Fernaud. I really, really need to find out exactly what happened. It could be important to a friend of mine. She's scared. Christ, I'm scared." He was leveling with her. "You must have lots of friends in the NYPD. I just need to find out what the police know and who they suspect. Who on Homicide is handling the case. Frankee, I know I'm asking a lot, but this could save someone's life."

"Okay, okay, I'll do it, but damn it, Jonathan, you better bring me something good one of these days. You owe me for this. And your timing stinks, as usual. These NYPD folks have pensions to protect, and they're running like scared rabbits since the mayor cracked down on leaks in the department last month. I don't know what I can get for you, but I'll try."

He heard a scraping on the other end of the phone. "Hold on. I need to find a pad."

"Sure." He waited.

"How do you spell the guy's name? First and last. Any middle initial?" She didn't wait for him to respond. "Give me everything you have. Who he was, where he was killed. The whole magilla."

Magilla? Jonathan gave it all to her. Chapter and verse. It took five minutes. He could hear her pen scratching at her pad.

"Give me a couple of days."

"Thanks, Frankee, call me as soon as you can." He thought she snorted. He gingerly put down the phone.

If Fernaud hadn't been killed, he and Nicole might have given up after Cunningham's confession. Jonathan somehow felt Fernaud's death could be the key to this whole thing. Someone had made a big mistake. He felt it in his bones. The only question was who.

He sat down in his chair and turned on the table lamp as he read. He had returned to the Carlyle to get Frankee's fax. He ignored the blinking message light.

"Pretty important is right." There were the names and descriptions of the Germans. He gave a whistle. Wolfgang Dietz, the first name on the list, was a politician and had been appointed to a cabinet position in the German government. He was being considered, according to the information, as head of the Central Bank for the European Union.

The other man was a prominent art dealer in Frankfurt. Nicole should know him, or at least know of him, he mused. Jonathan had another thought. He picked up the telephone and dialed Harry Kanter, an old banking friend at Chase.

"Harry, Jonathan Franklin here. How are you? It's been a while. Yes, to be honest, I love it up there, but it's good to get back to the city once in a while. Look, Harry, I need a favor."

Jonathan reflected that he was calling in a lot of chits today, what with Frankee Perone and now Harry. "Can you tell me how you would go about checking out the current financial status of someone? An individual. No, nothing too deep, but more than I can get from a financial reporting service." He pushed his glasses up on his nose and fiddled them into position. He reached for a glass of mini bar diet cola and took a sip.

"I just want to find out if there are any current financial problems. But it would have to be quiet. No, I don't have that kind of money to spend. You can? That would be terrific. This won't get back to anyone, will it? Good. The man's name is Henri DeSant." He set the glass back on the table.

"That's right, DeSant, D-small e-capital S-a-n-t. Henri is Henry with an i. A big art dealer. He has galleries here and in London and Paris. How long will it take? Great. I'll look forward to hearing from you then. I really appreciate this, Harry."

Jonathan felt a little uneasy going behind Nicole's back, but he was troubled by the coincidence that Henri DeSant possibly benefited from the trust reversion and also knew about their meeting with Jean-Claude Fernaud. *It's for her own good anyway.* An ugly thought crossed his mind. Where was Henri DeSant when Nicole's father died, and how could he find out?

He checked his messages. There was a call from Simon on his voicemail, as well as another call from the red-headed model in Boston. Jonathan didn't feel up to answering either of them. Instead, he settled down on the couch to read the accountant's report that Nicole had given to him at breakfast. He read through it once and started to reread it in detail, making notes in the margin of questions or matters he wanted to pursue. The rain outside had changed to snow. Jonathan looked out the window at the drifting white flakes. They were falling with such grace they made him drowsy. It had been a rough night.

The ringing telephone awoke him with a start. He had been dreaming of a candlelight dinner with Nicole. She'd been naked and her cheeks were streaked black with mascara. Her lips were bright red, as were her fingernails. It had been so vivid. She was running her hands over his naked body and kissing him everywhere. People were staring at the red lipstick marks.

He shook off sleep and reached for the phone. Wow, he hadn't been getting enough sex lately. He'd have to think about that dream.

"God damn it, Jonathan!" It snapped him fully awake. The bear was growling. "When I call you, the least you could do is call me back."

Simon Aaron was not happy. He had the tone of someone who was not used to being ignored. "I know you're concerned about Nicole, but when you agreed to take this matter on for me, I expected you to do it. You're behaving like some kind of lovesick schoolboy with a crush on his teacher, and I don't appreciate it. I have things I need to talk to you about."

Jonathan sighed and rubbed his sleep-tousled hair. "Sorry, Simon. You're right. I don't know what's gotten into me. What's up?"

Forty-one

He had slept late. His eyes were grainy. The stress of the last few days was taking its toll. Jonathan ran his hand over his cheeks and felt the bristles of his beard rough against his palm.

He vaguely remembered dreaming he was in the middle of a shopping mall. Nicole had been there too. Naked. Her body gleamed like it was oiled. Her cheeks were stained with mascara. She looked sad but beautiful. Her arms were around him and she was kissing him deeply. His body was responding. People were whispering to each other and turning around to point.

The grey drizzle outside didn't help his mood. He fidgeted over his room service breakfast, pushing at the poached egg for a while. He finally tossed his napkin on the tray.

The accountant's report on Cunningham lay tented on the coffee table, half notated. He looked over at it. Later. The room seemed cramped. It was going to be one of those days.

He had done everything he could think of, other than getting to the Germans. He was unsure how to do that yet. He stood up and reached for his raincoat. "I've got to get out of here and get some air," he said aloud to the empty room.

The rain had changed to a light snow. It was beginning to stick, covering the sidewalk in a thin white blanket. It crunched as he walked. He crossed Fifth Avenue to the park and put his glasses in his pocket. Everything was a little blurred.

He walked from 76th Street all the way down to 57th before he cut over to Madison and started back. He lifted his face to the cold, delicately-falling flakes and stuck out his tongue like a child. His mind wandered. He rubbed at the little silver snuffbox in his pocket.

Sam Cunningham was an issue. But Jonathan could probably get him to let them review the trust assets. Cunningham had to be concerned about what he'd done to Nicole.

An approaching man attracted his attention. He wore a faded red sweater held together with a bathrobe tie and short pants. He had on old black sneakers. There was a yarmulke on his head. He was mumbling to himself through his full black beard. As he passed Jonathan he nodded politely. New York! Jonathan shrugged and returned to his thoughts.

Anyway, from what he'd seen of the accountant's report, Cunningham had a real problem. Enough, maybe, to want Georges DeSant dead? Cunningham could lose his license. Certainly be thrown out of the firm. Even worse, maybe.

But then, why did Cunningham say it wasn't a suicide? Why make them start looking? Who knew? Maybe he'd embezzled from the trust and couldn't let it revert. He had to figure out some way to get at him. Maybe Nicole could help.

He became aware of a short, shabbily-dressed black man walking beside him. Rather, he smelled him. He looked over. The guy stuck out his hand. "Got a coupl'a bucks for some coffee?" Jonathan shook his head. "Asshole," the guy said and gave him the finger.

Jonathan walked on. He had to be careful. He couldn't let on to Nicole that he was still wary of Henri DeSant. Henri had become like a substitute father to her, and she was protective. But he had to make sure it wasn't all a front. Maybe it wasn't Henri De-Sant anyway, but one of the other beneficiaries, whoever they were. He'd have to find out.

He crossed the street at 62nd. He jumped to the curb when a taxi almost ran him down. "Asshole," the cabby shouted. Jonathan hadn't seen the light change.

I should pay more attention, he thought. But he didn't. He slipped back into his distraction.

He needed to get a copy of the trust from Cunningham. But at least he'd find out if Henri DeSant had financial troubles. And he'd be able to poke around some more once he had DeSant involved with Witten's as an expert witness. Simon had confirmed last night that DeSant had agreed to help. That was a piece of good luck.

He walked along lost in thought, rubbing on his silver box. The soft snowflakes were like a caress on his face.

The Germans were a tougher problem. God bless Frankie Perone for coming up with those names.

Getting to a German minister wasn't going to be easy. And how was he going to get the man to talk to him? Well, maybe he wouldn't want them to go to the press. That couldn't help his career or his chances to become head of the European Central Bank.

That art dealer, what's his name, should be easy to get to. He had to remember to ask Nicole. The guy might be willing to talk to them on a confidential basis if they approached him in the right way. It made sense to start with him.

"Professor Franklin." He was startled to find that he had turned back into the lobby of the Carlyle and was being addressed by the concierge. "A Ms. DeSant asked me to tell you that she is waiting for you in the cafe. She says you were to meet her there at ten."

He looked at his watch. It was 10:45.

"You mean you actually know the guy?" he exclaimed.

"Yes, I have talked to him many times. He has represented clients at several auctions over the last few years. Heinz Brauer is a well-known art dealer in European circles. He now must be close to eighty. A cheerful, bald little man with a good eye for art. I would never have guessed he was a Nazi. He seems so harmless."

Jonathan and Nicole were sitting at a little table in the Gallery. He had obliged with the appropriate groveling and explanations for his tardiness. It had taken fifteen minutes. Nicole didn't like to wait.

"You think he'll talk to us?"

Nicole angled her head and looked at him with those pale gray eyes. "I do not know, of course. But if I explain to him that it is important to me, and why, perhaps he will. At least he will listen."

He was struck by how different Nicole was. Different from his dreams, at least. Was there a mysterious, sultry side of her that his subconscious was observing? Was that good or bad? Or was it him? With an effort, he roused himself to address the present problem.

"It'll be interesting to see how he reacts," he said. "I would prefer to do this face-to-face, but there's too much going on right now with Simon's deal, and he's getting a bit testy anyway. I also have a feeling that time's important for some reason. Let's try reaching Brauer by telephone. Do you have a number for him?"

"Let me call my office and have my assistant open the contacts file on my computer. But I am sure that I took his telephone numbers last year when he was interested in some auction pieces that we were presenting."

"Here. Use my cell phone. Let's see, Germany is six hours ahead of us. It's around 11:15 now, so it's 5:15 in the afternoon there. We may still be able to reach him in his gallery if we're lucky."

"Ya, ya. This is Brauer. Who is calling? Ah, Fraulein DeSant. How nice to speak with you again."

They had gone up to Jonathan's room, where there were two extensions. They decided to be direct. It seemed like the only way to get any information. Since neither of them could figure out a more subtle approach under the circumstances, it wasn't too hard a choice.

Nicole introduced Jonathan and explained to Brauer the purpose of the call and how his name had come to their attention.

Surprisingly, Brauer offered a pensive laugh.

"Ya, those were very bad times. I have not thought of them in many years. I was a young man then, of course. I was an assistant in a museum in Munich. I was not a soldier. No, never a soldier. My life is art."

Brauer paused and seemed to reflect. "No. No, I have nothing to hide," he went on. "I never hurt anyone. I was never even a Nazi. I swear it."

No, Jonathan thought. *Of course not, there were only a few Nazis, and they were all executed at Nuremberg.*

"My father knew someone on Goering's staff. It was well known in the art world that Goering was an avid collector. Arrangements were made. I was sent to Paris. I was to advise Goering's adjutant, a Colonel Kurtzmann, on art that should be obtained. Once a picture was purchased for Herr Goering, I was responsible for making sure it was properly packed and transported to Berlin. That is all."

Purchased? Jonathan laughed to himself.

"Fraulein DeSant. I did not know your father. I never heard his name. Of course, I knew of the bank."

They had agreed that Nicole should lead the discussion, but Jonathan was finding it difficult to restrain himself. His mind bubbled with questions.

"Ya, I do recall the Matisse painting. It was exquisite. I was pleased that I could help to preserve it forever. I knew it would be safe in Berlin. So many of those Nazis were brutish thugs. They burned paintings, such beautiful paintings. I hated that. But Hitler had very unsound ideas about art. No one could talk to him. No one dared. It was hopeless. I did what I could."

"Bravo for you," Jonathan whispered to Nicole, holding the extension against his chest. She glared at him and put her fingers to her lips. She made a shushing sound.

Maybe he was becoming cynical. That thought amused him.

"But I am afraid, Fraulein, that I do not know more of what happened. The picture passed through my hands. I know nothing else. Full stop." He pronounced it "schtop."

"Herr Brauer." Jonathan spoke for the first time. "How long were you in Paris?" Nicole gave him a concerned glance.

"Let me see. Ya. We were there until October 1940."

"You seem to remember the date well, Herr Brauer. Why is that?" Jonathan said. He was trying to keep his voice light.

"I remember because it became so uncomfortable. Our entire group was ordered by the Reichsmarschall into Vichy, where a great deal of art was becoming available for acquisition. It was felt that we would have a better selection there, where others had not picked it over. But there were no decent living quarters, no decent hotels were available. I did not like it."

"Colonel Kurtzmann was the head of your group?" Jonathan asked. Now Nicole was making hand signals. He ignored them.

"Ya. He took all the best quarters. And the best food."

"Who else was in your group, Herr Brauer?" Nicole interrupted, clearly concerned that Brauer would be alarmed by Jonathan's aggressive tone. Apparently he hadn't achieved "light."

"There were eighteen of us. Several clerks to catalog acquisitions, a few workmen in charge of packing and hauling, and a communications man."

"How long did your group remain in Vichy?" Jonathan interrupted. Nicole gave an angry little shake of her head.

"We were called back to Berlin in early 1942. I was then assigned as an assistant curator of Herr Goering's collection. It was quite extensive by then."

"Did you see the Matisse again?" Nicole asked, cutting Jonathan off once more.

"No. No. I was told it had been shipped to his country home, which I never visited."

"Herr Brauer, did you know a Wolfgang Dietz?" Jonathan asked. He knew Nicole would be annoyed.

"Of course, I know Herr Dietz. In fact, he has been a client of mine from time to time. A fine man, you know. Very important to our country, and soon, we hope, to all of Europe."

"Was he involved with your group during the war, Herr Brauer?"

There was silence on the other end of the line.

"Professor Franklin," Brauer said carefully, "I am an old man. My memory is not so good as it once was. And I am afraid that I have become late for an important appointment. Please forgive me. I must go. It was nice to speak with you, Fraulein DeSant."

"Herr Brauer, don't ..." Nicole started, but the line was already dead.

Jonathan turned to Nicole. "What do you make of that?"

"His memory seems to have become bad quite suddenly," Nicole replied. There was a tinge of acerbity in her voice. "I do not think that he wanted to talk to you about Herr Dietz. Why, I cannot say. But you should have let me finish. I do not believe he responded well to you."

"You're right. Sorry."

She had expressed her annoyance. She might have gotten more out of Brauer. The thought took her by surprise. She was starting to feel like herself again. She liked it.

"Yeah, he sure didn't want to talk about Dietz," Jonathan said. "But it makes me want to know more."

Forty-two

"You don't have to threaten me."

"You're right, Cunningham, I don't, but let me do it again so I'm sure we understand each other." Jonathan's voice was quiet and cold.

They were sitting in the back of a coffee shop near Sam Cunningham's office. The weather had cleared, and the place was bright with washed sunlight. So different from the mood at the table.

It was three in the afternoon on Wednesday, and the coffee shop was empty. Jonathan had three large, addressed, sealed and stamped envelopes on the table between them.

"I'm going to ask you some questions. If you don't answer any of them, or if I find out that you lied to me in any way, any way at all, I'm going to mail these envelopes with the report from George DeSant's forensic accountants. One is going to the managing partner of your firm. The second goes to the ethics division of the state bar. And the third goes directly to the district attorney. Understood?"

This was really unlike him. But Sam Cunningham had trampled on his sense of ethics. Besides, Jonathan was scared. It made him more determined to squeeze Cunningham.

"Why are you doing this to me?" Cunningham's hand was trembling. Coffee dribbled unnoticed onto his white cuff from the cup he was holding.

"If you expect sympathy from me," Jonathan said, "forget it." His voice turned hard. "Let me put this to you straight. I know you're a liar, I think you're a thief, and you may be a murderer."

"Oh my God," Cunningham burst out. "Oh, no. No. Please, no." Tears trickled down his cheeks. He reached across the table. Jonathan drew back. "I couldn't. . . how could you think. . . oh, no."

"Now that we understand each other, let's get started," Jonathan said, his mouth set. He reached into his jacket pocket and produced a small black recorder. He stood it in the middle of the table. "I want a record of this, Cunningham. I don't suppose you object."

Sam Cunningham stared at it. "No."

He said it so softly that Jonathan repeated the word. "No?" Cunningham shook his head miserably.

Nicole had reluctantly agreed that Jonathan should meet with Cunningham alone, but only after Jonathan promised her a complete report. He snapped on the recorder.

"When was the last time you saw Georges DeSant?"

Cunningham's face collapsed into a mask of resignation. He started to speak haltingly, as if he were someplace else.

"The Thursday before his death. He came to get me to sign a resignation as the trustee of the trust. I pleaded with him. I told him I would pay back any money he thought was too much. I told him I would lower my fees."

Cunningham wiped at his wet cheeks. "He said it was too late. I literally got down on my knees and begged him to reconsider. He turned his back on me. He told me to sign the resignation or he was going to court to have me removed, and he walked out. That was the last I saw of him. I swear it."

"What happened next?"

"I tried to call him, to reason with him, to plead, but he wouldn't answer any of my calls. I was desperate."

"Desperate enough to commit murder?"

Cunningham's eyes went wide. "God, no. You must believe me. Not murder. Suicide. I thought about killing myself."

"Go on."

"Then I got a call. Mr. DeSant was dead. It was like a godsend." He crossed himself. "Heaven forgive me."

"Where were you when he was killed?"

"It's so ironic. I was at my law firm's annual retreat, probably my last one. The partners were acting strange, avoiding me as if I wasn't there." Cunningham spread his hands, palms up.

Jonathan leaned forward in his chair. This was important. He spoke carefully. "Why did you tell me you believed DeSant didn't commit suicide?"

"I told you before. I couldn't let the trust revert."

"Why, because you were embezzling money?"

"No. Never." He stared at the recorder. "I can account for every cent."

"Except for what you took by padding your fees."

"But that was different. I... I mean, I didn't."

"Remember what I said, Cunningham." He tapped the envelopes on the table.

"The firm was putting me under so much pressure to produce." Cunningham was almost whining. "I wasn't stealing. At first, it was just a few more hours. I spent time thinking about the trust. Really, I did. I was just billing for that time. Then there was more and more pressure. Hours. Billings. Sandra was on my back. It was driving me mad."

It came tumbling out. "I was going to offset the extra billings when the pressure was off. But it went on and on. I didn't mean to take anything." He curled his hands in front of him, staring at them. "I'm not a thief."

"Sure. Go on." The coffee was going cold in their cups.

"If Mr. DeSant committed suicide, the trust would revert. I would have lost the trusteeship. I needed the money. It would have been my only client if the firm threw me out. I was hoping you would find something. At least, I hoped it would delay the reversion for a time, maybe a long time."

"So, you have no reason to believe he didn't commit suicide. You were just trying to use me."

Cunningham shook his head. "No, I don't believe he did it, commit suicide, I mean. He was too strong. But I don't know anything else."

"Okay," Jonathan interrupted, reaching for the recorder and checking to be sure it was still recording. "That's enough. I'll check out what you told me. We may talk again. Here's what I need. I want a complete accounting for the trust and a copy of the trust agreement, as well as all of the correspondence files."

"I can't do that. It's privileged."

"Aren't you getting ethical a little too late? Besides, Nicole DeSant is the beneficiary of the trust if it doesn't revert. She's entitled to see the documents." Maybe she was and maybe she wasn't. Jonathan didn't care. "Make a copy of the last three annual accountings, the trust documents and the correspondence and have them sent to me tomorrow at the Carlyle. I'll fax you over a release from Nicole DeSant, but don't wait for it."

"I guess I can do that," Cunningham said. It was almost a whisper. His face formed itself into planes of despair.

"No, Cunningham. You not only can, but you will. Two men have been killed. I'm not going to fool around with you. If I have to, I can get the information, even if I have to go right through you. So get it for me, unless. . ." he gathered the envelopes and brandished them. He was having trouble controlling his temper. And he didn't have time to waste.

"Now," Jonathan continued, "what kind of investments were made through the trust?"

"Stocks and bonds," Cunningham said. "A few business deals that Mr. DeSant wanted to invest in. Real estate deals, usually. He had almost a sixth sense for a good deal. He amazed me."

"Were there any deals with people you were suspicious of? Or any deals that went bad?" Perhaps it was their intensity, but the waitresses were avoiding their table.

"Only one real estate deal went bad." Cunningham seemed to shrink around his own words. His responses were growing weaker. "But that deal was with some of the most important people in the city. Simon Aaron was heavily involved, as well as two of the big developers. We lost a good deal of money, but they lost a lot more money than we did. Mr. DeSant joked with me about it." The thought seemed to catch him off-guard. "No, there was nothing like that."

"Was there any situation you can think of that made Georges DeSant uncomfortable? Did he ever seem fearful or even uneasy?"

"No, I don't think so," Cunningham said, shaking his head. "He was a very strong-willed man."

Jonathan needed to cut this off before Cunningham cracked.

"All right, send me those files. And remember, if I find out that you lied to me, or held anything back, I'll have your hide nailed to the wall."

"What are you going to do with those letters?"

"Nothing for now. Later we'll see. Not that you deserve an answer." Jonathan clicked off the recorder.

"No, Nicole, I don't think he was lying to me. I think he was scared senseless." Jonathan sat across from her at the Drake, re-winding the tape he had just played for her.

"I called the hotel where Cunningham's firm had its retreat," Jonathan said, "and he was registered there the day your father died. It still doesn't mean he couldn't have come back into the city for a few hours."

"That poor man," Nicole said, shaking her head a little.

"Nicole, I really don't understand you. That 'poor man' stole from you. He might have killed your father."

"I do not believe that he is a murderer. He seems too small, somehow. I just feel badly, seeing his world falling down upon him. He seems so helpless. Like a little animal." This sense of compassion was new to her.

Jonathan shook his head in turn. "Let's put Cunningham aside for a moment. Assume you're right, he didn't do it. Where are we?"

They sat for a long time. Neither of them had any answers.

His cell phone rang as he was walking back to the Carlyle. He opened his coat and grabbed it from the inner pocket of his jacket.

"Jonathan, it's Frankee Perone. There's something screwy going on here." She spoke emphatically. "I got a personal favor out of one of my friends at the NYPD. I'm not going to tell you who it was or what I had to promise him." She gave a guffaw.

"Either the department has classified the information real tight on this Fernaud investigation, which would be very unusual, or their clerical staff has screwed this up big time. That wouldn't be so unusual. I'm assuming here you spelled the dead guy's name right."

He started to say something, but she cut him off.

"Anyway, my guy gets nothing out of the homicide files. I can't even tell you the name of the investigating officers yet. I don't know what's going on. And my guy is real spooked about asking a lot of questions with the mayor breathing down everyone's neck. Look, I'll keep trying. I'll call you if I come up with anything.

"Oh, and by the way, send me your check for $1425. And don't try to fax it to me."

"Frankee, I never. . ."

He could hear Perone laughing as she hung up the phone.

Forty-three

The telephone rang as Jonathan opened the door to his room. He pulled his coat off one arm and reached for the phone. "Oh, hi, Harry. Thanks for getting back to me so quickly." He shrugged off the other arm and threw the coat over the closest chair.

He listened to his friend from Chase as he tugged at his tie. "Really, that's very interesting."

"I think Henri DeSant was strapped financially," Kanter said. "It wasn't easy information to get. DeSant keeps a low profile, and he's a very private kind of guy." Jonathan shifted the phone from one hand to the other. He dragged a chair over closer to the phone with his foot and sat down.

"I know some guys over at J.P. Morgan," Kanter continued. "It seems like DeSant approached them for a loan and they turned him down. He told them a collector backed out of the purchase of a major picture that the DeSant firm had already bought in. It apparently left him illiquid."

"Interesting. Uh-huh." Jonathan listened for a moment more as Kanter continued to talk. "How bad a problem do you think he had?" he asked when Kanter paused.

"I don't know," Kanter said. "Besides, that was a few months ago. I can't tell you if he still has a problem, even if he had one then."

"Harry, many thanks. That's a great help. If I can return the favor, call." Jonathan listened. "No, you can't come live in my house and teach at the law school." Pause. "I do not keep a harem,

I don't care what you've heard." There was a tincture of male pride at the edge of his voice. "All those rumors are grossly exaggerated." He was enjoying the by-play. Pause. "Yeah, I don't care who told you. Hey, Harry, good to talk to you." He smiled as he put down the phone.

Well that was something to think about. He slipped into a sweater, grabbed his raincoat and the new Dortmunder mystery he had bought on the way back to the hotel, and headed out the door. He needed to find a small restaurant where he could have a quiet dinner with a good bottle of wine. Then he had every intention of coming back to his room, taking a sleeping pill and turning in early for a good night's sleep.

He bounded out of bed the next morning at 7:30. It was amazing what a good night's sleep could do. He showered, shaved, dressed and was whistling a fragment from Vivaldi's *Four Seasons* when he opened his door to go down to breakfast. He nearly tripped over a bulky package from Parks & Ellwood next to his copy of the *New York Times*.

Apparently, he had put the fear of God into Sam Cunningham. He took the package with him to breakfast. After he placed his breakfast order, he tore open the large envelope to see what he had. The sun warmed his shoulders.

The room was quiet, and he had a four-top near a bank of large windows. The sunlight was filtered through gaps in the taller buildings. It wasn't raining yet, but the clouds were moving in. He withdrew a three-inch-thick bundle of legal documents from the package.

Good, the executed trust documents, together with what, one, two, three amendments. He turned the pages, scanning quickly. Umm, it looked like the last one was executed about 1964, just after Nicole was born.

He put the trust documents aside and looked over the remaining papers. Three annual financial reports, together with monthly reports through last month. He thought Cunningham really wanted him to know he was clean. And the correspondence going back, let's see, to January 1, 1996. Great. Jonathan spread out the financial reports in front of him.

"Oh, sorry," he said to the waiter standing over him, holding his breakfast, "let me get these out of your way. Yes, more coffee, please. Can you bring me over a carafe, so I don't have to keep bothering you? I drink a lot of coffee in the morning. Thanks."

He turned back to the financial reports as the waiter retreated. He flipped through the annual reports and then spent a good deal of time on the latest monthly balance sheet, income statement and list of transactions.

Well, this is kind of interesting, he thought. *What do you know?* Something caught his eye. The trust owned almost 5% of Witten's. He shuffled back through the lists of transactions. It looked like Georges DeSant had bought it recently, when the stock bottomed out. No, there was another purchase. Over 9%.

And it looked like DeSant had bought a lot of subordinated debt too. At a discount. Over $4 million in face value. He'd have to ask Simon about it. He took out a piece of paper and made a note.

He noticed a carafe had appeared on his table. He didn't know how it had gotten there. That was concentration. He poured himself another cup of coffee. He continued through the pile of papers Parks & Ellwood had provided.

Nothing else was apparent, except that DeSant was a hell of an investor. It looked like the trust had sold one piece of property for a big profit. He should take a look at the back-up on that deal. He also should ask Cunningham to send him the list of investors for each of these deals. It might give them a lead.

He added some notes to his list, then turned to the correspondence. Not only was it uninformative, it was boring.

Now, let's see the trust, he thought, flipping through the bulky document. He stopped and put the document down and leaned back in his chair.

What was he doing? He took off his glasses and started to polish them with his napkin. Here he was playing detective, or maybe estate lawyer. He wasn't either. How had he gotten sucked into this?

Okay, it was Nicole. What did he feel? He hadn't asked himself that question in a long time. Events had swept him along. He certainly wasn't getting laid. That was evident.

Funny, that seemed okay. At least for the moment. He liked trying to help her. It made him feel good. Maybe that's what this was about. It made him feel good.

He put his glasses on and picked up the trust document again. An unusual structure. Originally the trust had reverted on death. But according to this last amendment, after Nicole was born, that was limited to suicide.

Now, if there's a suicide—oh, hell, he hated these kinds of documents. Page after page of meaningless legal verbiage. He ran his finger by each line as he scanned. He stopped abruptly, his finger poised.

He carefully parsed the formal legal wording. It looked like Henri DeSant didn't inherit, only the next generation did. And the trust continued in perpetuity with only its income being divided up among the beneficiaries.

He needed to find out who they were. Sam Cunningham had to have a list of everyone in case he needed to give notice. He wondered who knew about the terms of the trust. More importantly, its assets. He made another note. Then he started reading again.

Henri DeSant became the managing trustee upon reversion. Could that be important to him? Maybe the compensation was substantial? He flipped back through the pages of the document. No. Just a few thousand francs a year.

The documents were interesting, but not really helpful. He took a sip of coffee. He remembered he still had to figure out how to get to that German, Dietz, the minister who was up for that European Central Bank job. He jotted a note on his list.

His eggs had gone cold. He motioned for the check and signed it. Then he returned to his room to use the phone.

He left a list of the additional information that he wanted with Cunningham's secretary. She promised to get the material copied and messenger it over to his hotel. She had never seen a list of reversionary beneficiaries. She promised to look.

Then he rang up Simon.

"Jonathan who?" Simon queried. "How nice of you to occasionally think of those of us who are paying you. What's up?" Simon was a crappy camper this morning.

"I wanted to find out how Henri DeSant is doing. Are we meeting today?" Jonathan asked, sitting with his shoes off, rubbing the arches of his stockinged feet. He felt guilty about spending so much time on Nicole's matter. Well, not actually. He felt guilty about not spending enough time on Simon's. What was with this guilt thing? Maybe it was because his mother was Jewish. He reached into his pocket and fingered his silver snuffbox.

"Yeah," Simon said, "it still bugs me that he's going to cost me about twice what anyone else would. But you wanted the guy. We got the picture over to him last week, and I told him the time line. We set up a meeting at Whiting & Pierce for this afternoon. Five."

"Good, I'll be there. Any problem with the syndication of the ARMARs?" He was curious to see if his ideas were working. He loved these intricate securities puzzles. There was a neatness in ordering the pieces that he liked. The solutions were almost mathematical. He got a kick out of it when the pieces snapped into place. It was something he could see whole in his mind. Something he was good at. Nothing like real life.

"Sims called to say they're getting good soft circles on the pension funds," Simon said. "That seems to be going okay. But I think we're running out of time. I heard some rumors that Rollins is making headway on a new line of credit. We better get our ass in gear and get this deal closed."

"We will. I'll touch base with Sims and check with his syndication people. I'll also confirm with Harv Champlin that we've cleared all the legal hurdles and that the filings and opinions are on track. It should be a matter of days now." Jonathan got up and walked in a little circle, tethered to the phone.

"Good. The sooner the better."

"Simon, one question." He changed the subject. "Did you ever run into a German guy, maybe in his late 70s, named Wolfgang Dietz? Some kind of economics minister in Germany. His name's being bandied about for the head of the European Central Bank."

"Yeah, I've met him a few times. I don't really know him. Kind of a formal guy. Very reserved. Why?"

"Well, I need to find out from him what he knows about an incident during the war."

"Which one?"

"Oh. World War II."

"Could it be embarrassing to him?"

"Maybe."

"Then I think there's no chance of your getting to the guy," Simon said. "He's important over there."

"If he's so concerned, do you think he would speak to Nicole or me if we hinted that we would go to the press if he didn't talk to us?"

There was an ominous silence on the other end of the phone before Simon spoke again. "You haven't played this kind of game before." His voice was flat. "You're asking for major league trouble. If you intend to take a shot at this guy, you better not be bluffing and you better be real sure of your facts, because if you're wrong or you're not willing to go to the mat, some very powerful people in Germany and France are going to come after you and carve out your liver."

Jonathan resumed his seat. This might take a while. Simon was in full flood. "There are a lot of important men who want to see Dietz get that job. Believe me, it's going to be really ugly. You're in way over your head."

"Maybe you're right," Jonathan said. "Thanks for the good advice." Advice that he had no intention of following. The conversation, however, gave him another idea. "See you at five. Bye." He pushed the disconnect button and dialed Nicole's telephone number. He crossed his legs and leaned back.

"Well, you have to, unless you can think of another alternative, or do you think we should just drop it?" He had the phone cradled in his ear.

He had asked Nicole to use her family's banking connections in France to get them into a position to have a confidential discussion with Wolfgang Dietz. Some people had called Jonathan stubborn. He simply thought of himself as tenacious. He was finding out Nicole was tenacious too. He came forward in his chair.

"I know how painful it is for you, but you have a lot on the line here. Our only alternative, as I see it, is to hire Frankee Perone to do an investigation, and we don't have that kind of money. Anyway, it will be tough to get the information we want." He listened intently, his elbow on the chair arm and his index finger across his lips.

"I can see how reluctant you are," he said. "I understand. We can let it rest for a few days, but we have to make a decision. Maybe you should talk it over with Henri."

So where were they? Jonathan thought, hanging up. He started to rub his silver box again. It helped him think.

Henri DeSant was still a possible. He had financial troubles, maybe. But he didn't inherit.

Jonathan needed to wait for the information from Sam Cunningham to get all the names of the beneficiaries upon the reversion of the trust, if he knew them. Cunningham hadn't needed the information until DeSant was a presumed suicide. It could be a lot of work tracking them down. And Jonathan also needed the names of the investors in all those real estate deals. Every one of them was a long shot.

As for Cunningham himself, he tended to agree with Nicole. He was too weak to have committed murder. But it wasn't impossible. He labeled him a low possible, but not a probable. The art dealer, Brauer, hadn't seemed very concerned about exposure, and Dietz was a dead end for now. He hoped Nicole would get over her feelings about asking her family for help.

Basically, they were nowhere. And time was running out.

Forty-four

"Simon, relax." Jonathan laughed. Simon had rung Jonathan on his cell phone. Jonathan covered the cell phone and said, "Excuse me, Larry. I need to speak to Simon for a moment." He was sitting with Larry Sims. The investment banker made an open-handed gesture. Jonathan returned to his phone. "What's got you so excited?" His tone was light.

It had been a busy morning already. Harv Champlin at Whiting & Pierce had gone through the closing issues, and he was now sitting in Sims' small office in Midtown reviewing commitments for the debt. He also needed to spend some time talking with Nicole before the five o'clock meeting with Simon and Henri DeSant.

"Damn it, something's wrong," Simon said. "DeSant wants to meet you and me alone at the hotel at 11:30. He's cancelled the meeting this afternoon."

"Why?" Jonathan's smile faded.

"That's the problem. He won't say. He wants to discuss it face-to-face, without the lawyers. I don't like it."

"No. Neither do I. Look, it's 10:45 now. I'm at Aspen & Leach. I can meet you back at the hotel in about twenty minutes. I'll brief you on my discussions with Larry Sims and the lawyers while we wait for DeSant."

"Things look good," Jonathan said. He was in Simon's apartment at the Carlyle. He sat on the couch, leaning on the arm with his legs sprawled in front of him. Simon was sitting in one of the yellow-striped silk chairs across from him. The chairs and the matching drapes gave the room an air of luxury.

"We should be able to close on the ARMARs the first part of next week," Jonathan continued. It had turned gloomy again, and bruised sunlight came through the windows. It matched Simon's mood.

"I reviewed the investors list," Jonathan said. "Aspen & Leach has buyers committed for about 95 percent of the securities at par, and they still have a lot of prospects to circle back to. There are no big legal issues, but Champlin is having the usual back-and-forth on the legal opinion language with counsel for the lead investor." Jonathan brought his legs up under him and leaned forward on the couch.

"He assured me it's nothing serious, and Whiting & Pierce is doing its opinion research and back-up memos now, based on a worst-case scenario. We shouldn't have a problem with the Whiting & Pierce Opinions Committee."

"What the hell's that?" Simon asked.

"Actually, more information than you probably need or want." Jonathan clinked the ice cubes in his glass and took a sip of the Diet Coke Simon had produced at his request. He put down the glass. Simon moved it onto a coaster. Simon's fastidiousness amused Jonathan.

"All the big law firms have detailed procedures for issuing opinion letters," Jonathan said. "They usually require an independent review of all the legal issues by two partners other than the partner in charge of the matter. Haven't you ever wondered why getting an opinion letter out of one of the large law firms is so expensive?"

"No, I never wondered. Expensive, I knew. Wondered, I didn't, the damned leeches."

"No. They're the investment bankers."

"Huh? Oh, I get it. Aspen & Leach. Ha ha." There was no amusement in his voice. "They're damned leeches too. I hope those guys have to pay their own fees someday. But I probably won't live that long. And as for your sense of humor, I think you need more sleep."

There was a knock at the door.

"Well, that's probably Henri DeSant," Simon said with a detectable sense of apprehension. He put his hands on his knees and stood.

Henri DeSant was as poised and well dressed as when Jonathan had last seen him with Nicole at the Four Seasons. He was carrying a beautiful Italian leather folio. He shook hands with Simon and Jonathan and took the seat that Simon offered him on one of the silk-striped chairs. His face was serious.

"Henri, do you want to take your jacket off and make yourself comfortable?" Simon asked. DeSant shook his head. "Coffee? Anything?"

"No, thank you, Simon." DeSant's mouth hardened. "I needed to speak with you and Professor Franklin alone. The matter is serious."

"I gathered that, Henri. What's the problem?"

"The pastel you gave me to examine. The one that Jean-Claude Fernaud opined on."

"Yes."

"Based upon my research, and what I know of this painter's work, as well as my own examination of the provenance of this piece, I am not sure it is genuine."

"My God, that's awful!" Simon sat up straight, surprise showing at the corners of his eyes. "Are you sure?" He said it a little too loudly.

Jonathan had also leaned forward.

"I can only express my view," DeSant said. "But I do not do so lightly. If I did not feel certain. . . " He gave an open-handed Gaelic shrug.

"How could Fernaud be so wrong?"

"That I cannot say, Simon." DeSant maintained an almost stoic calm. His face was a poker mask of emptiness. "Perhaps he had other sources that were not available to me. Perhaps he came to a different conclusion based upon the same work that I did. Perhaps he just made a mistake. All these things are possible. But I wanted you to know my conclusion. You can understand why I wanted to do this without the lawyers present. You will need another expert. Obviously, I cannot be your expert witness. I am sorry. Naturally, I will return your fee."

That last bit struck Jonathan as unexpected from a man purported to be in difficult financial straits.

Simon had crossed his legs and his foot was fidgeting. He was nervous, Jonathan realized.

"Henri, can you run through your analysis?" Simon said. "This is important to me, and I want to understand how you arrived at your conclusion." He uncrossed his legs and leaned forward, making a little grunt with the effort. "Of course, you won't return the fee. You did the work, even if we can't use it."

"Thank you. I would be pleased to explain to you why, unfortunately, I am not able to vouch for the genuineness of this work. I brought my papers and photographs with me. Let me show you." He reached for his leather folio and withdrew a sheaf of papers and pictures. He spread them on the coffee table.

They spent the better part of the next hour huddled over the littered coffee table, reviewing DeSant's work and his conclusions. Finally they all sat back.

"Well, thank you, Henri." Simon was glum. "That was a very thorough analysis. We appreciate your time and all your effort. And thank you for coming here and doing this in private."

"Damn it, that's a poke in the eye," Simon said, turning to Jonathan after he closed the door behind DeSant. "Where does that leave us now?"

"No place we want to be, that's for sure." Jonathan stood up and twisted his head back and forth to loosen the muscles in his neck. He walked to the kitchen in the apartment alcove and opened the refrigerator. "Mind if I have another Diet Coke?" he asked rhetorically. He walked back into the room, clutching the can, and sat on the couch. He absentmindedly popped the can top. He poured some and put the can down on the table. Simon gave him a look, but didn't move the can.

"Did you understand any of that mumbo jumbo?" Simon asked.

"No. Not much."

Simon walked back across the room. "Me neither. Now what?"

"You're not going to like this," Jonathan said. That was an understatement. "But I think whether he's right or not, you need to get our lawyers to buy back that picture. Let them make whatever excuse they have to. But with the closing of the ARMARs so close, I don't think we want a problem out there that we can't control. That lawyer is liable to go to the press on the day before we're scheduled to close, particularly if she hears about the placement, and it would really bollix things up. Murphy's Law."

"Yeah, I knew him. Murphy's name was Moskowitz before he changed it." Simon dead-panned it.

Good Lord. Simon Aaron had a sense of humor. Morbid, but still. Jonathan eyed him in bemusement. Who would have guessed? Then he got back to work.

"We don't have time to postpone the closing. I also don't think we have the time to get another expert. So, as far as I can see, we have no choice. I guess it's just a deal cost."

"I have to agree with you," Simon said, grudgingly. Simon liked making money, not spending it. "But I just don't understand how this could happen." He looked at his watch. "I'm famished. Let's order room service."

"Sure."

Simon lifted the phone and dialed for some sandwiches. "About twenty minutes. I hope you're not hungry."

"Starved," Jonathan said absently. He had been distracted by a thought that had bolted into his head with all the talk about Henri DeSant. It was the name DeSant that triggered it. There was a loose end he needed to tie up.

"Simon, I didn't know that DeSant owned so much of Witten's. You never mentioned it to me."

"I haven't seen enough of you lately to mention anything to you," Simon said. "Besides, it didn't seem very important. Henri approached me a few days ago and offered to sell me his eleven percent stake in Witten's. I told him I was interested, but that I'd like to discuss it with him after the placement closed. We talked about a price, and it seemed fair. I didn't see a problem."

"Henri? Simon, I meant Georges DeSant. The trust owns about nine percent of your stock."

"I had no idea. There were no filings." Simon shrugged. "Well, anyway, that's good for us, isn't it?"

Jonathan had trouble keeping a straight face. He picked up his glass of Diet Coke and swirled it. *Oh, my God.* The thoughts stampeded through his head. *Have I missed a key piece of this puzzle? If twenty percent of Witten's stock fell into Rollins' hands, it would be devastating for Simon. He only owns twenty one percent of the stock.*

Could the DeSants have been playing a game with Simon? Witten's is important to him. He loves it deeply. Fiercely. Would he kill for it? The Diet Coke warmed in his hands. Were the DeSants dealing with Rollins? Did Simon know?

Simon was also the big loser in that real estate deal with Georges DeSant. Could there be something there as well? And Simon was one of the two people who knew that Nicole and he were going to see Jean-Claude Fernaud. *Is it possible?*

Now that it had entered his head, it was all he could think about. He just couldn't believe it. Not Simon.

Jonathan carefully put his glass down on the coaster and stood. "Yeah, sure, Simon, that's good for us," he said. "You know, I'm not really so hungry after all." He put on his jacket. "Let me call you later."

Forty-five

Jonathan was gone ten minutes after Henri DeSant. Simon was disappointed. He'd been looking forward to finding out what Jonathan was thinking. Jonathan had been acting strange lately. He ate lunch alone in the silent room, both sandwiches.

Jonathan had beaten a hasty retreat to a hole-in-the- wall coffee shop on 57th. An untouched hamburger was congealing on the plate in front of him. He was oblivious to the lunchtime chatter and bustle. A note pad was on the table by his right hand. His tie was loose. He was concentrating fiercely. But his mind was boggling at his train of thought. He was having trouble getting a grasp on the facts.

It couldn't be Simon, it just couldn't. He'd known him for years. He knew the man, damn it.

Georges DeSant had died when? Jonathan jotted down the question and thought about it. It must have been the 24th or 25$^{th.}$ He remembered it was Thanksgiving Day when Nicole flew in. So it was the 24th. He noted that, too. His concentration etched two parallel lines into his forehead. Where was Simon then? He wrote out the question. Of course, that's when they were meeting with Whiting & Pierce in New York. Henry Kent had blown Simon off. He was pissed.

But Simon wouldn't ever do something like that, he interrupted himself. *Come on, say it—kill someone—with his own hands. He would hire someone else to do it. And what better alibi than being with your lawyers?* And he'd made a big point of Jonathan being there with him.

"You want some more coffee?" It startled him.

"Uh. No, thanks."

The waitress shrugged and padded off.

Thinking back on it, Simon had seemed a little jumpy. Jonathan took off his glasses and put them on the table next to his plate. He squeezed the bridge of his nose. He looked down and pushed the plate of congealed hamburger across the table.

Jonathan couldn't figure it out. Why would Simon want to kill Georges DeSant? Why not kill Henri? Henri was an essential part of the scheme to accumulate the stock.

He tried to parse it. Henri had 11% of the stock. Georges only had 9%, plus a lot of bonds. Jonathan slapped his pencil down. This was stupid.

A couple of tourists at the next table looked at him like he was deranged and edged away. The man signaled frantically for a check. Jonathan ignored them.

He knew why it was Georges and not Henri. He just didn't want to admit it to himself. It was so cold. But it was starting to make sense.

Simon just needed to split up the voting block. Henri and Georges had almost the same number of shares. And Georges had been more accessible and more vulnerable.

Jonathan thought about who would have control of the shares on Georges' death. That would be who had the vote to determine the control of Witten's.

Simon couldn't have known about the suicide clause. So he would have been looking at Sam Cunningham. Now there was a guy whom Simon could have bought in a heartbeat, packaged and delivered. Could he have known about Cunningham and his problems? He paused again.

Sure. Simon would plan it meticulously. He always planned everything. He would have found out all there was to know about

DeSant and the trustee. Just like the analysis of a deal, and Simon was a master of that. Jonathan shuddered. The pieces were all there.

For that matter, Cunningham might have come to Simon if he thought Simon could be a way out for him, or even just to curry Simon's favor. He could have told Simon what was going on. It wasn't beyond Cunningham. Or Simon could have used Frankee Perone to find out what he needed to know. Jonathan picked his glasses up and tapped the corner of the frame on the table.

No, probably not, he backtracked. He looked off into the distance, his mind racing. Tap. Simon would have used someone else, and arranged it through some obscure corporation. There would have been some logical reason for the investigation. It would all be plausible. Tap, tap, tap. He set the glasses on the table with his hand cradling them.

And the investigators he would have used would be in a small firm, far away from New York. He wouldn't want anyone to see that article on Georges DeSant's death and put two and two to-gether. He slipped his glasses back on and nudged them into place. Then he sat back and looked vacantly out the front window.

It was possible. He couldn't believe it, but it was possible. Cunningham was the weak link. Simon would have had to wrap him up. So Jonathan needed to see Sam Cunningham again. He sighed. That wasn't a pleasant thought.

And it was time to see Nicole and get a few matters straight. She had some hard decisions to make. Now they would really need some help. Again, Jonathan had the feeling that time was running out. It wasn't just the trust reversion. It was something else too. Something hovered at the very edge of his mind, just beyond his grasp.

Why? What was that feeling? He flashed on a thought. Would the murderer strike again? At whom? Maybe the guy kicking up all the dust. Him. Jonathan's mouth went dry. That idea hadn't oc-curred to him before. He looked around at the faces of the people in the restaurant. No one looked back.

* * *

Jonathan and Sam Cunningham were again in the back of the coffee shop near Cunningham's office. Cunningham was practically shouting. The waitress was keeping her distance.

"I've told you everything I know. I've given you all the documents. My God, can't you leave me alone?" He had a day-old beard, and his suit looked like he'd slept in it. His eyes were rimmed in red, and there was a thin vein of hysteria deep in his voice. It flashed through Jonathan's mind that he might be cracking mentally. He would have to be careful.

"You've been very cooperative so far, Sam." Jonathan spoke with a gentleness he didn't feel. "I just need a little more information." He tried to smile but it didn't come off. "You told me that Simon Aaron was an investor in a real estate deal that the trust was involved in. Did you know him?"

Cunningham couldn't seem to concentrate. "What?"

"Did you know Simon Aaron?"

"Oh. Yes." Cunningham's eyes wandered. He couldn't seem to hold them on Jonathan.

Jonathan waited. "Well?" He said it a little too loudly.

Cunningham jerked as if he'd been slapped. "Uh, I did some work for him a few years ago." He spoke slowly, almost by rote. "Something he didn't want Whiting & Pierce to be involved in."

A warning light went off in Jonathan's head. "Did he know that you were the trustee of the DeSant trust?" He waited. "Sam?"

"I don't think so." Cunningham shook his head as if to clear it. He reached for a glass of water on the table and lifted it to his lips. He took a sip, then hesitated. He seemed to be remembering something.

"Sam," Jonathan prompted. "What do you remember?" He spoke soothingly.

"Mr. Aaron saw a bound volume of DeSant trust documents on my bookshelf. He asked me if it was the same DeSant family.

He said the daughter worked for him. I told him I was the trustee. I was proud of it." Cunningham shrank into silence.

"Did Simon ever ask you about the trust?"

"No." Cunningham's voice was starting to rise again. Spittle flecked the corner of Cunningham's mouth. "Why are you asking me all these questions? What does it have to do with anything?"

"Have you spoken to Simon Aaron lately?"

Cunningham shook his head in a distracted way. He got up, his chair scraping back. It was as if he didn't remember Jonathan was sitting there. He wandered out of the restaurant.

Jonathan sat a while, very still. Simon knew. Simon would have figured it out.

Forty-six

"Nicole, I feel like this is getting way out of hand."

Nicole and Jonathan were having dinner in a quiet neighborhood restaurant off Madison. The spare room was set off by deeply grained and polished wooden tables surrounded by custom-made ebony chairs. It created a sense of calm luxury. The linen-clothed tables held small bowls of floating yellow flowers. For a New York restaurant, it was quiet.

They were picking at their food. Neither had much of an appetite. Nicole put down her fork and looked up at him.

"There's just too much happening, too many possibilities," he said. "I think we need to go to the police."

"Jonathan, please, no." She spoke quickly. Stress fluted in her voice. "Is there no other way? Can we not use the investigating firm?" He noticed worry lines at the corners of her eyes. "Please. I must protect my father."

He was surprised at the strength of her feelings. Even in the face of two deaths. Wasn't she frightened?

"Possibly," he said reluctantly, thinking. "Maybe it would be better than going to the police. I'm not sure the police would believe us. And maybe it would be quicker." He put the tip of his finger to the corner of his lip and thought for a moment.

"I have a feeling we're running out of time. At least we can start there. But it'll cost a small fortune. How are we going to pay them?"

"I can ask Henri. I know he will help me. Let me call him."
She squeezed his hand.

"Sure, maybe that's a good idea." A darned good idea, from
his point of view. He could maybe get an insight into Henri's financial condition and perhaps ferret out something else useful.

"I can try him now." She was eager.

"Why not finish dinner?"

"I am not hungry."

"Do you want to use my cell phone?"

"I will be more comfortable if I speak to Henri alone. It is
embarrassing. Excuse me, please."

Nicole returned to the table. Her face seemed more relaxed.
He noticed the stress lines at the corners of her eyes had eased. He
stood and held out her chair.

"Jonathan, Henri asks that we join him for lunch tomorrow
at Les Cygnes. I am fortunate to have reached him." She sat back.
She turned pensive and her face softened.

"Why are you doing this?"

"Doing what?" he responded. A flash of guilt. "I don't understand?"

"Helping me. You have done so much."

He relaxed. "I hadn't thought about it." He had, but did it
make sense? "You're in trouble. It just seemed right." His hands
were flat on the table. He tapped a finger for a moment. "Maybe,
when you come down to it, it's the same reason you called me in
the first place." Whatever that was.

She sat still for a moment, reflecting on what he'd said. "Perhaps that is true," she responded, nodding her head. Her gray eyes
were thoughtful.

The restaurant in Midtown was just a short trip by cab from
the hotel. Jonathan joined Nicole and Henri there a few minutes
before twelve.

The tables were widely spaced, and the talk was murmured and sedate. The gray leather of the booths and the pale walls were washed with light that sparkled off the crystal. Menus lay undisturbed on the table. He quietly took his seat.

"Good afternoon, Henri," Jonathan said as he placed the starched napkin across his lap. Nicole smiled at him. Henri DeSant nodded but turned his attention to Nicole.

"Henri, thank you so much for making this time for us," Nicole said. "I know you are busy. I am grateful."

The maitre d' approached and stopped beside Henri DeSant, waiting quietly. Henri looked up.

"Would you care to order, Monsieur DeSant? I have a wonderful branzino today. Or perhaps the seafood salad you enjoyed yesterday."

"Thank you, Frederick, but we need a few minutes."

"Of course, *Monsieur*. Perhaps water?"

"Sparkling, please."

"Immediately." He departed with a small bow.

Henri turned back to Nicole. "*Cherie?*"

"I am embarrassed," she said. She leaned forward and spoke more softly. This was difficult for her. "I must ask you for a favor. A loan. I do not know when I can repay you. But it is very important to me. Let me explain."

Henri held up his hand. "No, Nicole. Please do not." Henri said it gently. "There is no need. You know I will do for you anything that I can."

They were interrupted by a tuxedoed waiter. He silently uncapped a bottle and poured sparkling water into each glass.

"Thank you," said Henri. As the waiter turned to leave, Henri leaned across the table to place his hand over Nicole's.

"Your father was dear to me, just as you are. Tell me how much you need, *cherie*."

Nicole turned to Jonathan with a quizzical look. Jonathan leaned back in his chair and guessed high. "No more than $200,000, I think."

She gasped. "Jonathan, you never told me it could be so much!" She turned toward Henri, flustered. "I did not realize," she said quickly. "I would not have come to you for so much money. Please forgive me."

Henri sat calmly, his face in repose, his hand still over Nicole's. The amount had not startled him. Or he was a wonderful poker player. "Nicole, *cherie*. I have known you for all of your life. You are as dear to me as my own daughters. Never have you asked me for anything. I will need to make some arrangements, but such a loan is not a problem. I must speak with Simon Aaron."

"Simon mentioned that you were discussing the sale of your shares of Witten's," Jonathan interposed. He reached for his glass and took a sip. "He's very interested, you know," he said over the half-lowered glass.

Henri turned toward him. His gaze held onto Jonathan. "Yes, we have discussed it. I would not choose to part with them now, but these things have their own time. And it will be helpful to Mr. Aaron."

"Oh, how is that?" Jonathan asked.

Henri DeSant sat back in his chair and straightened his French cuffs, one at a time. The diamonds in his cufflinks blinked with the movement. He never took his eyes off Jonathan. They were a steely gray and held Jonathan almost physically.

"I am surprised you do not know," Henri said. His voice was flat. It made Jonathan shift in his seat. "I had believed that you were closer to Mr. Aaron," Henri said. "You know, of course, that Witten's has had financial difficulties and that Mr. Aaron has been concerned about a man named Vincent Rollins."

Jonathan nodded. He had overstepped himself, and this man was a lot smarter than he had assumed. *And I'm stupid*, he thought.

"I was approached by this man, Rollins," Henri continued. "He even tried to force Nicole to become involved." Nicole nodded. "A most unpleasant man. Apparently he had been looking into our affairs, Professor Franklin, something we do not appreciate."

Jonathan thought DeSant stared at him with those piercing gray eyes for just a little too long. He couldn't possibly know, could he?

"This man suggested that I sell him my Witten's shares. He offered me a very large premium for them. And more if I would approach Georges. He suggested that he knew of certain financial problems that I was having, and he had the temerity to suggest that he could cause me harm if I did not comply. I laughed at him." A trace of anger still lingered in DeSant's voice. His mouth was set in a thin line.

"Then I called Mr. Aaron. Is that what you wished to know, Professor Franklin? Or is there something else?" Henri's emphasis was on the last sentence.

"I apologize if I offended you," Jonathan said. He had just gotten a glimpse into the DeSant family and how hard a man Henri DeSant could be beneath his veneer of European politeness. It was a lesson, and it stung.

Henri turned to Nicole, and his face relaxed into a look of concern. "*Cherie*, I will have your loan for you this afternoon. Please do not trouble yourself. And if there is anything else I can do for you, or—" he turned to look directly at Jonathan "—Professor Franklin, please allow me to help." DeSant was scrupulously polite, but Jonathan felt the bite.

Henri DeSant looked at his watch. It was a thin gold Brequet. An unusual one. "Now if you will excuse me," Desant said, "I must leave for an appointment. Please order. The lunch has been placed on my bill. Do not hurry. Forgive me."

Jonathan signaled the waiter for more water as Henri DeSant left the restaurant. He and Nicole sat quietly while the waiter refilled their glasses. "I guess we should order." He sounded sheep-ish, even to himself.

No one spoke. A half-finished lunch lay on the table. Finally, Jonathan broke the awkward silence. "I apologize if I seem to be mumbling. I have my foot in my mouth."

"You should not play Henri for the fool," Nicole said, more gently than he had expected. "He is what we call in French *'formida-ble.'* The same word is in English, but it has a very different nuance."

"Indeed," he said, then sank back into silence, lost in his thoughts.

Well, there's good news here and bad news, he realized. They had just eliminated both Simon and Henri as suspects. That was a reve-lation. He hadn't even consciously realized it until this moment. It startled him.

There was no way Henri DeSant would kill for money. Not considering the way he'd responded to Nicole. And it was clear the DeSants weren't dealing with Rollins. Rollins was trying to lean on Henri to get to Georges. And DeSant had called Simon and told him.

So, thank God, Simon wouldn't seem to have a motive either. He wasn't at risk of losing Witten's. And Henri would have never called Simon if the DeSants were going to make a run at Witten's themselves.

The bad news was that he had made a fool of himself, and now they were back to square one. Everyone else was a long shot. Not one of them had any reason to know they were going to see Fernaud that day. He didn't know where to take this.

Nicole touched his arm and broke into his thoughts. "Do not be upset. At least we may now engage the investigating firm." She smiled at him.

"Yeah," he said with a resigned tone. "I'd better try to speak to Frankee Perone. I'll call and see if she can see me tomorrow morning. Let's meet after that."

"I must go to my office tomorrow. Perhaps we can meet at five."

"Fine. I'll pick you up at Witten's."

"My goodness, Jonathan Franklin again. I must be living right. Or wrong." Frankee Perone, squarely cut with short gray hair, rose from behind her spare desk and extended her hand. "Tell me, Franklin, what's with the tweed jackets? Don't they pay you enough as a schoolteacher to buy some decent clothes?"

"Come on, Frankee, quit hassling me. It's like baseball. You change teams, you change uniforms. Besides, I like tweed jackets. They make me look professorial."

"Well, I'm glad for you. But to what do I owe this honor? I like you, but if you're looking for another handout, you've got the wrong girl."

"No, ma'am. I come, checkbook in hand and heart on my sleeve. I need you to check up on the movements of two guys between November 23rd and 25th. One's Samuel Cunningham. He's a lawyer here in town. Parks & Ellwood."

"Slow down, big boy. Would you spell those big names for me? Slowly. I'm just a humble detective. Not a Harvard professor."

"I could buy you a tweed jacket, Frankee." It drew a smile. Not a big one, but a smile. He spelled the names.

"Cunningham claims to have been at his firm's retreat in upstate New York," Jonathan said. "The other's a German, Wolfgang Dietz. He's one of the guys you put me onto. If they were in New York City, I need to know when and where. Who saw them, the usual stuff."

"What's the big deal about the dates?"

"That's when George DeSant was killed. He's supposed to have committed suicide, but I think he may have been murdered. These two are a long shot, but I need to be sure."

Frankee Perone burst out laughing, catching him completely off guard.

"This Dietz, he's the German minister?" Frankee asked, hardly able to speak.

"Right."

She swiped a tear from the corner of her eye. "I don't know about Cunningham, but I can pretty well tell you that Dietz didn't kill DeSant."

"Oh, and how can you do that?" He felt a little annoyed. He hadn't been laughed at a lot.

"Hey, don't get angry. Have you ever seen this guy Dietz?"

"No."

"Do you know what he looks like?"

"No."

"This isn't a guy who can just sneak around unnoticed. Dietz was wounded in World War II. I ran into him during a visit he made to Chicago when I was with the FBI. He's paralyzed from the waist down. He gets around in a big black motorized wheelchair. And he lost an eye. He wears a patch."

Perone could hardly continue, she was laughing so hard. "Believe me, he didn't do it. Unless, of course, everyone overlooked a guy in a wheelchair with an eye patch." Jonathan had a picture in his mind of Dr. Strangelove wheeling around New York City.

She finally regained some composure. "Sorry, Jonathan. I'll run a check on the movements of both of them for you. It should be pretty straightforward. We'll see. But how do you know they didn't hire somebody to do it?"

"I don't."

"If they did, you know we've got no hope of turning anything up. That's pure police work. Anyway, why're you so sure it wasn't suicide?"

He paused a moment. "Well, I guess when you come down to it, it's Jean-Claude Fernaud's death."

"That's the guy you had me check the police on. Who is he?"

"Head of Impressionist art at Witten's. He and Nicole De-Sant worked together."

"That's the daughter? Good looking?"

"Yes."

"And you like her, right?"

"Frankee, come on."

"Uh-huh. And how do you know Fernaud's death and De-Sant's are connected?"

"Nicole and I were on our way to see him."

"So what? Were you going to see him about DeSant?"

"Uh, actually, no. We were going to see him about Nazi war loot."

"Oh? And how's that connected to DeSant's death?"

"I don't know."

"If you can't be sure it's not a suicide, and you really have no reason to believe otherwise, how come you're doing all this?"

"It's important, Frankee."

"Why?"

"It's important to Nicole."

Frankee Perone cocked an eyebrow. "I'm not your mother and it's your money, but when something walks like a duck and quacks like a duck, in my world, it usually is a duck."

"Yeah, I know."

"Well, let's get on with it. You know my retainer."

He wrote out a personal check for $25,000 and handed it to Perone. He made a note to get himself reimbursed.

"Oh, I need one more thing," he said. "DeSant had a trust. These are the potential beneficiaries." Jonathan passed across a list, the list that had finally come from Cunningham's office. "I just need to know where they live and what they do."

"No big deal. I'll put some of my people on it today. We should be able to track down a lot of this stuff on the Internet and over the phone. I can probably have something preliminary for you by noon tomorrow."

"Gosh, Frankee, I just gave you $25,000. That's a lot of money."

"Hey, a girl's got to live, you know." She leaned back in her chair and brushed aside his complaint with the back of her hand. "Besides, you owe me one." A benign smile spread across her face.

It was eleven o'clock, and there was nothing else to do until five. Jonathan figured he should swing downtown and see how Whiting & Pierce was doing on the closing of the Art Market Participation Certificates placement.

A least Simon will be happy, he thought. *And I know what I'm doing down there.* He felt lost.

He could pick up Nicole at Witten's on the way back. Jonathan shivered involuntarily. There was that feeling again, like a shadow passing over him.

Forty-seven

The bloodshot eye of the answering machine was blinking when they opened the door to Nicole's apartment. The mist-soaked twilight barely illuminated the living room overlooking Central Park, dimming the cheerful décor and intensifying the blinking light. "I have no idea who would be calling me," she said, flipping on the light switch. "I will not be a moment."

She returned to the living room almost at once. From the set of her mouth and the tension around her eyes, agitation was written plainly on her face.

He got quickly to his feet. "Nicole, what's wrong?"

"That policeman, Lieutenant Wayne. He called. He wants to see me as soon as possible. He sounded very urgent. He said he could come here this afternoon or tomorrow. Jonathan, please see him with me." She reached out and touched his arm. Her gray eyes were dark with stress. "I do not want the police involved." There it was again.

He gave a helpless shrug. "There's really no way we can stop him. All we can do is listen and hope that it's nothing. If you want, I'll call and see if I can catch him now. Maybe we can get this over with."

Maybe Wayne had something. It might not be such a bad idea to have the police involved anyway. He didn't feel nearly as certain as Nicole did.

He returned to the room after a few moments. "We missed him. He left word that if you called, to tell you he could be here at two o'clock tomorrow. I confirmed. I'll come over around 1:30. Shall we catch a quick dinner?"

They made their way to a small bistro on a little side street three blocks from Nicole's father's apartment. The rain was a soft mist falling around them. The long zinc-covered bar that spread along the left side of the room dominated the space. No one sat on the wooden stools. Only one of the dark wooden tables was occupied. "You're sure we'll survive the food?" Jonathan said, hoping to get a smile from Nicole. He didn't.

The hostess showed them to a table in the back and left them with menus. "You could use a glass of wine," Jonathan said.

"That would be nice." Her voice was laced with the tiredness of intense emotion.

He beckoned over the waiter skulking on the far side of the bar. "A wine list, please." The waiter returned with a large loose-leaf book. Jonathan opened it. It was one of those wine lists where each page is taken up with the wine label and an effusive description of the wine. Not a good sign.

Jonathan quickly perused the list. "We'll have a bottle of the 1990 Montrose," he said, pointing at the page. It was too young, but it was the best he could do.

The waiter looked sullen. "We're out of that. We have the 1992." A truly terrible year in Bordeaux. Jonathan grumbled his disappointment. He settled on a 1994, second- rate Cabernet from Napa. Their last bottle.

Nicole seemed lost in her thoughts. "It's not so bad, you know," Jonathan said. "I mean, even if the police are involved, we'll deal with it together."

She looked up at him and gave him a weary smile. "You are a very dear man." She reached across and took his hand. "I do not know how I could have done this without you. So many things. It must be very hard for you."

"A little. I've never been involved with anything like this. But I'm okay. I want you to be okay too." Her hand remained in his. He liked it.

They were interrupted by the waiter. Nicole removed her hand and sat back. The waiter held out the bottle without revealing the label. Jonathan reached and turned the bottle. It was a 1995, not the 1994 he'd ordered. "This isn't a 1994," he said.

"They must have sold the last one," the waiter said with a shrug. "This is all we have." Jonathan surrendered with ill grace. He motioned with his hand for the waiter to open the bottle. It was as poor a wine as he had imagined.

"Not the best we've had," Jonathan said, more for something to say while the waiter poured the wine than for any other reason.

Nicole picked up her glass and looked at the wine. Her gaze was more trained than interested. She raised her glass and sipped. "Fine," she said without passion. Jonathan didn't even think she noticed.

"Would you like to order?" the waiter asked.

"We need a little more time," Jonathan said. The waiter took a book of matches from his pocket and struck one. He applied the flame to the small candle on the table. It flickered, and the small light picked up the red of Nicole's fingernails. The waiter wandered off.

The restaurant was slowly starting to fill. Jonathan opened his menu. "What would you like?" He leaned close to Nicole so as not to raise his voice.

"I am not really hungry," she said.

Women. A small thing like unexplained deaths and the police put them off their appetite. Maybe that's why they were so thin. As for him, he was hungry. "Would you like to split something? Maybe the caprese and the steak frites?"

"Let us have whatever you like." Kind but unenthusiastic. He signaled to the waiter, who made his way slowly to the table. "Sir?" he said.

"Do you use buffalo mozzarella for the caprese?" Jonathan asked.

"I think so," the waiter responded.

Oh, well. "We'll have the steak frites and the caprese, please. Not too much olive oil on the caprese." The waiter scribbled.

"Would you like another bottle of wine with your dinner?" the waiter asked.

Jonathan glanced at the bottle. It was three-quarters full. "No, this will be adequate." He had rarely hit on so perfect a description. He turned back to Nicole.

"I miss my father so much," she said. A totally new thought.

"How could you not?"

She lifted her glass and sipped thoughtfully. "This has become so complicated," she said over the rim of her glass.

"Yes."

"Will it ever end?"

"If we can hang on a while."

She sat back, rubbing her index finger along the side of her wine glass. Something in her eyes changed. The gray seemed deeper. In the flickering candlelight, her face resolved into an ease Jonathan hadn't seen before.

"Jonathan."

"Yes."

"Will you stay with me?"

"Of course."

She smiled for the first time that evening. It was dazzling, as if the sun had emerged. "No. I mean, will you come home with me tonight? I do not want to be alone."

He wondered if she was feeling lonely. Or maybe scared. "Sure. I'll sleep on the couch." He surprised himself.

She reached for his hand and took it in hers. She drew it across the table and kissed the knuckles tenderly. "I do not want you to sleep on the couch. I want to be with you."

"Isn't this rather sudden?" What was he asking questions for? Was he out of his mind?

"No, quite the contrary." The smile lit up her gray eyes. "I have always been whole, you might say complete. I have been successful. I took pride in that. I thought I didn't need anyone else."

"Okay," Jonathan said. He was totally lost, but listening closely.

"It has taken me far too long to understand."

"Understand what?" he said. He tipped his head sideways in a quizzical manner as he spoke. He wasn't aware of any of the noise or the movement around him.

"I can be complete on my own and yet better with another."

"You've lost me."

"I hope that is not the case." Her laugh was far from innocent.

They lay on Nicole's bed, covered by a sheet. Muffled horns sounded on the street below. Rain patterned the windows. Her head nestled against his shoulder. Her warmth folded into his.

Their lovemaking had been gentle, so different from the first time, as if they knew each other well. Yet there had been passion there that filled the space between them.

"You're terrific," Jonathan said, turning to look into her closed eyes. A gentle smile touched the corners of her mouth.

"Umm," she said, cuddling in closer to fit her body into the curves of his.

The room was dark except for a puddle of moonlight that spilled onto the floor. A sense of warmth suffused Jonathan. He reached over and stroked Nicole's hair. "Thank you." It seemed inadequate. "I want. . ." he started but Nicole lifted her finger to his lips.

"Shhh," she said. She put her arm across his chest and hugged him. She opened her eyes and whispered into his ear, "I have never known a better man."

"How about handsome?" he said, his sense of humor re-asserting itself.

She elbowed him playfully. "I seem to know you so well. As if I have known you all my life. How strange." There was a tinge of wonder in her voice.

Jonathan remained still. He wanted to hear what she would say next. All he heard was her rhythmic breathing as she fell asleep.

He awoke the next morning with a feeling of well-being. Nicole was still cuddled into him, her arm over his chest. He looked at her face, innocent in sleep, and he smiled.

What an extraordinary woman. She had been knocked about. God, that was an understatement. Yet after all that had happened, she seemed to be growing stronger. He wasn't sure he could have done as well.

Nicole shifted beside him and blinked her eyes open.

"Good morning, pretty one," he said.

"Good morning," Nicole said through a yawn, nuzzling his neck with her nose. Her hand started to rub his chest and sink lower.

He turned and kissed her lightly on the lips and took her roving hand in his. "Alas, we can't play." He rolled over and gave her nipple a light kiss. "We have a full day. I have to meet with Aspen & Leach. You've ruined me, woman, but I have to attend to business." Nicole gave a derisive mew.

"First, it's the Carlyle for me," he continued resolutely. "I have to change. And Frankee may have left me something on her investigation. Then we have to meet with Lieutenant Wayne at two."

At the mention of Wayne's name, a doubt shadowed his mind. He was again beset by the feeling he had missed something important, but he couldn't quite put his finger on it.

"Do you think the police will become involved?" Nicole said. There was anxiety in her voice.

"You know, I don't think so," Jonathan said. His analytical mind was clicking in. "Wayne asked to see you. He didn't insist." He paused and looked at her. "No, there's something else going on." He said it with a certainty he didn't feel. Seldom right but always certain. Simon had said something like that.

He rolled out of bed. "Come on, Adam," he said.

"Adam?" she echoed.

"Sure, you must be Adam."

"You are very confusing."

"Why? I'm up. That makes you Adam, right? Up and Adam." With that he pulled off the sheet she had wrapped herself in.

The pillow hit him in the face.

Forty-eight

The taxi ride to the Carlyle was pleasant. Jonathan would have preferred to walk, but he didn't have an umbrella. The rain tattooed lightly on the roof of the cab. He wanted to concentrate on the closing issues he would be discussing at his meeting with Aspen & Leach. But his mind kept wandering back to Nicole. He felt a sense of wonder at how things had turned.

For once the ride across the park was easy. Even quiet. He asked for his key at the front desk and was handed a heavy legal-sized envelope from Parks & Ellwood and a fax from Frankee Perone.

He flipped on the lights, shed his raincoat and draped his tweed jacket over the back of the chair. He flopped onto the couch, holding the fax and the thick envelope. He wanted to shower, but he was anxious to see what new information was at hand.

First he tore open the envelope from Cunningham's office. There were six complete limited partnership agreements in it, each for a different piece of real property. Jonathan flipped through the signature pages. One was missing. That was suspicious. He'd have to call Cunningham. He recognized many of the names on the other signature pages from his lawyering days or from the society pages. Nothing obvious there.

He turned to the fax from Frankee Perone. It was thick enough to be promising.

"Let's see what's here," he murmured aloud. He ran a finger down the typed report, reading as he went. Nothing was new with the NYPD on the Fernaud homicide. It was suspicious. But why?

He was having difficulty concentrating. Thoughts of lying with Nicole in that quiet interlude after making love overtook him. He could feel the softness of her body and luxuriate in her smell.

Then an old thought jolted him from his reverie. He had missed something. But what? It was frustrating. Maybe if he didn't think about it.

He picked up the fax and flipped the page to a copy of a group of Internet research pieces on Wolfgang Dietz. Dietz apparently had been the good German bureaucrat all his life, never venturing to seek elective office. Respected. A lot of awards. Some quotes from people who knew him. Certainly nothing either startling or suspicious. He had not been in the United States in six months. So much for Dr. Strangelove.

The next couple of pages were about Sam Cunningham. Snippets of telephone interviews with upstate hotel people and copies of hotel bar tabs and restaurant receipts. Cunningham had signed chits or credit slips several times throughout the days surrounding Georges DeSant's death. Each was stamped with a time and date. It would have been nearly impossible for him to get to the city and back.

It reminded him he had to call Sam Cunningham about the missing signature page. Maybe Cunningham was hiding something. Jonathan thought he had put the fear of God into him, but he couldn't be sure. Maybe he was more afraid of someone else.

The final four pages of the fax were a list of the present addresses of reversionary beneficiaries under the trust, all 42 of them. By many of the names were the person's age and a notation of what he or she was doing now. Jonathan ran his finger down the names.

The youngest was 25, and she was studying for a graduate degree in design at the École des Beaux-Arts in Paris. Of the 42, 24 seemed to have real jobs. Two of the men worked in New York in major positions with the DeSant bank. A total of six lived in the United States. It appeared that two of the women were married to men in the city. *I didn't know she was a DeSant*, he thought, recognizing one of the couples.

Nothing there.

On the last page, in bold writing, was a note from Frankee Perone and another bill for the matter that Jonathan had asked her to undertake on an hourly basis. "Shit," he said out loud. "That much?"

He put the fax aside and reached for the telephone. He knew Sam Cunningham's number by heart.

"Mr. Cunningham's office." Cunningham's secretary. Jonathan recognized her.

"May I speak to Mr. Cunningham? Jonathan Franklin calling."

"I'm sorry, Mr. Cunningham isn't here, Mr. Franklin." There was something amiss in her voice.

"When will he be back?"

The woman started to sob. "Are you okay?" Jonathan said. He was getting a bad feeling.

"Mr. Cunningham was struck by a bus yesterday," she said between sobs. "He was killed instantly. He was such a good man." She burst into tears. He hung up quietly.

Another death. He was glad they were going to see that policeman at two. Now Nicole couldn't possibly object.

Forty-nine

"Lieutenant Wayne," Jonathan said, opening the door of Nicole's apartment and extending his hand, "I'm Jonathan Franklin. We met a few weeks ago." It was 2:15.

Wayne was wearing a rumpled suit over a mismatched plaid shirt and tie. "Yeah, I remember." He didn't seem pleased.

Jonathan showed him into the living room, where Nicole was seated on the sofa.

Wayne turned to him. "Franklin, I'd like to see Ms. DeSant alone."

Jonathan saw a look of panic rise in Nicole's eyes. "Actually, I need to be here, Lieutenant. You see, I'm acting as Ms. DeSant's lawyer for the purpose of this interview. As you're well aware, Ms. DeSant is entitled to counsel."

Wayne grimaced. "Does Ms. DeSant need a lawyer, Franklin? Maybe I better be lookin' at this whole thing different."

"Not really," said Jonathan, "but you scare her, Lieutenant. And it would be better for all of us if I stay. Perhaps we should get on with it. Can I get you something cold to drink?"

"I thought this was Ms. DeSant's place," Wayne said dryly. "Anyway, no thanks." He brushed away the offer with a move of his hand.

Wayne sat down in the chair opposite Nicole. "Did you know a . . ." Wayne took out a notebook and riffled through the pages. "Jean-Claude Fernaud, Ms. DeSant?"

Jonathan moved to stand behind Nicole. He put a hand on her shoulder. He could feel the tension. Nicole nodded, but remained silent. She was sitting very erect. The position of the sun shadowed her face.

"Did you know he was dead?"

Again, Nicole nodded, but then looked up at Jonathan with concern.

"Lieutenant Wayne," he said, "we were at Monsieur Fernaud's hotel when his body was taken away. We had an appointment to see him."

Wayne turned his head to look at Jonathan. "I know that, Franklin." His voice was gruff. "We found Fernaud's appointment book. That's how we tied this to Ms. DeSant. What I wanna know is why?"

"It was a business matter. We wanted to consult Fernaud about a piece of art that had been found in Germany. As you probably know, Fernaud was an art expert. He and Ms. DeSant worked together at Witten's. We never got to see him, Lieutenant."

Wayne turned back to Nicole without responding. "Fernaud also knew your father. That right, Ms. DeSant?"

Before she could respond, Jonathan interrupted again.

"I don't understand how any of this is relevant to finding out who murdered Fernaud."

Wayne shifted his body to look directly at him. "Murdered? What're you talking about, Franklin?"

"We . . ." Jonathan started to say, but was silenced by the look on Wayne's face. He felt a warm flush climbing up his neck.

"That's what I came to tell Ms. DeSant, Franklin. Fernaud killed himself."

"What?" Jonathan exclaimed. "Are you sure?"

"He blew his brains out. The gun was in his hand. He left a note. I wanted to bring it to Ms. DeSant. It took us a while to get the two cases hooked up. Sorry it took so long, but it's a big city.

We woulda gotten there a lot sooner if you'd a come and told us about the connection."

Wayne turned back to Nicole. "We got it wrong about your father. And I gave you a pretty hard time. I thought I owed it to you to bring you this."

He handed Nicole a copy of a handwritten letter.

"I think Fernaud addressed it to you," he said.

She started to read it, then she handed it to Jonathan, her eyes filling with tears. "Could you read it to me, please?"

He looked at the letter. "Nicole, I'm sorry, the letter's in French. My French just isn't that good."

"Wait a minute, Franklin," Wayne said, patting at his coat. "I got a translation here." He reached into his inside coat pocket and took out a piece of folded paper.

Jonathan unfolded the sheet of paper and started to read.

> *Nicole, please forgive me, I did not mean to cause you pain. Everything I want in the world is gone.*
>
> *I loved your father, but in some ways I also hated him. As you know by now, it was I who copied the Matisse that your father passed on to the Nazis. It was perfect. Can you imagine that, perfect. My greatest work of art. A copy. I knew then. Perhaps I always knew. There was nothing creative, nothing original, in me. And it was your father who sought me out. Who did this to me.*
>
> *I had seen the article that was published in the Herald Tribune. I knew that the Matisse they had discovered was mine. I had to find out if your father knew, and what he was going to do about it. So much depended upon it. So much.*

Jonathan leaned forward with the letter in his hand, as if to immerse himself it.

> *I had worked so many days, so many years for Witten's. Every day, touching the genius of those great artists. And feeling the deepest humiliation, knowing that I had none. That I was nothing. All I had*

left were my little pleasures. And what would I have when I was pensioned off? A pittance. I had spent everything. I had no savings. Almost a pauper, shuffling in the streets. I could not stand it.

When I saw your father, he was ebullient. He wanted to open a bottle of champagne. He wanted us to have a toast. "The picture has survived," he shouted, holding out the newspaper article. "Now it is no longer just our word. Now we can prove that we are heroes, patriots, not vile traitors. My name will be mine again. I can hold up my head."

His face was shining. Until I told him that I could not, I would not, support him. I told him that in my position in the art world, such a revelation would ruin me. A forger, the head of Impressionist art at Witten's.

Nicole wiped a tear away with the back of her hand.

I lied to him. "Please," I begged him. "You will only make the scandal worse." I offered to give him money if he had need of it.

My words infuriated him. I had not seen such anger. He raised his hand to strike me. I brushed his blow aside and pushed him away. He lost his balance and fell. He struck his head on the corner of the table. I tried to revive him. You must believe me. I did not mean to kill him.

I knew that I must not be associated with his death. I was desperate. My only hope was the money from the sale of the Van Gogh study that I had created. It also was perfect. It had taken so long. It was my whole future. Placing it in the Klyberg sale was my last opportunity.

God forgive me. I dragged him to the window and pushed him out. I did not think of you. I was thinking of no one but myself.

You must help me. Do not let the Van Gogh be sold. It will be discovered now. I must not be remembered as a forger. Please, for me, find it and destroy it.

I could not stand to be poor. That is my crime.

Jean-Claude

"My God." It escaped from Jonathan involuntarily. The letter hung limply. Nicole was sobbing quietly, her face in her hands.

Wayne got up to leave, but turned back at the door, holding on to the knob.

"Ms. DeSant. Look, it's none of my business. But I been doing this for a lotta years now and seen lotsa guys get caught. If I were you, I wouldn't believe half of the crap, pardon the expression, in that letter. If he coulda gotten away with it, he'd've taken the money and run and you'd've never known. Only cared about number one, as far as I can see. And, oh," he paused for a moment, "this apartment here had been straightened up and wiped clean. Don't figure, does it? Sorry, just mouthin' off. See you."

Fifty

Past the hand-painted jockeys and down the three steps. Simon, Nicole and Jonathan were alone at "21." Simon had taken over the entire restaurant.

It was four days after Christmas. The day was unusually bright and breezy. Clouds pranced across the sky, their edges silvered in sunlight. Jonathan's tweed jacket felt a little warm.

They were seated in the Bar Room. The entire ceiling was covered in toys. Toys that bore the corporate logos of great American corporations. A model of an American Airlines jet dangled from a wire above Jonathan.

Simon chuckled to himself. "Do you know," he asked, "the famous story of the night Clare Booth Luce and Dorothy Parker arrived at the front door at the same time?"

"I do not," said Nicole. Jonathan smiled Simon onward.

"Well, Luce stepped aside for Parker when the doorman opened the door. She bowed and made a sweeping gesture. 'Age before beauty,' she said." Simon mimicked the gesture. "Now Dorothy Parker was legendary at the Algonquin for her razor wit. Her bark was far worse than her bite. Without missing a beat she responded, 'Pearls before swine, dear.' " He burst into laughter.

Nicole held her hand to her mouth to stifle an unladylike giggle.

"God, what a woman," Simon said. "I wish I could have met her."

Jonathan was absorbed in his own thoughts. *The regulars must really be pissed off.* He was sure he could hear the media types snuffling and rooting around outside the door like wild bores. Jonathan chuckled to himself at his own play on words, echoing Dorothy Parker unintentionally. Unfortunately, without the same wit.

Simon was in full bay. "See that table over there? That was where Groucho used to sit whenever he was in New York."

"Was it a private club then?" Nicole asked.

"Never," Simon said. "But you couldn't get in during Prohibition without an introduction. It was a speakeasy. The best in New York."

"How strange," Nicole said, not exactly sure what was prohibited. "Was that illegal?"

"Not here," Simon said. "They had a secret wine cellar. Still do. You could only get in by sliding an eighteen-inch wire into a specific crack in one of the bricks."

He grasped a bottle of Cristal champagne by the neck and stood, brandishing it in front of him like a scepter, a wide smile creasing his face. "The Feds could never find it. Believe me, they tried. Good thing. That's where Jimmy Walker used to drink when he was mayor."

Simon stopped talking long enough to pour champagne until everyone's glass was full. Then he put down the bottle, stood and picked up his own glass. He held it out ceremoniously.

"I want to propose a toast to Jonathan and to the Good Lord. Thank the Good Lord that Jonathan is a better lawyer than he is a detective."

Jonathan let out a guffaw. "I resemble that remark," he said, quoting one of his favorite TV characters.

"Simon, that is not fair!" said Nicole. "I. . ."

"Hold on, Nicole," Simon said, raising his hand. "I was only kidding. Maybe it's just a guy thing. Seriously, Jonathan. Your ideas were brilliant. The pension funds closed on $230 million in Art Market Participation Certificates. They ate them up. The investment bankers told me we were $80 million oversubscribed. They were beside themselves that we wouldn't take more money. And we finally got the amendment to our loan covenants."

He bounced up and down on his toes in elation. "Witten's paid off the subordinated debt. You were right about that too. Our agent bank came up with another hundred million dollars when we paid down our credit line."

Jonathan shifted in his seat. A little smile pulled at his lips. He still had it.

"And you two—" Simon said, holding his glass and moving it to encompass both Jonathan and Nicole. "You two saved Witten's from a catastrophe. We could have sold an $8 million forgery. My God, do you know what that could have done to our reputation— and our balance sheet? We might have had to buy back the damn picture." He clinked each of their glasses and drank a sip of champagne. They joined him.

"Fernaud had it all arranged," Simon said. "The police found the papers for a Swiss bank account he opened in the fake name of the owner of the picture. He set it up over a year ago, with his signature on the account. I wonder how many other paintings he passed off through Witten's? It gives me nightmares to think about it. Well, anyhow," he said, returning to his toast, "here's to the both of you." Simon raised his glass, drank deeply and sat down.

"Nicole," Jonathan said before Simon could get started again. He had to be quick. When Simon picked up a head of steam, he was unstoppable. "There's something I don't understand. Why did Fernaud think you knew he was the forger? We had no idea."

Nicole tapped thoughtfully at her lower lip, then brought her hand down and placed it on the table. "I cannot be sure. I have been thinking about this. When I called him, I was still very upset. I told him that my father talked to Henri about the forgery and I asked him to see us right away. He must have believed that we knew, or at least suspected."

Her gray eyes seemed to turn inward. She lowered her voice. "He must have misunderstood. I believe he was wracked with guilt. I have known him for many years. He was, at heart, a good man, I think. He did so much for others. And the mutilation by the Nazis. I cannot believe that he ever intended to harm me."

Simon and Jonathan both spoke at once. "How can you. . ." started Simon. Jonathan said, "You can't be. . ." Both stopped at the cacophony of sound.

Simon started again. "Nicole, really, how can you think that? Damn it, the guy was a thief. He didn't care about your father. I don't believe he cared about you. He was terrified of going to jail."

Before Nicole could respond, Jonathan cut in.

"You only see the best in people. I just don't buy it either. I think Lieutenant Wayne was right. Maybe we'll never know for sure if he was a murderer, but whatever he once was, Fernaud was a bad guy. He was totally possessed by his desires. All he cared about was himself. He was even trying to use you with his suicide note, to protect his memory. No way."

Everyone sat quietly for a moment. Nicole was pensive.

"Perhaps," she finally said. "But what a great irony. A forgery that was made more than 50 years ago, created to help others, caused the deaths of three men and so much trouble. *Quel dommage.*"

"Well," Jonathan said, lifting his champagne glass toward Nicole. "Anyway, here's to your father. He was a hero. A patriot. A man whose bravery I can only imagine. I don't think I would have had his courage."

"Thank you, Jonathan," she said, leaning against him in the banquette. He felt her soft body through her thin dress.

"And to Nicole." Simon rose from his seat and lifted his glass again. "To your happiness, to your inheritance and to your good fortune. It's well deserved."

"Hear! Hear!" added Jonathan.

"And speaking of your inheritance, Nicole, what do you intend to do with all that money?" Simon asked.

"Simon, I am going to buy an auction house. Henri and I have decided to become your new competitors."

Simon's jaw sagged. He looked funny with his mouth open.

"We have heard that Sotheby's is for sale," Nicole said with a pleasant smile. Her pale gray eyes sparkled. "Henri and I have been approached by a man named Taubman who is interested in making a joint offer. He desires that I run it."

"Nicole, you can't do this to me," Simon stammered out. "What about all our years together? What about loyalty? What we've meant to each other? I need you."

"But, Simon, as you have told me, this is business."

"Isn't there anything I can do?"

She paused with her face down, apparently in thought. She remained still. Finally she raised her head. Her eyes flashed and a smile threaded her lips.

"Perhaps." She let the word hang in the air. "If we choose to bid on Sotheby's, I will have to sell my Witten's stock. That could prove difficult for both of us. . ." She hesitated with her lips pursed just for the moment necessary to raise Simon's level of anxiety. It was masterful. "Do you, by chance, need a managing director?"

"What do you want?" Simon said, a note of resignation in his voice.

"Only what you have promised me. I will be appointed managing director of Witten's. You will become non-executive chairman. And I believe a salary of 200,000 pounds a year would be fair. Plus, of course, stock options and a bonus based on profits."

She leaned back, folded her graceful hands on the table and smiled at him. The small smile of a feral cat.

"Would you consider 150,000 pounds?"

"No."

"Ah. Well, then. I guess we have a deal." Simon smiled too and stuck out his hand.

Jonathan smiled as well. But for a different reason. He had just seen the great Simon Aaron taken to the cleaners. And by a woman, nonetheless. His woman.

Simon turned to him. "Since we're talking business, why don't you quit wasting your time at that law school? Come back and be my partner. I could use the help. I'll guarantee you $2 million a year, minimum."

Nicole reached over and covered his hand with hers. With her other hand she put a finger across his lips. He could feel her small breasts pressed into him.

"I need a partner too," she said. "And I will make you a *better* offer."

Her smile was beguiling.